I0637506

SHADOW FRACTION

BOOK 2 OF SHADOW TRILOGY

H.G AHEDI

"Hell is empty and all the devils are here."

William Shakespeare

First edition published in 2022
Copyright © H.G. Ahedi 2022
All rights reserved.

ISBN: 9780645505603 (eBook)
ISBN: 9780645505610 (paperback)
ISBN: 9780645505627 (hardcover)
Book cover concept by H.G. Ahedi
Book cover designed by Rebecca covers (fiver.com)

❀ Created with Vellum

CONTENTS

1

THE BEGINNING OF THE END

17th April 2020 (Present Day)
Willow's Heart

The wind was chilly, and the sky clear. The thick canopy of tall trees dominated the valley. Roots of trees were almost as old as the land itself sprouted out from underneath the soil. The plateau was a vast land partly turned to ashes and partly covered by unkept grass. The moon shone high above, illuminating the enormous mountains and dense forest surrounding the plateau. A group of vultures circled an old fortress. Far from the structure, within the valley's wilderness, a soft rustle broke the pin-drop silence. Something moved in the dark—slowly, hiding within the bushes.

Sheriff Norris Cunningham had to stop crawling to catch his breath. Nightridge, his hometown, was miles away. He was sweating, tired, and breathless. His feet were aching, his knees sore, but he had to keep moving. Norris's clothes were covered with filth, his hands soiled as he laid his head on the ground. For a while, he had eluded his nemesis. But soon, his assailant would catch up. Peering above the dewy grass, he checked if he was on the right path. The muddy truck stood twenty yards away. The cracks on the side of the windshield were still there, and the wide dent near the front tire was unmissable. Once in his truck, he planned to call for help. He might be able to save the others. Struggling, he stood up and limped toward the vehicle.

The creepy forest intimidated him, like a predator watching his every move. He was unarmed and lost in the valley. With his palm, he wiped the sweat dripping down his face. His heart raced, pounding loudly in his chest. Norris heard a rustle and froze. Out of the darkness emerged a tall figure resembling a demon from another world. It had two large horns, stony bloodshot eyes, and a wide jaw. The bipedal creature stepped forward, drawing a curved sword. Norris wanted to believe it was a nightmare. But it was not. The creature was hunting him. Scared to death, he ran. But he tripped over a twig and fell on his face.

17th April 2020 (Present Day)
Willow's Heart

It was a void night without stars; a shadowy impenetrable dungeon that invited the devil itself. A foul odor made the air unbreathable. A steady plip, plip, plip of water leakage broke the silence. From a hole in the ground, little black creatures jumped out. Little feet scuttled through the damp, grimy ground. The group of rats followed the scent of blood. They came to a stop, and the lead rat sniffed the air, its whiskers flaring. The rodent pounced ahead, and the others followed.

The scent of blood was getting stronger. Scurrying closer, the rats ripped the flesh off the woman's hand.

Detective Tom Nash opened his eyes. Coughing, he spat out a mouthful of dirt. Pain rippled through his leg. He slowly stretched, and the pain subsided. The overwhelming stench made him want to vomit, but his throat remained parched. Tom squinted as his vision adjusted to his murky surroundings. "Where the hell am I?" he muttered, shivering.

He felt a strain on his wrist and realized his hands were bound. He looked around, petrified. His pulse rose as pure blackness surrounded him. He was cut off from the beauty of twinkling stars, serenity of the birdsongs, and fresh air. He was a prisoner in a deep hole, and if he did not escape, no one would ever find him.

SEVEN HEADS

2nd April 2020
Two Weeks Ago
Springfield, Massachusetts

Underneath an old tree, Sheriff Norris Cunningham grieved in silence as he gripped a cremation jar in his hands. The white ceramic urn adorned with a silver design held his son's remains. Another victim of the pandemic.

Norris was the tallest of the group of mourners. His copper-colored eyes were swollen, lifeless, and full of tears. Norris felt far older in the last six months than he had ever felt in the last decade. He was losing hair, and it was turning gray. His eyesight was fine, but the black circles underneath his eyes refused to go. Age had caught up with him, and he felt a pain in his joints now and then.

The priest began the sermon, and he remained speechless with his head bowed. His son's face popped in front of his eyes, and he felt his presence. Mary, his daughter, stood beside him like a statue—pale and speechless. Her face showed no signs of hope or despair. She was a portrait of her mother. A petite woman with jet black hair, soft skin, almond-shaped eyes full of kindness. Mary was a nurse, and in the last year, she had seen too many people die. Including her own family. Kim Cunningham, his daughter-in-law, stood along his side with a jar in her hands, a smaller replica of the bigger urn. She was broken, her hazel eyes were still like stone. He had known Kim for over ten years. She was a cheerful, kind-hearted, hardworking businesswoman who had won his son's heart. Norris loved to talk with her. But today, she hadn't said a word, and he wondered how she would survive these dreadful times.

A significant part of his family was gone. He gaped at the second hole in the ground. His heart crumbled. As if losing his son was not enough, his grandson was the second fatality in his family. Born during the raging pandemic, the infant did not stand a chance. One of his deepest regrets was that he didn't get the chance to meet his grandson. Anger stirred inside him. There was nothing he could do. No one to blame, arrest, or even incriminate. The victims of the pandemic may never get justice.

Norris cursed the pandemic for ripping his family apart. How many more would die? When was this going to end? The lockdown had lifted. But the virus prevailed, and chaos followed. According to the current rules, funerals could include a few people. Honestly, he preferred it. It gave him more private time with his son and grandson. More time to say goodbye. More time to express how much he loved and missed them. He did not have to share this moment with anyone. He did not want to.

The sermon finished, and Norris buried the ashes of his loved ones. He had thought of where his son would prefer to be buried. Dispersing the ashes in the field was one option, but he remembered his son loved old trees. He smiled at the enormous oak tree standing tall above them. It was perfect. When the burial concluded, the priest left them alone. For several minutes, he stared at the plaques.

Finally, Mary spoke. "Dad, let's go."

"Yes, it is time," he replied, putting his arms around her and kissing her forehead.

After lunch, he said goodbye to his family and drove toward Nightridge. The drive was smooth, calming, and although his heart was full of grief, he was glad to have the opportunity to say goodbye. The pandemic had shaken everyone, but the situation was slowly returning to normal. But he was edgy. Uncertainty lingered in the air. No one knew what would happen next. Fortunately, so far, he hadn't contracted the virus, but tomorrow was a different story. He had to be careful.

The situation in Nightridge was finally improving. After the Shadow Pandemic put the entire village into a murdering rage, it had taken time for things to settle. They had rebuilt the bridge and most of the houses. But several households still lay in ashes, and many villagers never returned. He felt layers of unsettling emotions as he drove past the burned fields and broken, neglected houses. Norris swayed the steering wheel and entered the premises of a little one-story cottage. Spring was here, and colorful flowers encircled the house. The trees he planted years ago had grown tall. He parked his truck and stepped out. For a moment, he marveled at the beautiful sky and enjoyed the scent of jasmine and gentle breeze. He was home.

In the late afternoon, he began fixing the fence behind his house. Just a few months ago, during the craziness of the Shadow Pandemic, someone had driven a car through his fence and broken all the windows. Fixing the windows was easy. The fence was another story. Repairing it was tiring and frustrating. He had not done such a physically laborious task in a long time.

Hours passed, and Norris touched his arm, trying to ease the pain. A cluster of orangish clouds sat over the horizon, hiding the sun. He hammered the last nail in the fence and smiled with satisfaction. It was done before nightfall. The wind picked up, and the birds sang in the woods. Another day was gone. With his work done, Norris retired for the day.

After a long shower, he ate his dinner. On the porch, Norris smoked a cigar, staring into obscurity and thinking about his life. The last three months had been quiet, and he preferred it. But once more, he sensed it. Something was coming.

3rd April 2020
Meadow Cottage, Nightridge

The yellow golden bright light fell on Nightridge. It was serene, just like a painting. The trees stood still; the swamp was silent and mysterious, and the houses remained quiet. A new day had begun. Norris was awake, but he didn't want to go anywhere. Glancing at the other side of the bed, he sensed his wife's presence. He saw Martha every day, even though she had passed away three years ago. Her scent still lingered in the room, and her soft, loving voice echoed in his mind. Norris had not parted with her clothes or any of her belongings. It was as if she still lived in the house. In the last twelve months, he had accepted the fact that it was her time. One thing gave him some comfort. Martha didn't have to witness this chaotic world that snatched away their son and grandson.

Sulking, he forced himself out of bed. As he brushed his teeth, he studied his face in the mirror. His eyes were swollen, and his face was pale. It was no use sobbing. He had to accept that he would feel the loss for the rest of his life.

Dressed for work, Norris cracked two eggs in the pan and pushed the toaster button down. He prepared coffee and soon made himself comfortable at the dining table. With the radio blaring in the background, he ate his breakfast. The phone rang, and he got to his feet to reach for his cellphone on the kitchen bench.

"Hello…" he said.

"Morning, Norris," replied an unfamiliar voice.

"Good morning. Who is this?"

"This is Edgar. How are you?"

Norris was stunned. *No way. No way.*

"Edgar Thobe?" he said.

"The one and the same."

"Oh, it has been a long time," Norris said, feeling confused and excited. They had fought together in the war.

"I know. How have you been?"

"I'm good. On which base are you located?" Norris asked.

"I left the Army ten years ago."

"I see. I didn't know," Norris said, recalling the good old days. If one could call them that. Wars were ugly, but he had met good people and made lifelong friends.

"It's my fault. I should have stayed in touch."

Norris tilted his head, thinking not all friendships last. They are not meant to.

"So, did you retire?" he asked sarcastically.

Edgar laughed. "No. No. Retirement is not for me. But I have left the military and am now a sheriff."

Norris was shocked. "Oh... Congrats. Where are you stationed?"

"Willow's Heart."

"Oh really? That's not too far from here," Norris said, trying to remember if he had a map lying around.

"You are right. I never realized we were in neighboring counties until I read in the papers about the incident at Nightridge."

Norris gulped uncomfortably. A shiver ran down his spine. It was more than just an incident. It was a nightmare.

"I see," Norris replied, not able to think straight.

"I am glad you are all right."

"Thanks."

"I think you handled it admirably," said Edgar.

"Thank you," Norris replied uncomfortably. A tingling dread crept through his body. Flattery was not Edgar's style. The line became silent. He returned to the dining table and sipped his coffee. "So, are you coming down to Nightridge for tea?" he said, trying to break the ice.

"Thanks for the invite. But was wondering if you could come to Willow's Heart?"

Norris sensed something off in his tone. "What happened?"

"We have a little situation down here," said Edgar.

"The pandemic," remarked Norris.

"Uh, that's a mess, and we can't do anything about it. This is something… different."

"Well, you are the sheriff. I am sure you can manage it," Norris said, not wanting to get involved.

"I think I could use your insight."

Norris raised his eyebrows. "What happened?"

"Just drive down here, will you? Please. For old time's sake."

Norris finished his breakfast. He wore his jacket and placed his hat on his head. For a couple of minutes, he stood in front of the mirror, touching his jaw. It had been over a decade since he had spoken with Edgar. Out of the blue, he had contacted him. Norris was pleased and worried. Was he meeting an old friend or an old nemesis? Reluctantly, he stepped out of the house and closed the door behind him.

On the drive to Willow's Heart, Norris thought about the old days. It seemed like a lifetime ago. The year was 1990. Technology was in its infancy. Landlines and VCRs were the most advanced gadgets in the market. They were simpler times. Perhaps happier times. In those days, people actually met up in person, and like today, social media did not dominate human life. That was how he had met Edgar.

He and Martha had traveled to Norwalk to see her

brother, Richie. They had planned to have dinner and drinks at a local bar. Norris was eager to please his new bride's family. They were now his family, and he wanted to be a part of it. He had just returned from military service, but his duty to his country was not over. Norris knew he would have to leave soon.

The dim bar was crowded, stuffy, and a strong smell of smoke and alcohol dominated the air. Several men sat puffing cigars. Waitresses in yellow dresses carried drinks and food on trays. The bartender was busy serving one drink after another. Norris and Martha found Richie drinking a beer at a table.

"Hey!" said Martha

Richie jumped to his feet and hugged her sister.

"Congrats again!"

Martha smiled.

Norris shook hands with Richie and bought everyone drinks.

Richie drove trucks for a living. He was a short, stout man who took small steps. He often spoke very little, had challenges remembering things, and was very gullible. Martha often worried that people took advantage of Richie. They had met a few of his so-called friends, and they didn't like them. That summer evening was no different, and Richie was eager for Norris to meet his new friend. A friend who had come out of nowhere. In a few minutes, a man of Norris's age, wearing a military uniform, joined them at the table.

"Hey, Edgar, thanks for coming!" said Richie, shaking his hand.

After brief pleasantries, everyone settled in their chairs.

Edgar's sharp blue eyes sized him and his new bride. Something reflected in them. Perhaps a thirst, ambition, or pride. Norris didn't know. Edgar smirked, crossed his arms, and sat back in the chair. Unlike Richie, who appeared pale and sickly, Edgar was gifted with good looks and health.

Norris broke the silence. "Will you be deployed soon?"

"Yes. In the next few weeks," answered Edgar.

"I see."

"I wish you didn't go. You are my only friend," said Richie.

Norris felt a bit hurt. He had been trying his best to get close to Richie and supported him from time to time. Richie had met up with Edgar just a few weeks ago, and they were best friends already. As if sensing his disappointment, Martha placed her hand on his lap.

"Oh, I will return. Don't worry!" Edgar said, patting his back.

"No. No. I wish I could go with you," Richie insisted.

"No, Richie," said Martha.

Norris would have encouraged him too, but he knew better. Richie wouldn't survive the grueling and competitive army training. It was both physically and mentally demanding. The journey of becoming a soldier needed strength, willingness to push boundaries, and being able to think on your feet. It was not a good fit for Richie.

"I agree with your lovely sister. You are good at what you do. Stay with it," said Edgar.

Richie bowed his head. "I want to be more."

"There are other ways of doing that," said Norris before Edgar could.

Edgar eyed him, and Norris didn't look away. Both had

subtle smiles on their faces, but their smiles were fake. Norris would never forget the coldness in Edgar's eyes.

"Well, I got into the military without any trouble. You know, several of my friends applied. All of them failed, and I got an ASVAB score of eighty."

Norris nodded. "Well done."

The Armed Services Vocational Aptitude Battery was a test to assess if a candidate was fit to join the military. Norris remembered how hard he had to work to get a good grade.

"You know what's funny? I didn't even study that hard!" said Edgar, laughing.

Richie put his arms around Edgar and shook him. "You are so smart."

"Yeah. I was the smartest in the class. Everyone struggled. I passed with flying colors. Everyone loves me and I am breezing through my combat training. I am ready for battle!"

Norris smiled.

"When did you finish your training?" asked Edgar.

"Six months ago," replied Norris.

"Where are you based?"

"Nevada."

"Great. I am based in Alabama. I am having the time of my life. What have you been doing?"

"Nothing much. Just the usual training," Norris replied.

That was a lie. Norris had been hard on training, especially martial arts. Not that he liked to kill. He enjoyed the physical endurance.

"So, you haven't been involved in an actual war," said Edgar.

Norris said nothing.

"I am sure I am going to enjoy it," said Edgar. "This

would be my first deployment. It's exciting. I am going to crush our enemies! Nothing will stop me…"

Edgar's excitement was evident, and Norris had met several men with the same attitude. He just nodded.

"So, Martha, what are your plans now?" Edgar asked.

Martha smiled. "Oh, I am a simple woman with simple needs."

Norris was proud because he knew her. Martha was not a simple woman. She was smart, and a better person than Norris. During her lifetime, not only had she brought up two great kids, but she became a powerful pillar of the community. She volunteered in schools and community centers. All her life, she worked with underprivileged families and children. Seeing her passion, Norris decided never to let her down and provide for his family. And fortunately for him, it worked out well.

"Oh really? Why would you want to do that?" said Edgar.

Norris's eyes fixated on him, and he had an urge to punch him in the face.

"What I do with my life is my business," Martha replied, smiling.

"Oh, but there should be more. What about living your life? Traveling, seeing the world… marriage sounds like the end of all fun," he said, sipping beer.

"Yeah. It's boring. I never want to get married," added Richie.

His words sadden Martha.

That evening, Norris decided not to be friends with Edgar and tried to keep Richie away from him. But it did not work.

They remained friends for a long time. To be fair, as far as he knew, Edgar didn't take advantage of Richie. But his visits caused friction and disturbed the peace in his family. Edgar would encourage Richie to drink, and he got hooked on drugs. Martha had to put her brother into rehab. Edgar felt like a dark shadow on his family, and Norris did not like it.

A week after their drinks, they were deployed to Iraq. Saddam Hussein had invaded Kuwait. The Coalition retaliated, and the war was waged for over a year. Norris and Edgar were in the same platoon. They fought with thousands of soldiers and many never returned to their homeland. Norris could still hear screams and the explosions. It was horrible. A nightmare that took Norris's years to forget. He particularly recalled the men huddled together, smoking, and hoping to get home safely. No soldier was happy to take a life. It was a duty, not a liberty. But Edgar was different and spoke animatedly about the men he had killed and how they deserved to die. He seemed to be made for the military, while Norris always questioned his role.

In late 1991, they returned home, and Norris did not look forward to another war. Even the peacekeeping missions in the Middle East were risky. After ten years of service, Norris had had enough, and although he had risen to the role of lieutenant, he was done. His military service had lost meaning, and he resigned. Edgar had visited him the day he was leaving.

"How could you do this?" he demanded.

Norris didn't need to explain his decision to anyone. "Because I can," he said.

"But what about the war? We have to win this. We must rule!"

The young, free-spirited man he had met in the bar was long gone. This man was heavier, with some gray hair and tanned skin.

Norris said nothing.

"What are you going to do?" Edgar demanded.

"I haven't decided yet. But it has been ten years, and I am done. My family needs me."

"But we have to serve our country. Preserve our future. Perish our enemies. We have to be the best!"

Norris eyed him. "There are other ways to preserve our future. I am done."

"You are a traitor!"

Norris remembered how those words had hurt him. But he knew Edgar. He took things too literally. Everything was black and white, and he minimized the human elements. Wars had no meaning. Norris loved his country and its people, but he didn't want to be a pawn in a political game. He picked up his bags and left without another word.

Norris had returned home, and he would never forget the sparkle of joy in his wife's eyes. His children were thrilled, and as time passed, he forgot about Edgar. Until he received a letter from him six years later. Edgar apologized and gave him the good news that he was appointed a lieutenant in the Army. Norris didn't believe in holding grudges. He had replied to his letters, and for a short while, they became pen pals. Then he had vanished from his life, only to reappear amid a global pandemic. It bothered Norris. Edgar was a proud, arrogant man. Asking for help was not his style. What did he really want?

The drive was long, but Norris was used to it. Driving was

a part of county life. Willow's Heart was linked to Nightridge by Route 9. While Nightridge was near the coast, Willow's Heart was positioned west and mostly dominated by a dense, unexplored forest. The hilly county had a population of over two thousand people. A handful of modern houses were on the outer edges of the county, including the Sheriff's Department. Houses with lawns and farms were scattered over the land. The valley that formed the heart of the county was ancient. Several people migrated from the valley a long time ago, and the old houses still stood as remnants of the past.

The straight, barren road was slightly wet because of recent rain. Norris glanced at the time. It was 10.00 am. The GPS showed his destination was close. The sheriff's truck turned right and drove on a rough road. Thick trees engulfed the path, and he slowed down when he saw a police car. Driving around the parked car, he pushed the brakes, turned the key, and hopped out of the truck. With his hands in his pockets, he strolled toward the clearing. Icy terror gripped him.

"What the…" he said but lost his voice.

With his mouth still open, he approached the field and joined the three deputies, who appeared as stunned as him. Crows cawed in the surrounding trees and vultures dominated the sky. He glared at the seven wolves' heads on wooden crosses. Two heads were white, three gray, and the last two were black. He stepped closer and looked closely into the dead eyes of a wolf. Blood had flowed down the wood, painting it red. Flies and mosquitoes buzzed around the decapitated head. Norris's pulse raced. He stared into the next pair of haunted eyes. The second wolf's head was white and of a similar size. Its eyes were dark, and the head was cut off with great precision.

"Hi," said Edgar Thobe.

Edgar had changed little, except his hair was grayer, and he was heavier and muscular. The lines around his hazel eyes and his forehead showed signs of aging. But the coldness in his eyes remained.

"Good to see you."

They shook hands.

"Thanks for coming," said Edgar.

"No problem. I-I am wondering. What happened here?"

"I was hoping you could shed some light on this."

Norris eyed him. "Me? I know nothing about beheaded animals."

"I didn't know who else to call."

Norris noticed that one of the wolf's eyes had been gutted out. "Has this ever happened before?"

"Not on my watch. What do you think?" Edgar said.

Norris tilted his head. "It could be a warning, or it could be the work of a madman."

"What do we do?" asked one deputy.

"We start with testing the blood," Norris replied.

All eyes turned to him.

"It's likely to be animal blood," said Edgar.

Norris studied the heads. "Whoever did this... wants to tell us something. Maybe he left a clue. I suggest calling the crime scene unit."

"Are you serious?" said Edgar.

"You asked for my help," Norris replied sharply.

"Fine, fine..." Edgar signaled one of his deputies.

Norris noted that all the crosses were made of the same

type of wood. White oak. The gray wood was cut perfectly by a machine. The butcher had hammered the crosses into the ground and bloodstains on the wood were unremarkable. He kneeled and examined the ground. There were no signs of blood. It meant only one thing—the wolves had been killed somewhere else. Norris saw several partial footprints in the dust.

"What's your plan?" Norris asked Edgar.

"After the CSI is done, I plan to send the heads to the county morgue," Edgar replied.

"Are you sure that is a good idea?"

Edgar raised his eyebrows. "What do you suggest?"

Norris did not like Edgar, but the mystery intrigued him. He smiled. "What do you want, Edgar?"

"I want answers."

"Then don't send the heads to the county morgue."

Edgar eyed him curiously.

3

THE HUNTER AND THE HUNTED

17th April 2020 (Present Day)
Willow's Heart

Pain ripped through Norris' body. He tried to pick himself up, but the ache in his knee made it hard. He glanced behind, and the figure still stood in the distance. The creature had no real eyes, but he sensed it was watching him.

They enjoy the hunt.

If he stood up, it would hunt him down. Maybe it had not seen him yet. Norris used his hands to drag himself toward the truck. The vehicle was within his reach. He glanced behind again. The figure was gone. Norris felt a sharp bolt of fear. He knew it would come for him. Pushing himself, he crawled as fast as he could. A pair of feet appeared, blocking his way. Norris lifted his head. A strange figure stood over him.

"Going somewhere?" it said in a horrid voice.

Raising its sword, the creature attacked. Norris quickly

rolled away, missing the blade by inches. His heart was racing. The creature roared. He pulled himself to his feet, almost tearing the wound in his knee. The creature swung the blade. Norris ducked, dodging the blade by inches. He grabbed a thin piece of stick, struck him hard on the knee. It screamed. Taking his chance, Norris sprang on him. Both men dropped to the ground. If Norris thought he could win, he was wrong. The creature grabbed his neck. It overpowered him, hurling him to the ground.

"This is going to be your end," it said as it smothered Norris with its hands.

Norris's legs fluttered in the air as he fought to breathe. He grabbed its hand and tried to pull it away. He threw a punch, but it had no effect. Norris sensed his willpower shutter. The creature laughed. Norris tried to push the creature off him when he felt a handle. He pulled out the knife from the creature's belt and rammed it into its chest. Screams filled the valley. Blood flowed over Norris. With all his strength, he pulled out the knife and plunged it back into its chest. The creature collapsed to the ground, screaming in pain. Holding his injured leg, Norris moved away and watched it convulse in torment.

"Die, you son of a bitch," he muttered.

17th April 2020 (Present Day)
Fortress, Willow's Heart

In the dungeon somewhere in Willow's Heart, Tom stretched his legs to relieve the cramp. He was getting old. The spasm passed after a few minutes, and he shut his eyes, trying to think clearly. It was hard. He was tired and hungry, and his throat was dry. It was tough to focus on this dreary, unholy place. He felt he might never escape. He immediately pushed such thoughts away.

"I need to get out of here," he whispered.

He flung his hands, trying to free himself, when a muffled noise reverberated. Tom looked in the sound's direction. It was pitch dark. He tried hard to pinpoint its source but failed. Using his hands, he felt the soft and wet surface underneath him. He moved further, extending his hands as he touched the ground. Suddenly, he felt something. It was soft and felt like skin.

"Hello? Who is there?"

Silence.

"Hey, answer me!" he said, reaching further. His heart stopped in his chest. He lifted the dry, frigid flesh and realized what it was. A human hand.

"Ah!" he cried out, dropping it.

He moved to a corner, bracing himself, expecting the killer to emerge anytime. How would he protect himself? He was unarmed and tied down. A clatter distracted him. He heard a low gasp.

"Who is it?"

The breathing became louder.

"Who is it?!" he demanded.

In the darkness, a vague figure appeared. He opened his mouth and let out a blood-curdling scream.

4

RISE OF THE DEAD

3rd April 2020
Nightridge

The sheriff's office was in an old building made of yellow stones. It had a rectangular hall with six desks equipped with computers. Two rooms were allocated to records, evidence, and storage. Three deputies sat at their desks, working quietly. Norris's office was at the end of the hall. He marched in and shut the door behind him. As he got seated, he glanced over the monitor to view the entire hall.

Norris shifted to his right and opened the window next to his desk. Fresh air filled the stuffy room. He turned on the computer, which let out a long mechanical groan as it came to life. He relaxed in his chair and flipped through the stack of messages piled neatly on a tray. The aroma of coffee flooded the office, and he smiled.

The door opened, and Mrs. Terresa Flores stepped in. "Good morning, Chief."

"Morning," he said.

Mrs. Flores was a bossy, blunt woman who marched around the office as if she owned it. With her commanding personality, she single-handedly managed the administration.

"How are you doing?" he asked.

"Fine. Another day... another long to-do list," she replied.

He laughed. She always found ways to make him smile. She handed him more messages and left. He quickly flipped through them and put them aside. They were not a priority. He began scrolling through his emails and deleted the ones that needed no response from him.

Mrs. Flores returned and gave him his first cup of coffee. "I heard you went to Willow's Heart."

"Are you keeping tabs on me?"

She smiled slyly. "Someone has to look after you."

Norris wrinkled his nose. "Yes, Edgar called me to Willow's Heart."

"Who is Edgar?"

Norris became thoughtful. "An old friend."

She studied his face. "If there is a problem in his county, let him deal with it."

"He needed my help... well... advice."

"Some sicko beheaded animals and put their heads on crosses. The pandemic has brought out the worst in people."

"People are who they are. The pandemic has little to do with it," he muttered, sipping his coffee.

"So, what did you do?"

He waited for her to explain.

"What did you do with the wolf heads?" she asked.

He smiled, not saying a word.

Excitement flashed in her eyes. "Oh, no. You sent them to Dr. Death, didn't you?"

He laughed.

"Dr. William Sterling is a fine medical examiner," said Norris.

"And I should say... rather cute," Mrs. Flores replied, winking.

Beams of golden rays penetrated through multiple thin bands of white clouds. The day was about to finish.

The wind rushed through the windows. Norris rubbed his eyes and turned away from the screen.

One day, all this paperwork is going to kill me.

He logged off the computer, stood up, and stretched. His phone rang. It was a video call.

"Well, it's about time," he murmured.

He accepted the call, and Dr. William Sterling's face appeared. "Hey."

"How are you doing?" Norris asked, wearing his jacket and hat. He picked up the phone and left the office.

"I am good. Thanks for sending me more weird stuff."

Norris cackled. "I am sure it grabbed your attention."

"Well, I am used to receiving human heads," William mocked.

Norris didn't think it was funny.

William cleared his throat.

With the phone held in his hand, Norris stepped out of the office and into the empty hall. Everyone had finished the day and gone home. "How are things in New York?" he asked, continuing their chat as he exited the building.

"I wouldn't say they have improved."

Norris got behind the wheel and placed the phone on a mount attached to his dashboard. "Uh-huh. So, did you find anything? Just wolf heads and animal blood, right?"

"I examined the wolves thoroughly. There were no traces of human tissue in their mouth or teeth. From what I can gather, the animals were healthy."

The engine came to life. Norris put the vehicle in first gear and pushed the accelerator. "Where did they come from?"

"The zoologist is still gathering information. My assistant got curious and called in all the zoos in New York. No animals are missing. What about Nightridge?"

"There are wolves in the forest, but I am sure no one is slaughtering them," Norris said, turning the truck. There were no other cars on the street.

"Are you certain?" asked William.

Norris sulked. "Okay. What else?"

"I found human blood…"

Norris released his foot on the gas pedal. The truck slowed down. "Really?"

"Yep."

"There is more, isn't it?" Norris muttered.

"Oh, this is where it gets interesting."

"Ah-huh?"

"The blood is fresh, probably from a cut, and it belongs to Mr. Gail Clegg."

Norris became silent. The name didn't ring a bell. It wasn't linked to any major cases he was working on, and Gail wasn't a resident of Nightridge.

"What is special about him?" he asked.

"Oh, he is quite special. He is supposed to be dead," replied William.

Norris pressed the brakes, and the truck stopped in the middle of the road. "You're kidding me."

"Nope, looks like our dead man is out there slaughtering wolves."

"How did Gail die? Did they find a body?"

"Well, according to the police report, he is dead. Gail was a suspect in the ritualistic murders of three children. They had circumstantial evidence against him, and he was psychologically unstable. Officer Kain Botkin paid him a visit on 10th June 2010. Out of the blue, Gail became violent and shot Kain."

"Jesus," Norris said, gripping the steering wheel.

"According to the report, an officer followed and gunned down Gail."

Norris turned to the camera and leaned closer. "Who?" he asked.

"You will never guess. It was Officer Tom Nash."

5

CREATURES OF THE DARK

17th April 2020 (Present Day)
Willow's Heart

The creature's blood soaked the ground. Norris waited with a rock in his hand. He tried to ignore the longhorns, the devilish wide-eyed mask, and the bizarre outfit. It was just a man; he told himself. The men they called hunters. The adrenaline rush wore off, and he felt the ache in his leg and his throat. A part of him wanted to unmask the figure and unravel its identity. But he had no time.

I have to get out of here before the others track me down.

He grabbed the bark of a tree and stood up. A sharp pain ran through his leg. Ignoring it, he headed for the truck. For the first time, it occurred to him they might have tampered with his vehicle. If that was true, then he was stuck here. He needed to get help. Otherwise, this madness would never stop. Norris caught his breath and noticed a hollow log. He was about to walk when he heard a cracking noise. He stopped dead on his feet. Something was coming. The moonlight crept through the canopy, and not too far away, a gigantic shadow appeared. He ducked and crawled into the hollow log. A family of spiders rushed out of the log, making a home for its new tenant. Norris became motionless. Through a small hole, he witnessed the massive shadow materialize into a strange figure. Shabbily dressed, carrying a large, curved sword, its enormous evil-looking head moved side to side. Norris quivered, pushing aside the thoughts of what they would do to him if he were captured. A hissing noise echoed, and a snake slithered into the log. He stiffened. It hissed over his arm and crept over his back. The hair on his arm rose and sweat gathered on his skin. The snake slithered away. Norris sighed. He peered out of the hole. The figure had vanished. Unsure whether he was alone, Norris waited.

The minutes passed painfully. Crickets chipped loudly, and frogs croaked. When he thought it was safe, Norris crawled out.

He got to his feet. He was alone, and the body of the masked figure lay where he had left him. Turning, he limped toward the truck and swung open the door. A loud growl stunned him. From a distance, a four-legged creature with red eyes darted toward him.

"Damn it!"

Norris jumped in and shut the door. The wolf bashed against the door, shaking the truck. The beast stared unblinkingly at him, blood dripping from its jaw. Its bloodshot eyes were larger than any wolf he had seen. The wolf lowered onto all four limbs, growled, and viciously lunged at the vehicle. Its claws dug into the metal, leaving marks. Its master emerged from the darkness. With trembling hands, Norris turned the key. The truck failed to start.

17th April 2020 (Present Day)
Fortress, Willow's Heart

Cornered in the dark, Tom's heart drummed. Millions of thoughts rushed through his mind. These people were killers, and they would not hesitate to torture him before finishing him. He wished he had called for backup sooner. The scary figure he saw had vanished. But he knew he was not alone in this dungeon. He blinked several times. After a few moments, he had the guts to ask, "Who is it?"

Something moved, and Tom glued himself against the wall. He was tongue-tied. Surely, being a detective, he could defend himself. But he had his limits. A muffled sound echoed, as if someone was trying to speak underwater.

"Who's there!?"

The muffled noises continued, and he felt something bump against his leg. He cried out, moving away.

"Rats, I hate rats!" he screamed. "Stay away from me!"

The muffling noise returned. This was no rat. Tom sat in the corner, wondering who it could be.

"Norris? Is that you?"

Thinking this could be a friend, Tom moved toward the noise.

"Okay, okay…" he muttered, trying to reach with his hands. Soon he felt fresh. It was warm and soft. He moved his hands upwards, feeling a cloth-like material.

"Hey, are you okay?" asked Tom, realizing there could be

another prisoner. It might be Norris. Soon his hands reached the chest. It was a man.

"It is okay. I am trying to help," he said, moving upwards.

He now understood how it felt to be blind. It would be terrible not to experience all the beauty life offered. Soon he felt a smooth, rectangular surface, which felt like tape. The man shook his head, and the muffling sound resumed. Tom traced the ends of the duct tape and ripped it off.

"Ah!" a voice cried out.

"Norris? Norris? Is that you?"

The man released a loud moan.

"Are you okay?" Tom asked.

"Detective…"

"Kyle?" Tom muttered, feeling a sharp pain as if someone had pierced a dagger through his heart. He felt ashamed for forgetting about the young deputy. Since he had awakened, he had just thought about himself. A loud clang startled them, and a stream of light emerged from the top.

6

REMNANTS OF THE PAST

3rd April 2020
Tom's Apartment, New York

Detective Tom Nash stretched on the bed. It was 6:00 am, and soon he had to head for work. He grumbled. Work had become a pain. Most of his ten-year career as a cop had been exciting. He had enjoyed cracking cases and getting answers for the victims and their families. Fighting for justice made him feel like he was doing some good for society. Of course, he loathed the administrative work and the bureaucracy, but his job had several perks.

But since the pandemic, it had become just another damn job. Like everyone else, Tom blamed it. It was the reason for all the chaos nowadays, and it was an easy target. A virus had plagued the world. As if humans did not have enough problems already. Growing population, failing economy, global warming, and lack of proper leadership. The list continued. The widespread pandemonium was cruel and unforgiving, and it was here to stay.

The alarm rang, and Tom hit the snooze button and slid under the blankets. It was getting warmer, and all signs of winter were fading away. He wished it also took all his worries and anger with it. But perhaps it was too much to ask.

It was a typical NYC morning. Shouts in English and other languages echoed through the building. The smell of cigarette smoke seeped into his bedroom. His neighbor was smoking on the balcony again. Tom reached for the remote and turned on the reverse cycling air conditioner. Joys of technology. The odor vanished, but then there was something else, and it was far worse. The stench of garbage. Tom rubbed his nose and missed the Indian restaurant, which used to open early in the morning and fill the neighborhood with smells of exotic oils and spices. Thanks to the pandemic, it had closed.

After a struggle, Tom got out of bed and stood in front of the mirror. Feeling sure he had put on some weight; he touched his stomach.

"I need to exercise," he said.

Words he had told himself far too many times. He noted his ruffled light brown hair and the black circles around his baby blue eyes. Tom thought he looked all right. He had inherited his mother's eyes. She was kind, a gentle soul who was taken before her time. He had inherited his rough brown hair and small round face from his father. Tom hung his head. He had not called him recently.

Did it matter? He does not remember me, anyway.

Alzheimer's was prevalent in his family, and his father had showed symptoms around six years ago. Now in a nursing home, Richard Nash lived a solitary life in a world of dreams and disappearing memories. He hardly interacted with anyone and acted like a child most of the time.

Tom came to the window and glared out. He had to mend for himself all his life. He was a good cop, but unlucky in love. Duty came first. Claire, his ex-wife, did not like it and left. After her, he had decided not to invest time in relationships. But when Jenny came along, everything changed. It was like he was a new man. Someone who needed to be more than a cop. Feeling satisfied with his life he left the bedroom.

Tom's day progressed slowly, and he stepped into the messy kitchen in search of something to eat. Unwashed dishes were piled in the sink. Memories flashed, and he remembered how good it was to have breakfast with Jenny. But they were now separated. Jenny Garrison was a financial consultant and had left for the United Kingdom for a project. She was supposed to return in two months, but then the pandemic struck, and the borders closed. It had been six months since he had seen her, and he was tired of waiting for things to return to normal.

After a shower, he began making breakfast. The news blared on the TV. The blame game continued, and so did the rise in the death toll. Feeling depressed by the news, he changed the channel and searched for a replay of the Knicks game. Tom stopped at an unexpected channel. The headline "Seven Heads" attracted his attention. He increased the volume.

"This is devastating," said Ursula Caddle. "They slaughtered these animals for no reason."

Tom knew her. Ursula was a passionate animal activist with millions of followers. She ran campaigns against animal cruelty and was fighting for animal protection rights.

"What are you talking about?" Tom said, talking to himself.

As he read the rest of the headlines, he got his answer.

"Oh my god," he muttered.

"It is unbelievable. These animals have a right to live and thrive on this planet as we do," continued Ursula. "Just because we are on top of the food chain doesn't mean we can mistreat other species."

"You are damn right. Who the hell did this?" stated Tom.

"Have the police found anything?" asked the reporter.

"Well, the incident occurred in Willow's Heart, a county about twenty-five miles from the city. The sheriff is investigating the incident."

The news reporter nodded. "Are any animals missing from the zoos?"

"Not that we know of."

"Could these be wild animals?"

"It is possible, and we should find out who killed them. Just because it did not involve humans doesn't mean we should not prosecute people who kill animals for pleasure! It has to stop!" said Ursula.

"Willow's Heart…" Tom tried to remember where it was.

A map appeared on the screen, and Tom's face flushed. Willow's Heart was close to Nightridge. The news reporter reappeared on the screen and continued, "The animal slaughtering at Willow's Heart is being investigated. If you have any information, please email us or call the number below."

Tom was not listening anymore. He got up and searched for his phone. When he found it, he saw that there were five missed calls from Norris.

3rd March 2020
NYPD Precinct, New York

Tom did not expect his day to go this way. After he chatted with Norris, he left for work within ten minutes. The drive to the precinct was uneventful. He took the elevator to the sixth floor. The cop on duty greeted him. Terry Elrod wore a face mask that barely covered his thick beard. The enormous man reminded him of the heavy-weight champions. Tom touched his face. He had almost forgotten he was wearing a mask. It had become like a second skin.

"Hey, Terry. How are things?"

"Good. Detective, what can I do for you?"

"I need all the case files and the evidence box for Mr. Gail Clegg," he said, handing over a piece of paper with the case number.

"Please fill in this form."

Tom nodded. He took a seat and filled out the form. A minute later, Terry appeared with a box and placed it on the table. Tom signed the form and handed it over.

"Here are all the copies of the files. You will have to wait for the evidence box."

"Why?"

"It's not in this precinct."

Tom remembered he was not the lead detective in Gail's case, and all the evidence was stored elsewhere.

"I will put in a transfer request," said Terry.

Tom nodded and left with the box.

.   .   .

The aroma of fresh-brewed coffee and donuts flooded the precinct. Tom stopped by the lounge to refill his mug. He needed the caffeine. As he returned to his small office on the fourth floor, he spotted cops huddled around a cooler talking. Through the glass partition, he noticed a group of patrol officers rush down the corridor, talking animatedly. Another group was gathered around a computer. Six months ago, everything had come to a halt, but slowly, life had begun to move forward. The office he shared with his partner, John White, was simple, with two desks, chairs, and plenty of cabinets. Files and books towered over the cabinet, and the dustbin was overflowing. John was in the courthouse, giving testimony on a case. Tom didn't want to stay in the office alone. He finished his coffee, left the files on his desk, and took the elevator to the parking lot.

3rd April 2020
City Morgue, New York

The late afternoon drive to City Morgue was quiet, and traffic was scarce. He noticed people were waiting in a queue for takeout food and drinks, but days of sitting and enjoying food in a restaurant were still to come. Tom parked his car parallel on the street and entered the gray building. He did not need to introduce himself to the receptionist. Even when he was wearing a mask, she recognized him. He headed for the elevator. The offices on the ground floor were open, and he heard phones ring and people chatting. He found his way down to the morgue and walked by several small offices. Tom stopped at a glass door and saw Dr. William Sterling examining a wolf's head. William wore a quarantine suit. Before the pandemic, scrubs were enough. But now, extra caution was a part of life. He held a scalpel in his hand and bent over a black wolf's head on the table. Tom preferred not to watch and turned around. He folded his arms and waited.

When William was done, he stepped out.

"Hi! I didn't think you would drop by," William said.

His friend had changed little. The last time they had met was a few days after their return from Nightridge. William was broken. Not only because so many people had died but also because Joan stepped out of his life. Relationships were hard. As far as Tom knew, she had not returned.

"I thought it would be a good idea. I had a chat with Norris, and he told me they sent the heads to you. Have you found anything?"

"Not much. I have just finished examining the seventh head."

"And?"

"I spoke with a zoologist. According to him, they were around five to six years old and wild. As for their origins, white wolves are rare in these parts of the country. They are native to Canada. It might be possible they could have migrated, or the murderer snatched them from an animal sanctuary."

"We can contact all facilities that keep wolves," Tom said. "Hopefully, we will find out if any of them are missing."

"That's a good idea. The gray wolves, also known as Canis lupus, are found in Northern America and are likely native to counties like Willow's Heart."

"I see," Tom said.

Keeping their distance, they headed for the locker rooms. Tom waited as William changed and sanitized his hands.

"The two gray wolves belonged to the species Alexander Archipelago," said William as he applied a clean face mask.

"Never heard of it."

"Very rare and found in Alaska."

They reached the elevator, and William pushed the button.

"What are they doing down here?" Tom asked.

"I have no idea. The killer could be a breeder."

The elevator door opened, and they stepped in.

"This killer has to be a hunter and someone with knowledge of wildlife," Tom concluded.

"I agree. Edgar's deputies didn't find any fingerprints. There were several footprints around the crosses, but they are not useful."

They left the elevator and to enter William's office.

"What about Gail?" William asked.

Tom scowled. "I have his files… but let us talk about it somewhere else. I want to get out of here."

"Pubs make me uncomfortable," William said.

Tom hung his head.

"There is a place better than any pub…"

Tom felt excited. He wanted to hang out with friends. He had been deprived of company for far too long. But still, he wanted to be sure he wasn't imposing. "Are you sure he won't mind?"

3rd April 2020
Cranston House, New York

Tom steered his old Ford and stopped in front of an iron gate. William rolled down the passenger side window and entered the codes on a panel. The gates opened with a loud clang. Tom parked beside a gray Audi. Stepping out, he admired the vehicle.

"Why does he always get the best toys?" he remarked, winking.

William laughed.

The Cranston house reminded him of old Victorian houses. It was a beautiful white mansion with a well-manicured lawn encircling all four sides. Tall trees provided privacy from the outer world. Tom always felt serene when he came here. He wished he and Jenny could find a place like this to spend their lives together. All they had to do was survive these crazy times. They strolled toward the main door and knocked.

"Does he know we are coming?" Tom asked.

"Yep, I texted him."

"Excellent. So, did you buy a new car?"

During the Shadow Pandemic, William's car was burned down. Tom thought since it had been several months, William would have bought a new one.

"No. No. I haven't."

"I see," Tom replied, not knowing what else to say.

The door opened, and Roumoult welcomed them into his home. "Hey!"

"Hi...how are you?" Tom asked.

"I'm well. Thanks!" Roumoult said.

They didn't shake hands, and hugging was out of the question. The pandemic had made physical contact taboo.

He had expected Roumoult to appear fragile. Show signs of the deadly illness he had tackled. But he looked as sharp as ever. Well dressed, fit, and with no signs of fatigue.

Perhaps the lockdown had forced him to rest and had helped him recover. Tom was glad his friend was feeling better. No one would believe he had COVID-19 and spent a week in the ICU. To make matters worse, when it happened, he and his father were in Canada. Tom had never felt so helpless. His friend was miles away, and he could do nothing to help. It was a horrible week, and he remembered expecting the worst. To everyone's relief, Roumoult recovered. Tom wondered what he would do if he got infected. The thought sent a chill down his spine.

Roumoult led them to the living room. After months of isolation and being under pressure, Tom felt calm. There was something about this house. Perhaps it was the décor. Very fashionable and elegant furniture completed the living room. The air was fresh, and soft music played in the background. A family portrait hung above a fireplace to his right. Roumoult's mother had an extraordinary taste, and it appeared she took pleasure in decorating her home. Unfortunately, she was gone. Tom would have loved to meet her. He often wondered from whom had Roumoult inherited his immense curiosity, cockiness, wit, and blind courage.

"Have a seat. What would you like?" Roumoult asked Tom.

Tom made himself comfortable in the oversized chair and said, "A scotch would be lovely."

Roumoult nodded and turned to William.

"I'll take the same," said William.

The study door opened, and multiple barks caught Tom's attention. "Bob!" he cried out joyfully.

The dog charged toward him. Bob was a wire fox terrier with coffee-colored hair, small ears, and adorable black eyes.

His tail was small and bushy, and he weighed around eight pounds. Bob jumped over Tom and licked his face.

"Woof! Woof!"

"Ah...he missed you," Roumoult said and vanished into the study.

"I missed him too," Tom said, rubbing the dog's ears. "How have you been, buddy? You are gorgeous!"

He barked, bouncing, and hopping around the living room.

"Where are the rest of them?" William called out.

Tom felt a jolt of excitement. "Rest of them?"

Four little pups rushed out of the study and into the living room.

"Oh my god!" Tom cried out.

The pups sniffed him as if making sure he was friendly. Wagging their tails, they pounced over him.

"They are so cute!" Tom said, lifting one of them over his head. "How old are they?"

"Around six weeks," Roumoult replied, re-entering the room with the drinks.

Tom didn't remember feeling so excited or happy. He didn't know which one to play with. They were all adorable. All the pups, except one, hopped off him and rushed toward Roumoult. The last one sat on Tom's lap and licked his paw.

"Are they Bob's?" Tom asked, accepting his glass of scotch.

"Yes," Roumoult said and handed over a drink to William. Bob joined Tom in the chair.

"When did that happen?" Tom asked, patting Bob.

"When Dad and I were stuck in Canada, Charles took Bob

to Grandpa's place. It appeared they made friends with an old lady who also had a fox terrier."

"Really? Oh, you lucky boy!" Tom said to Bob.

William chuckled. The pup stood up and attempted to reach for the drink. "No… no, this isn't for you," Tom said to the pup.

"Maybe you should adopt one," William suggested.

Tom gazed into its adorable eyes.

"Oh…I am not sure," Tom said. "Hey, has anyone heard from Angelus?"

William and Roumoult glanced at each other. The private detective had become an enigma.

"No. He has become a ghost. Three weeks ago, he was working on a high-paying gig. I tried to contact him, but he didn't answer my calls. I guess he is busy," replied Roumoult.

"Right, so the vampire case he was trying to solve hit a dead end," said Tom.

"The trail has been cold for months," replied Roumoult.

"And for the record, I don't think it has anything to do with vampires," William said.

"No! We just like to call it that," joked Roumoult.

Fred Cranston stepped out of the study. Roumoult's father was as tall as his son. He remained cheerful, and his bright blue eyes twinkled even in these dreadful times. Two pups bounced toward him.

Tom smiled and got on his feet.

"How are you doing, Detective?" Fred said.

"Quite well. Yourself?"

"I am well, thanks," Fred said and turned to William. "It's good to see you again."

"Good to be here," William replied.

Fred joined the group, and the conversations shifted to politics and the global pandemic.

After finishing their drinks, Roumoult invited them to the dining table, where a spread of steaming dishes awaited them. Tom had forgotten the taste of home-cooked meals. He enjoyed every bit of the roasted chicken. Being around people he admired was great. They had animated conversations and told each other stories about work and life. Once dinner ended, they returned to the cozy living room with their drinks. Bob sat on Roumoult's lap. The pups slept together in the basket, looking like a ball of fur.

Tom enjoyed his drink.

"So, severed wolf heads," Roumoult said, smiling.

Tom eyed William. "You told him."

"I tell him everything," he answered.

"And somehow it's linked to you," Roumoult remarked.

"Yes. Gail Clegg. It's interesting, William, that you found traces of his blood on a wolf. It has been years since I have thought about him," Tom said.

"Trust me, I was not expecting human blood," William answered.

"What can you tell us?" Roumoult asked.

"You never forget the first time you pulled the trigger," Tom replied. "It doesn't matter how much you train. You are never ready, and no one can prepare you. No one." He paused, then continued, "It was about two years after I finished the academy. I had never drawn my gun, didn't need to. I had used the taser a few times. It was just another day. I was patrolling Brunswick Avenue in East Williamsburg. I heard gunshots, and I rushed to the scene to find Kain Botkin bleeding to death."

"Did you know him?" Roumoult asked.

"I had never met the man. We were not from the same precinct. I called the ambulance and radioed headquarters. Then I heard a woman scream. Expecting the worst, I rushed down the street and spotted a man running with a gun in his hand."

Tom sipped his drink and took a deep breath.

"I ran after him. The suspect entered a building which turned out to be an orphanage."

Roumoult held his head.

"I followed the screams and shouts, and finally I reached the hall on the first floor. A woman was shielding several African American children. She was begging Gail to stop and to let the children go. I had to act and stood in between him and the group of children. He was holding a gun on a little girl's head." Tears gathered in Tom's eyes as he still felt the pain in his chest. Roumoult leaned forward and waited for him to continue. "I tried to reason with him. But he kept screaming about his destiny. He claimed it was God's way. It was what he was made for. He kept justifying why he had to take a child's life. It would free him from sins because the child's blood was pure. She had to be sacrificed so that he could be a free man."

William huffed, and his face reddened. "Bastard."

"The little girl shivered, sobbing, pleaded with me for help. I had a clear shot, but at the academy, they taught us to give the perpetrator a warning. I tried to talk with him, but it was useless. Gail was about to pull the trigger when I shot him."

Bob's ears were erect, as if he understood every word Tom said.

"So, he died," William concluded.

"No. Gail collapsed. I kicked away the weapon and rushed to the girl. Once she was safe, I checked Gail's pulse. He was alive. A part of me wanted to let him die. But that would be too easy. I thought he should face the consequences of his actions." He paused, sighing. "I called an ambulance. He was rushed to the hospital. The doctors did their best, but he died within a few hours. Trust me. No one misses that lunatic."

"But why did he attack Kain?" asked Roumoult.

"Gail Clegg was a suspect in ritualistic child murders. Two weeks before the shooting, three children were kidnapped. They found their bodies in a basement of an abandoned building. The forensic scientist unearthed a black powder, which led them to several suspects, including Gail. The cops suspected him because of his unstable condition, and he had no alibi."

"What condition?" Roumoult asked.

"His doctor diagnosed him with psychosis. Gail had a history of fits, hallucinations, and violence. The doctor's notes showed Gail had difficulty accepting reality and believed he was better than others. He deeply believed in spirituality and often said he could hear God."

"Oh, that is just great," Roumoult muttered.

"He was on antipsychotic drugs for years and was hospitalized many times. According to his doctor, he was stable for many years on medicine, until those three kids were murdered."

A pup yawned, stretched, and hopped out of the basket. It

walked haphazardly toward Tom. The detective lifted the puppy and placed it on his lap. The puppy yawned again, made himself comfortable, and closed his eyes.

"Have you thought about keeping a pet?" Roumoult asked.

"Ah…I'm not sure."

"Maybe you could adopt one," said Roumoult, winking toward William.

"Don't tell me you are giving them away?" Tom asked.

Roumoult spread his hands. "I can barely take care of Bob, and you know Dad, he doesn't like dogs."

William laughed.

"Wrong!" Fred yelled and stepped out of the study.

Tom tried not to laugh.

"Dad, we can't have so many dogs running around the house," Roumoult said.

Fred stood with his hands on his waist. "Well, since I don't have any grandchildren, no thanks to you, I have to settle for dogs!"

William chuckled, and Tom joined him.

"Oh, thanks, Dad!"

"You and Emma better get married soon…"

Roumoult sulked. Emma Myers was his current girl-friend, and it had been an utter surprise to everyone that their relationship had lasted. Fred's face turned soft, and his eyes fell to the floor. William and Tom stayed silent, knowing there was no use adding fuel to the fire. Roumoult was head-strong and wouldn't listen to anyone except his heart. Knowing his words would have no more impact, Fred left the room.

"Okay," William said, "about the case. What do we do?"

"You are absolutely sure the blood belongs to Gail Clegg?" asked Roumoult.

"Without a doubt," William said.

"That puzzles me. The doctors said he died. How could he be alive?" said Tom.

"Maybe the reports were doctored," Roumoult suggested.

7

HIT AND RUN

17th April 2020 (Present Day)
Willow's Heart

Norris was shaking. The hunter and his wolf would not give up. The engine started with a loud groan, and the truck shook. The wolf charged at the door again.

"Come on," he muttered, changing gears.

The wolf howled, and he floored the accelerator. The tires screeched. Swinging the steering wheel, Norris gained control as the truck skidded sideways. The wolf lurched behind the vehicle. Out of nowhere, the figure reappeared and flung a sword. Norris ducked. It hit the windshield and bounced over the roof, leaving an enormous crack. Perspiration trickled down his neck. Norris increased speed, and the vehicle raced ahead, disappearing into the fog.

After several minutes, Norris slowed and glanced behind. No one was following him, and for now, he was safe. He eased the pedal, and the truck came to a stop on the road-side. The pain in his knee returned, and he clutched it with his hand. Blood flowed out of the wound and soaked his torn clothes. He waited, but the ache did not subside. Leaning forward, Norris frantically searched the glove compartment. It was full of documents, and he didn't have any painkillers.

"Damn," he muttered.

Ignoring his pain, he picked up the radio and turned up the volume.

"Hello? Is anyone there?"

All he heard was static. He tried another frequency. Again, there was no reply.

"Damn it!"

He had no other means of contacting the outside world but had to find a way. He could not handle the Shadow Fraction by himself. Taking a deep breath, he wondered what to do next. Suddenly, an idea occurred to him. He restarted the truck and drove into the night.

17th April 2020 (Present Day)
Fortress, Willow's Heart

Tom shook with fear in the terrifying dungeon. The light fell from the roof, and a ladder slid down. A tall, vague figure slowly came down the ladder. In the dim light, he saw Kyle Torres near his feet. His hands and feet were tied.

"Kyle… are you okay?"

"No, I am not," he muttered, watching the dark figure approaching them.

Tom quickly assessed his surroundings. It was an underground cave. Water dripped from the soiled walls. He gasped when he saw two human skulls not too far away from him. A group of rats gnawed at the human hand. He wanted to move away, but he didn't want to show any weakness. Tom wished he could shield Kyle. He was young, innocent, and had a family. But what could Tom do? He was a prisoner himself. The man approaching them did not look like someone who would listen to reason. A gigantic shadow fell on him, blocking the source of light. The hefty, tall man glared at them through his wolf's mask with curved, long horns. Tom gulped. He couldn't predict what would happen next. The shadowy man grabbed Kyle's leg and began dragging him away.

"No. No!" Tom shouted, scuffling to save his friend.

Kyle cried out, flinging his arms as he tried to free himself. "Let me go! Let me go!" he shouted.

The hunter shoved the deputy against the wall.

"Let him go!" Tom shouted.

His words fell on deaf ears. The hunter tied the deputy's hands and punched him in his face. Kyle winched. The hunter stepped away, letting go of his prey, and a wave of relief rushed through Tom. Maybe they would survive this. The hunter gazed at him, as if recognizing him. Tom wondered; did he know him? Perhaps it was someone he had put away? Maybe it was Gail Clegg. He would worry about Gail later. Right now, they had to get out of here. The hunter turned, climbed up the ladder, and shut the trapdoor. Darkness loomed again. The foul smell made the air unbreathable. It reminded him of the open sewers of New York. Tom closed his eyes, and he could hear the screeching of the rats and the dripping of water. Fear gripped him. Rats were relentless—what if he was next? All the hunters needed to do was leave him half dead in this filthy place. He broke into a cold sweat. "We have to get out of here," he muttered.

8

THE UNFORGIVING DEAD

6th April 2020
Meadow Cottage, Nightridge

Norris sat on the porch drinking coffee. He thought about the wolves on the crosses. As if finding human blood wasn't intriguing enough, the blood belonged to a dead man. Edgar was as surprised as him.

Three days had passed, and he hadn't heard from William. It meant only one thing—there was nothing to report, at least not yet. He wondered about the origin of the wolves and assumed they were from the valley. It was a playground for wild animals. But capturing wolves and decapitating them was hard. Maybe these people were hunters. He frowned. He needed more information, and for now, things were moving too slowly.

Nightridge was silent, and the wind was colder than yesterday. He enjoyed the sunshine and wondered when he would get the time to paint the fence. The phone buzzed in his pocket. Kyle was calling him. He was the youngest of all the deputies who worked with Norris.

"Morning, Kyle," he said, wondering why he was calling.

"Morning, Chief."

"I should be at the office within an hour," he stated, sipping his coffee.

"That is not why I called," said Kyle.

Something in his voice alarmed Norris. His thoughts turned to the people of Nightridge. "Oh, what happened?" he asked, gripping his cup of coffee.

"Sheriff Edgar Thobe called."

"What does he want?" he asked, relaxing a bit.

"He was trying to get in touch with you."

"Why?"

The line went silent.

"What? What happened, Kyle?"

Kyle cleared his throat. "Edgar didn't tell me much. But he wants you to return to Willow's Heart."

6th April 2020
Willow's Heart

It was past midday when Norris exited Route 9. He drove past the village and took a road toward the heart of the valley. The narrow road was full of potholes. Kyle grabbed the dashboard as the truck jolted. Norris flashed a smile toward the deputy. Norris liked his company and thought it would be good to bring him along. Intelligent and dependable, Kyle had surpassed all his expectations. Born in Nightridge, Kyle lived with his wife and son in a house built by his father. Kyle's parents had passed away a decade ago.

His features were not remarkable. An average-sized young man with black hair, small brown eyes, and a friendly face. Even-tempered, the man hardly argued or got into fights. Given his disposition and appearance, no one would believe Kyle was a cop.

In a few minutes, they reached their destination. Norris leaned on his vehicle, adjusted his hat to shield his face from the sun shining just above his head.

"Are you sure this is the spot?" he asked Kyle.

"Yes, Chief," Kyle said, putting on his mask.

Norris reluctantly did the same.

Dust flew in every direction. They stood in front of a barn surrounded by vast fields on both sides. Just beyond the field, he spotted an old house. Norris noticed the mountains and thick forest that hemmed them in.

Edgar left the barn, looking gloomy. "Ah... Norris, you are here," he said.

"Hello again, Edgar. What happened?"

"Nasty business..."

"Another wolf?"

Edgar's face turned white. "If only."

Norris felt a lump in his throat and followed Edgar inside. The barn was full of haystacks and smelled of manure mixed with an intense metallic odor. It occurred to Norris what it was—blood. The CSI unit was taking pictures. He peered over the two men. Cold fear gripped him.

"Oh, my god."

Between the bundles of hay sat a butchered, headless body. Norris covered his mouth with his hand, and his eyes met Edgar's.

They waited for the forensic unit to finish taking pictures.

When they completed their work, Norris took a step forward and noted the legs and hands of the victim bore several bite marks. He kneeled and observed the body. He assumed the man was around five feet, six inches tall and a hundred and eighty pounds. The cause of death was clear. He noticed the base of the neck. The spine was clearly visible within layers of thick muscle. Norris gulped.

"Rats," said Norris as he stared at the multiple small puncture wounds on the victim's legs.

"You think rats did this to him?" asked Edgar.

"It appears the killer fed him to rats, and then he chopped off his head."

Norris continued observing. "What about this?" he asked, pointing toward a massive bite mark on his left leg visible through the torn pants.

"A dog...maybe."

"Or a wolf," suggested Norris.

Edgar nodded.

"Have you found the head of the victim?" Norris said.

"No. We are looking for it."

"Anything to identify him?"

"There was no wallet. We have taken his fingerprints. He might be in the system."

Norris nodded, standing straight. Leaving the body behind, he followed Edgar outside of the barn.

"Who discovered the body?" Norris asked.

"Eddie Warner. It's his farm," Edgar replied, pointing at a man sitting on the ground with his head in his hands.

"When?"

"About two hours ago."

Norris neared Eddie and sat beside him on the ground. "I am so sorry," he said, dusting his hands.

"It's horrible! Horrible!" Eddie yelled.

"Have you seen this man before?" Norris asked.

"Didn't you notice! He… he has no head! Oh geez! This is crazy. There is a madman out there!"

"Let's not get ahead of ourselves," said Norris calmly. "When did you last enter the barn?"

"Ah… three… four days ago. Look, I rarely go in there."

"Is it locked?"

"No! No one steals anything in this village."

Norris nodded.

"Have you seen any strangers?" Edgar asked.

Eddie gave it a thought and shook his head.

"Does anyone else live around here?" Norris asked.

"There are several houses in this valley. Jacob is the nearest to me. His farm is ten miles down the road," replied Eddie.

Norris turned to Edgar.

"The victim is not Jacob. He is in his early sixties and weighs around two-hundred pounds," Edgar replied.

"This is not right. Not right. Oh my god! What am I going to do?" cried out Eddie.

"Stay calm," said Edgar.

"Easy for you to say!" shouted Eddie, getting on his feet. "Just get him out of my barn!"

"It's a crime scene. You shouldn't enter the barn until we finish our investigation," Norris said.

"What? That's ridiculous!"

"Eddie, it's okay. We will take care of it," said Edgar.

Eddie cursed under his breath and left.

Sulking, Norris stood up and dusted his hands.

"Do you think this has something to do with the heads?" Edgar asked.

"A couple of days ago, we found wolf heads on crosses, and now we find a headless man half-eaten by rats. This is not a coincidence."

Edgar appeared uncomfortable.

"I think we should arrange a small team of officers to search for the victim's head."

Edgar looked at his three deputies standing near the gates. "I don't have the manpower."

"I can assign two of my deputies," Norris said, peering at Kyle, who nodded his head in agreement. "And I think we should send the body to Dr. Sterling."

Edgar eyed him. "Why?"

"This is something more than just a headless body."

It was late afternoon when a search party of six police officers marched in different directions from the barn. Norris couldn't stay long and returned to Nightridge. He left Kyle in charge.

6th April 2020
St Mary's Hospital, New York

After his dinner at the Cranston house, Tom couldn't shake the feeling he might have missed something about Gail's case. The next day, he paired up with his partner, John White, and drove to the hospital where Gail was admitted after getting shot.

As Tom parked the car on the street, John yawned. He was a skinny man with dark brown eyes and rough black hair. John was a silent man, hardly noticeable. Tom often wondered if he spoke with anyone else at the precinct except him. He was so content that it appeared he needed no one else. John wasn't married, never had a girlfriend—not that Tom knew any about his relationships. He had considered if his partner was gay, but something told him he wasn't. John was born and bred in the Bronx. His father was a librarian, and his mother a teacher. He had a brother who he never spoke about. All Tom knew was that John's brother ran a shop in Lower Manhattan.

Tom had received the box containing all the files on Gail Clegg, but his medical file was missing. Tom stepped out and waited on the roadside. John stood beside him, sipping coffee from his tumbler. They entered the hospital, which was ten times busier than usual. They had to wait in the queue for over thirty minutes. Finally, when it was his turn, Tom approached the receptionist and explained that he needed a medical report.

"This happened twelve years ago?" said the receptionist, an elderly overweight woman with thick curly hair.

"Yes. It was a shooting. Technically, the hospital should keep a record," said Tom.

John remained silent.

"Yes, and technically, they send a report to the police as well. I think you would find it's an exact copy," she replied.

"It's missing. I need another copy."

The receptionist got to work. As Tom waited, he examined the hospital, realizing it had changed a bit over the decade. They had renovated the reception area with abstract paintings, new comfortable chairs, and door frames. But more or less, it was the same.

Half an hour later, the receptionist returned with the medical records. "Here you go."

Tom reviewed the file, and something caught his attention. He leaned over and asked, "Does Dr. Pete Coleman still work here?"

She shook her head.

"Do you have a phone number or a forwarding address?"

"Sure."

"What about the nurse, Mrs. Ella Morgan?"

"What about her?"

"Do you have her contact details?"

"Well, what a surprise," she muttered and began typing.

6th April 2020
Brooklyn

Tom reread the address in his notebook and then glanced at the ten-story building. They were in the right spot. It was late, and he wondered if Dr. Coleman was at home. Climbing a few steps, they entered the building and took the lift to the ninth floor. The elevator shuddered to a stop, and they stepped out. The corridors were wide, painted cream with white circular ceiling lights. He knocked on the door labeled 4B. As he waited, he sanitized his hands and adjusted his mask. An old man wearing a face shield and thick glasses opened the door.

"Yes?"

"Dr. Pete Coleman?"

"Yes," Dr. Coleman replied, taking a step back.

They flashed their badges. Tom placed the man in his late sixties. The doctor looked ill, skinny and wore a loose white

T-shirt and oversized gray pajamas. He noticed his left hand shook slightly.

"Evening, Detectives. I am sorry, I don't think we should shake hands. Please don't mind."

"We understand," Tom replied. "It will take only a few minutes. Do you remember a man you treated by the name of Mr. Gail Clegg?"

Dr. Coleman's face turned thoughtful.

"It was over a decade ago. The paramedics brought him to the St. Mary's Hospital with a gunshot wound to his chest."

"A shooting? There are so many of them. You can't expect me to remember them all."

Tom nodded, showed him a picture of Gail, and handed him over the copy of the medical file. The doctor studied the report.

"Oh, I remember." Dr. Coleman's face turned solemn.

Tom felt better. "What can you tell me about him?"

"Nothing much. I didn't know him personally. He was brought into the emergency room, and I pulled out the bullet and did an emergency procedure to stop the blood from entering his lung. Unfortunately, I had to attend to another emergency. As soon as his vitals were stable, the nurses took over, and I attended to the next patient. But before I finished for the day, I heard he was gone."

"Did you see his dead body?" asked John.

"Of course, I signed the death certificate."

Then how did Gail's blood get on the wolf's head?

"Are you sure he died?" Tom asked.

Drawing a breath, Dr. Coleman said, "Detective, I am not in the habit of lying!"

Tom raised his hand. "I am just following a lead. What about the nurse? Ella Morgan?"

Dr. Coleman referred to the file. "Of course, I knew Ella. We worked together for many years," he replied, returning the file to Tom.

"And she was present during the surgery?" he asked.

"Yes. She was."

"Are you in touch with her?"

"No. Not really."

Tom smiled, thanked the doctor, and left.

It was late in the evening, and Brooklyn was busy. People swarmed the streets, some wearing masks and keeping their distance, while others simply did not care. Several homeless people queued up on the walkway, waiting to get a bed for the night. Since their next destination was not far away, Tom and John elected to walk down the road. They entered a tall, old building and climbed several steps to reach the sixth floor. Breathless, Tom knocked on flat number 10C and waited. A young woman in her twenties opened the door. They showed her their NYPD badges and stayed out of the apartment. It seemed the lady preferred it.

"I am Detective Tom Nash, and this is Detective John White. We are looking for Mrs. Ella Morgan."

"Ella, she…she is gone."

"Gone? You mean dead?" Tom inquired, feeling weary.

"No. I am sorry. Let me clarify. She moved a long time ago."

"Where?" John asked.

"Florida. She wished to retire."

"Retire?" Tom asked, knowing Ella was thirty-eight years old.

The young lady just shrugged her shoulders.

"May I ask who you are? How are you related to Mrs. Morgan?" Tom asked.

"I am her niece, Janice."

Tom referred to his notes. "According to her file, Ella had a daughter."

"Oh yes. My cousin Helen. She is… gone."

Tom waited for her to tell him more. But when she remained silent, he said, "Gone? Did she move with her mother?"

Janice's eyes lowered. Her demeanor changed. "No. She committed suicide," she replied sadly.

The detectives exchanged worried glances.

"I-I am so sorry. We were not aware. Do you know why?" Tom inquired.

"No. It just happened. We didn't think she would kill herself. It was dreadful. Just dreadful," Janice replied, crossing her arms and looking away from the men.

"When did it happen?" John inquired in a soft tone.

"About eleven years ago."

That was before Tom had shot Gail in the orphanage.

"Why did Helen take her life?" John asked.

Janice's face turned solemn. "I don't know. And I don't want to talk about it."

"Was there a police inquiry?" said John.

"I don't believe so… she hung herself…"

Tom felt a knot in his stomach. They thanked Janice and walked down the corridor. Tom came down the stairs, and he wondered about Ella. Losing a daughter would be devastating. She had no other family except a niece with whom it appeared she hardly communicated. Perhaps the daughter's death was too much and persuaded Ella to move.

6th April 2020
Sheriff's Office, Nightridge

Norris returned to his office and spent hours working. Paperwork was a nightmare. It felt like he was an administrator rather than a sheriff. Although he had Mrs. Flores, there was not much he could delegate. He thought about his visit to the neighboring county. A crime in Willow's Heart. Perhaps the first in many years. The truth was, a decapitated body was not something he had dealt with often.

As the day wound down to night, Norris picked up the phone and called Kyle. The young deputy sounded tired.

"How did it go?" he asked.

"Not good. We found nothing! No trails or footprints to lead us to the murderer. Neville's head has vanished into thin air."

"What about the barn?"

"Except the victim's blood and some black powder, it's clean. Chief, I have a bad feeling about this."

"Me too. Are you heading home?"

"I am already on my way."

"See you tomorrow."

Norris closed the door behind him and hopped in his truck. He drove home and then took a shower. As he dried his hair, he heard the phone ring. He glanced at the display and smiled.

"Good evening, William," he said, answering the video call.

"Evening. I received the unidentified body from Willow's Heart."

William's office was dimly lit, and the doctor rubbed his eyes as he stacked files on the corner of the desk.

"I thought it would be best for you to have a look," Norris said.

William nodded, stretching. "I can try to do the autopsy tomorrow."

"No problem," Norris said, opening the fridge and looking for leftovers.

"By the way, I have identified the victim."

Norris straightened, "Already?"

"He is in the system," William replied.

He looked blankly inside the fridge. "Who is it?"

"Neville Easton."

Norris struggled to remember if he knew the man.

"He was a thirty-six-year-old man, Caucasian who worked in a bar and as a janitor. He was born in the Bronx, his parents passed away ten years ago, and he married Claire Easton and has a son. They now lived in Queens."

Norris shut the fridge door and looked at his feet. "What was he doing down here?"

"Beats me."

Staring into the camera, he asked, "Why is he in the system?"

William bowed his head. "He was one of the primary suspects in a sexual assault case three years ago."

Norris felt his stomach twist. "Who was the victim?"

William referred to his computer screen. "Ms. Angela Vince claimed Neville raped her on June seventeenth, two-thousand-seventeen."

Norris bit his lips. "What happened?"

"He was acquitted."

"Why?"

"Neville had an alibi when the crime was being committed, and there was no additional tangible evidence to prove he had hurt her."

"Did they ever catch the real culprit?"

"No. It's a cold case."

"Do you have the victim's contact details?" Norris asked.

William studied his face. "What are you thinking?"

"If this man got away with rape, someone might look for redemption," said Norris.

9

NIGHT DRIVE

17ᵗʰ April 2020 (Present Day)
Willow's Heart

Norris had a tough time focusing on driving. Exhaustion was slowing him down, and he felt like he would lose consciousness. The pain in his knee intensified by the minute. Running out of options, he reduced speed and parked the truck on the side of the road. He rested his head on the steering wheel and tried to relax.

You can do it. Stay awake.

The silence was comforting. Norris's shoulders slumped, and he exhaled. With a heavy heart, he restarted the truck. If he remembered correctly, there was a house five miles west of his position. But he knew it was the first place the hunters would search for him. To elude them, he drove east.

The road was rocky, and the vehicle shook and bounced. The valley was full of rough pathways interconnected with each other. He was hoping he could use them to get to his destination undetected. The radio was still not working.

Perspiring, he assessed both sides. The drive through the valley in the gloominess was terrifying. The hunters could be anywhere. He turned off the headlights and reduced the speed. But he could not silence the engine. The roars of the motor echoed, and he wished he had a quieter vehicle. Despite feeling fatigued, he noticed movement in the bushes to his left. He immediately slammed on the brakes. The truck skidded to a stop. A deer jumped out of the bushes and galloped across the rough road. Norris pouted, rubbing his tired eyes. He changed gears and kept driving.

After at least an hour, Norris arrived at his destination. He parked his truck in a corner and stared at the enormous house with a sloping roof and rectangular wooden-framed windows. A barn was on one side of the house, and a huge stable stood on the other. There was no gate. A simple wire fence marked the boundaries.

He bit his lip and wondered if it was a trap. Most old houses in the valley were abandoned. But the hunters could hide in them, waiting for him. It was their domain. But he had to take a chance. Norris put the truck in first gear and cautiously drove into the stables, ensuring his vehicle was out of sight. As soon as the engine died off, he heard the horse's bray.

With his hand on his injured leg, he stepped out and limped toward the exit. A small outdoor pinned area held a slew of snorting pigs. The animals rushed to a corner at the sight of him. Norris ducked, hiding behind a stack of hay. He had to make sure no one was following him. The mist masked the vast mountains which surrounded the valley. The fog descended downwards, and he watched as the road vanished.

Satisfied they did not follow him; Norris made his way to the empty house. Making sure he was alone, he hurried to a window and peered in. There was no one. One by one, he started checking the other windows. The pain in his leg escalated as he tried the last window facing the backyard. It budged and slid open with ease.

He entered the shadowy house and shut the window behind him. His eyes soon adjusted to the interior. He crossed the living room, avoiding the edges of the furniture, which resembled dark shadows.

The house was cold, dark, and unwelcoming. It was neglected, and the torn carpet and cracked walls told him a sad story. Walking through a narrow corridor, he found himself in the kitchen. He spun around and noticed a door to his left leading to a neat compact bedroom. There was someone living here. But who? He hoped he wouldn't show up. On returning to the corridor, he found the door to the master bedroom. The bed was undisturbed. He was glad no one was home and hobbled to the bathroom to open the cabinet above the washbasin.

In the moonlight that crept through the windows, he read the label on the white bottle and popped two pills of naproxen. Placing the painkiller bottle in his pocket, Norris returned to the kitchen and searched all the drawers and cabinets. Most of them were empty. He stopped when he found a bottle of vodka. Norris found some bandages, a suturing kit, and a Betadine bottle.

By the time he came to the living room, the pain was unbearable. Sitting on the couch, he tore the pants around his knee to expose the wound. After thoroughly washing the multiple cuts with vodka, he began. The war had taught him many things, including sewing wounds. This night reminded him of the day he was shot in the arm. Medical help was far away. His comrade had removed the bullet, but Norris had to stitch the wound himself because it was so painful. Tonight, he had to repeat the process.

It was agonizing and slow. His hands trembled as he pushed the needle into his skin. It took five stitches to stop the bleeding. When it was done, he covered the wound with a bandage. He got up, walked to the bathroom, and washed his hands and face. He returned to the couch and drank from the bottle, waiting for the medicine to act.

The house was silent, and he felt safe. Norris knew he could rest here. At least, for the time being.

As soon as he felt like it, he headed for the kitchen. In a drawer filled with cutlery, he spotted a knife, and after digging further, he located a flashlight. One by one, he checked every room. Minimum rations and wine were stored in boxes. Women's clothes in the closet were neatly folded. He found a dead landline but no computer.

"Damn," he muttered.

He rubbed his temples and wondered how to get help. He glanced at the time. It was almost 11.00 pm.

I am running out of time. If I don't get help, they will kill them.

The thought of Kyle and Tom being prisoners filled him with dread. If he did not get help, his friends would meet the same fate as others. He thought about his options. Fatigue was his enemy, and he had to stay awake. He could always drive to Nightridge. But would he make it? The hunters were guarding the two main exits. He had to do something unexpected.

17th April 2020 (Present Day)
Willow's Heart, Fortress

The dungeon was getting colder. The rats sculled on the muddy ground, knowing a feast soon awaited them. Tom did not want to die here. The life of a detective had been hard, and he considered himself lucky. But perhaps today, his luck had run out. He heard the rats feeding on the dead woman's hand. Maybe he would be next. Norris might have escaped, and Tom hoped he could find help.

"How are you holding up?" he asked Kyle.

Kyle had removed his duct tape. "I am scared to death. They are killers…insane! What is going to happen to us?"

"Something tells me we will find out soon."

Kyle's chains clanged as he attempted to move.

"Do you know what the time is?" Tom asked.

"Gosh, the last time I looked at the watch, it was around eight o'clock."

"How many times have they come to check on us?"

"Only once, I think," Kyle replied.

Tom gave it a thought. The hunters did not think it was necessary for them to monitor the prisoners all the time. They probably thought there was no way out of here.

"What do you remember?" he asked.

"The hall…" Kyle said gravely.

Tom's heart sank. "Yes, I remember it as well."

There was no use wondering. They had to figure out a way to escape. Tom yanked his hands under his thighs. He felt the metallic cuffs underneath him. After several attempts, he successfully bent forward, and his legs easily passed through. He let out a relieved breath.

"What are you doing?" Kyle whispered.

"Trying to get us out of here."

"Do you have a plan?"

Tom thought about the times he had been captured, attacked, and ended up in the hospital. He had learned to be prepared. The hunters had taken their phones, keys, and wallets, but they would not have checked everywhere. He touched his shoes, and a smile spread across his face.

10

EXPERIMENTS

6th April 2020
Withering Heights Apartments, New York

Wiliam's apartment building, once stylish, had lost all its luster. Grime had gathered on the bricks, layers of dust covered its windows, and the corridors were dim because of the broken lights. The building's super was uncaring, and the tenants didn't bother to complain anymore. William didn't mind. He didn't like buildings that glittered in daylight and were awkwardly shaped. For him, the buildings that stood years after their builders were gone were priceless and formed an integral part of the city. But things never remained the same. Change was inevitable.

William was alone in his two-bedroom apartment. He watched the city from his living room window. A strong cup of coffee helped. It was early in the morning, and he needed to feel as awake as possible. There was a lot of work to be done.

William felt he had let himself slip. Just last year, he had been fit, exercising, and having the time of his life. In the last few months, he had been eating out—mostly deep-fried food. The weight gain was not helping his morale or his health. But food was like therapy and the only thing he seemed to enjoy these days. In the bathroom he gaped at his own reflection. His hair was long and unevenly cut. His French beard was losing shape. He flung open his closet. The closet contained a set of white shirts and black trousers. He got dressed and looked at himself. He had been wearing this attire for the last three months. It had become a uniform, and it surprised him that no one had noticed.

William was struggling to keep his head above water. The battle to keep the fear at bay, the fight to stay alive and remain positive in the growing darkness, was hard. The pandemic was not only killing people, but it was also eating away the souls of the living. But for him, it was worse. The one woman he had truly loved had left him, and he was the problem. She did not give up on them; he did. He thought he was done with the relationship, but he was wrong.

"It could be the lockdown," he muttered.

But deep down, he knew it was a lie. He returned to the living room and began wearing his shoes. He continued to think about Joan. The lockdown had brought them closer and tore them apart. Unfortunately, after the breakup, neither of them had reached out. He had hoped Joan would return, if only to fight or argue with him. That hadn't happened. Was he to say sorry? Call her back? It was harder because he was the one who had pushed her away.

He stood up and picked up his backpack from where he had left it last night. Locking the door behind him, he strolled to the elevator with his head bowed. He didn't know what to do, and his friends told him he had made a grave mistake. All couples fight, and they must find common ground to work out their differences. Nothing was perfect.

6th April 2020
NYPD Precinct

Tom sat in front of the computer, going through Gail Clegg's file. The first man he had shot. The man he had thought was dead. There was no record of a family, and Tom had followed up with his close contacts. They confirmed he was dead. Gail was cremated, and his wife had dispersed his ashes in the river. Mrs. Clegg had lived a quiet life for the last decade. He couldn't find anything on her. Tom bit his lips. The information was inadequate. They had called all the animal sanctuaries and zoos in New York, and none of the wolves were missing. His inquiries about people who breed or could train wolves were in vain.

The door opened, and John White entered the office.

"Hey!"

"Hi, how are you doing?" Tom asked.

"I am well." John took a seat on the other side of the office.

"Any luck with finding Mrs. Morgan?"

John ran his hands over his face. "Not yet. The address she gave to the hospital and her niece was correct, but she left a long time ago."

"Oh, why?"

"I haven't got the slightest idea," John replied, raising his hands.

Tom sat back. "Okay. I have contacted Norris and asked him to find out if anyone in Nightridge or Willow's Heart has experience dealing with animals."

"That's a good idea. Are there any animal reserves around those counties?"

"Only one. I called the reserve, and the administrator reported that they have a dozen wolves in their care, and they are safe and sound."

"I wonder, aren't these animals registered? Can someone just slaughter a wolf?" John said.

"Unfortunately, people do," Tom replied, shaking his head. "There are hunters, collectors, and traders who capture and kill innocent animals for pleasure or decoration."

"I hate that."

"That's the world we live in."

John leaned forward. "He mounted the wolf heads on the crosses for the police to find...what does that tell you?"

"He's a showoff," Tom said.

"Exactly," John said, smiling. "He could have hidden those heads anywhere, but he didn't. We should ask another question. What else is happening in Willow's Heart?"

6th April 2020
Sheriff's Office, Nightridge

The sheriff's office was silent. Most of the deputies were in Willow's Heart, searching the territory. The last time Kyle had reported in, he sounded frustrated. The search party had acquired three police dogs who had not picked up the scent of the body. Norris was afraid they might have lost the trail.

He sipped his coffee while Mrs. Flores read a case file.

They were rechecking to see if the paperwork for last year's cases was complete. Another bureaucratic task. He signed at the bottom of the report, closed the file, and then placed it over the stack.

The phone rang, interrupting them. Norris pushed the green button, and William's face appeared on the screen.

"Hello there," Norris said, picking up the next file.

"Hey, Mrs. Flores, how are you?"

"I am well, thanks!" she replied.

William smiled. "I thought I should give an update on the case."

"May I say something? I think you two should stay out of this," interrupted Mrs. Flores.

The men looked amused.

"Ah… we are invested," said Norris to Mrs. Flores. He leaned closer to his phone screen. "You have something for me?"

"Yes. As you know, the heads were cut off clean. We found several traces of rat hair and droppings. Rats probably ate the flesh on the legs and hands, but the bite mark on his left leg was definitely from a wolf."

"Okay, did you find anything else? A fingerprint, a human hair, footprint, anything that leads to the killer?" Norris asked.

"Not yet," William answered. "The zoologist traced the origin of the rats. According to him, it's the Norway rat, AKA Rattus norvegicus, also known as brown rats. They are very common in North America."

"That doesn't give us much."

"No. Any luck tracing the wolves?"

"Not yet," Norris replied.

Both men were quiet for a moment.

"I'll keep you updated," said William.

"Sure. Thanks for the call."

Norris felt a bit disappointed. He half-heartedly completed his paperwork. He remembered Tom's message. They had to investigate what else was happening in Willow's heart. He couldn't go there himself without drawing attention. But perhaps someone else was more qualified for this job. They heard a loud noise of an engine. He peered out of the window to see Kyle bang the door shut. He shoved his hands into his pockets and kicked a stone off the pavement.

"Kyle! Would you come in here?" he called.

Kyle became alert. "Coming, Chief..."

He stepped into the office.

"How did it go?"

Kyle scoffed. "We wasted three days... found nothing," he complained, removing his hat.

"Don't worry. What about the others?"

"Ah... they were exhausted, so I sent them home."

Norris did not mind. "I have a job for you."

"But we still need to find Neville's head."

"Let the others do that. I need you to follow another lead."

The deputy flipped open his notebook and stood ready with a pen.

"I need to know what else is happening in Willow's Heart."

"Like what?"

"I think you will know when you see it,"

Kyle raised his eyebrows, grinned, and left.

. . .

Mrs. Flores left the office. He got himself a cup of coffee. Norris studied the map of Willow's Heart. The county appeared an interesting place to visit, but he had never set foot on the land. It reminded him of the first time he had come to Nightridge. After he was done with the military, they were looking for a better place to bring up their family. He would not have considered living here, but Martha fell in love with the village. While she searched for a house, he found an opening in the local sheriff's department. His military training came in handy, and he got a job as a sergeant. He moved to Nightridge with his family. He smiled as he reflected on his past. Their children grew up and relocated to the city for further studies. Soon after, he became the sheriff. He refocused on the map and noticed the fortress surrounded by thick forest. They had been looking for Neville's head, and he knew the fortress had not been checked. Not wanting to stay in the office, he decided to check it out. He grabbed his phone to call Edgar, but decided against it. Norris stood up and armed himself. His eyes became fixed on a photo. It was a picture of him with his wife on their thirtieth wedding anniversary. Norris ran his fingers over Martha's face, realizing how grateful he was to have her in his life.

Norris drove for at least over an hour. The route was rough, narrow, and surrounded on both sides by tall trees and thick vegetation. There were no streetlights, and the truck left a trail of dust behind it. His feet lifted from the accelerator as the road widened. To his left, he noticed another rough road leading to the fortress. He slowed the truck and eased it to a stop. Norris left the truck behind and marched towards the fortress.

It was unique. This kind of building was rare in this region. The short information on the map revealed the natives had built it in the 1900s. The four rounded pillars supported the thick wall made up of gray stones. Each stone measured roughly around thirty by twenty inches. There are stairs leading to an oak door. He marched up the hill and spotted fresh footprints. He took the stairs and tried the door. It did not budge. He came down the steps and marched through the tall weeds and bushes. A flock of birds flew over the structure. Crows sat in groups over the pillars and crocked loudly. As Norris walked around the structure, he saw no other entrance. When he reached the back of the fortress, he spotted a balcony on the first floor with broken windows and another door.

"This is useless," he muttered, deciding to return to his truck.

With eyes still fixed on the fortress, he got behind the wheels and wondered if it was connected to the murders. It appeared as if no one had lived here for a long time. He wanted to look inside, but since it was private property, he could not act without a warrant. Shaking his head, he turned the ignition on.

6th April 2020
NYPD Precinct, New York

Tom made inquiries about Angela, the alleged victim in the Neville Easton vs. Angela Vince case. She lived in New Jersey, and her file had not been updated for a long time. Tom had contacted the local police department and tried to find out if Angela's family had been inquiring about Neville. Till now, all his inquiries led to nothing. Neville or Angela had never come to Nightridge or Willow's Heart. They had not been in touch with each other after the trial.

He then checked if there was a connection between Gail, Neville, and Angela. Three hours later, he hit a wall. These people were strangers. They lived in different parts of the city and worked in different areas. One drove a car, the other took the subway. The cases had different witnesses, lawyers, and judges. Cops from different precincts had handled the cases and had left detailed notes. There was no link between them. Tom felt like pulling his hair.

After a tedious day at work, he headed home. Tom parked his car below the building. A short flight of stairs took him to his small and comfortable flat. He closed the door behind him. Fatigued, he took a quick shower and then went straight to bed.

He slept for a while until his phone cruelly woke him up. It was William Sterling. Half asleep, he pushed the green button.

"Yes," he said.

"Tom, you need to come down to the morgue."

"Ah, why?"

"Just do it!"

"Oh…fine…"

Tom ended the call and tossed the phone on the bed. He had the powerful urge to ignore that call, but now he was curious.

"Oh, I hate that guy," he muttered.

7th April 2020
City Morgue, New York

At 1:00 am, he parked his car in front of the City Morgue. Stray dogs ran on the street, and several homeless people slept on the pavement. He knocked on the main door, and the security guard let him in. The morgue felt like an abandoned hospital in a zombie movie. Wishing he was somewhere else; Tom stepped into the elevator and pushed a button.

As the hefty elevator ascended, he wondered why William had asked him to come to the fourth floor. He usually visited William in his office on the third floor or at the morgue. The lift shuddered to a stop, and the doors opened. A strong smell confronted him. It was formaldehyde. Tom was confused. He was standing in a vast hall divided by a plastic screen hanging from the ceiling. He saw shadows behind the thick screen. Tom moved the screen to the side and stepped in. White sheets covered the floor and walls. He noticed a long bench with a computer and monitors. On the other side was another bench full of objects. William and his assistant Johnathan Wright stood in front of the computer wearing white suits.

"What is going on here?" Tom demanded as he approached them but halted when he saw the bodies of five pigs hanging on hooks on a stand.

"Ah! Good morning, Detective! You made it," said Johnathan, waving toward him.

William's assistant had not changed. Tom feared that the

scrawny man with a weather-beaten face would one day wither away. First, he had thought perhaps Johnathan starved himself, but one day he saw him consume three burgers at a time with two packs of fries. He wondered what happened to all the calories. If he ate at that much, he would certainly have a heart attack.

Flabbergasted, he wondered what was happening. His eyes set on a wide collection of swords on the long table. Two of the long knives and short swords had blood on them. He eyed the Jian sword with a golden hilt and a pair of double-edge straight swords. Tom bent over and examined the elegant handwork on the hilt. Next to it sat a hefty silver sword, which Tom knew was a two-handed sword.

"This can't be good," he muttered, eying the curved one-edged swords with one sharp edge and the other with a zigzag design.

"Hey, Tom, good morning," William said, holding a curved narrow sword.

"What are you doing?" Tom asked, worried.

"Do you want to find the murder weapon?"

"Yeah. Sure… but what are you…" Tom said, but his voice trailed away. He noticed a carcass of a pig sitting erect on a stand. "This can't be happening… William!"

William swung the weapon, slicing through the meat. The blade stopped midway.

"Shit," he muttered, pulling the blade out.

"Not this one," William said, placing the sword on the table. "Let's try the next one."

Tom hung his head. "Guys…you woke me up for this."

"Yeah, because it's fun!" William replied.

"You can do computer simulations, right?"

But William was not listening. Tom knew he was frustrated with his relationship with Joan, but there were other ways of resolving emotions.

"So, it's not a narrow sword. It must be something wider," he said thoughtfully.

"Where did you get these?" Tom asked.

"You can get anything on the internet these days," William said.

"I'll pretend I didn't hear that," Tom responded.

"Do you think animal slaughtering is ritualistic?" Johnathan answered.

"Yeah," Tom said.

"I am testing what type of sword was used to commit the crime," William explained.

"I can see that. And I think this is a terrible idea."

William bent forward and picked up the broad, curved sword with a zigzag design on one side.

"That looks dangerous," remarked Tom.

Something moved behind him. He saw Johnathan setting up a fresh specimen.

"Oh, good lord."

William observed the second pig's head. "The pigs' dimensions are similar to the wolves we found."

"Okay," Tom said, taking a step back.

Johnathan did the same.

Getting ready, William took a deep breath and swung the weapon. The blade cut through the flesh, and the severed head fell to the floor.

"Yes! Success at last!" Johnathan said excitedly.

Tom rolled his eyes. "Exactly how long have you guys been here?"

"We haven't left the morgue since yesterday morning," answered Johnathan.

"You guys seriously need to get out more," Tom said.

William picked up a high-definition camera and stepped close to the beheaded animal. Tom watched him take pictures. He waited as the medical examiner loaded the images to the computer. In a second, the close-up image of the base of the pig's neck was displayed on the monitor.

"Look how clean the cut is. It has gone through the vertebra, separating the head from the neck. I would bet the murder weapon looked something like this," William said, looking at the sword. Then he focused on the picture of the base of the human head and the pig's head.

"It is a close match of the sword that decapitated Neville," he added.

Tom regarded him. "We need to find who bought these swords."

William smiled. "And you have your lead."

"Tell him about the heads!" shouted Johnathan excitedly.

Tom eyed William, whose face brightened. Once more, they shifted their attention to the monitors. Tom waited as William arranged the images of the base of the wolves' heads on the monitors.

"Note, there is a slight difference in the angle of each cut."

"So?"

"The killer stood over the animal, raised the sword, and then swung it. But I think a different person butchered each wolf, although they used the same type of sword."

Tom's face turned gloomy. "Are you sure?"

"Definitely! Let's get to the second part of the experiment," William said, glancing at his watch.

"Second part?" Tom asked, surprised.

A creaking noise echoed, and he turned. Horror-struck him as he watched Johnathan push the stand with four dead pigs.

"Oh no, this can't be good," Tom muttered. "Did you actually slaughter those animals?"

Both men seemed offended.

"We are not barbarians," argued Johnathan.

Tom gulped and felt his stomach grumble.

"So, here is our plan. We will stick sensors in various parts of the specimen and record the force and impact of each strike," William explained.

Tom just gawked at him.

The detective waited as the doctor's inserted sensors into the different spots of the first specimen. Footsteps echoed, and he turned to see Jack Calvin. Jack was a computer engineer who worked with Roumoult. He ruffled his hair and walked with the swing as if he was on a beach with a smug smile and his keen eyes surveyed the hall. He was almost thirty years old but looked like a college student. His physique undermined his experience in computer programming and his other talents, which included designing programs, extensive coding, and creating new algorithms. But this was just on paper. Tom was sure he had other talents.

"Jack, what are you doing here?" Tom asked.

"William called and said it was urgent," Jack replied.

"Jack! Great, you are here. Stay with the detective."

William handed them plastic protective suits, and Tom quickly wore one.

"Okay, ready?" William asked.

"What are we doing?" Jack asked.

"Slaying pig heads," Tom replied sarcastically.

"What!?" Jack yelled.

"I'll start," William announced.

Johnathan ensured the sensors were working and recording.

"Ready?" William asked.

"Ready!" said Johnathan.

In one stroke, William cut off the pig's head. Blood splashed over him. Streaks of meat flew in every direction, and the head landed on the floor with a thump and rolled away.

"Whoa!" cried out Jack. He rushed to the monitors and added, "That was awesome!"

Looking at the chopped bleeding head, William said, "I thought it would be harder."

Tom glared at him.

"I'm next! I'm next!" shouted Johnathan.

Tom shook his head. "What am I doing here?"

William and Jack recalibrated the sensors and prepared the second specimen. No one bothered to clean the blood. It was Johnathan's turn. He balanced the weapon in both his hands, raised the blade and swung. The head fell to the floor. The men hurled close to the severed head. Tom noted the muscle fibers and bits and pieces of the spine. William took a few pictures.

"Ah! Damn!" Johnathan shouted.

Jack rushed to the monitor, "You used twenty Newton less force compared to William," he said.

"Oh, this sucks! I thought I would do better," said Johnathan.

William smiled. "That's okay. Tom, you are next," he said as he clicked pictures of the bottom of the detached head.

"No. Leave me out of it," Tom said, raising his hands.

"Come on. It's fun," William said, facing him.

"Your definition of fun is very different from mine," Tom replied.

"Tom, give it a shot," William insisted.

Reluctantly, Tom stepped forward. He held the sword in his hands and waited for the doctors to reset the sensors and place them in the third specimen.

"Go," Johnathan said.

Tom took a deep breath and slashed through the flesh. The head dropped to the floor. The adrenaline rush was exhilarating. He smiled and looked at the sword. He hadn't realized he would like it.

"Wow...you beat me by thirty Newtons!" William shouted.

"I don't believe it. That felt good," Tom murmured.

Johnathan snapped photos.

"Jack, you are next!" William said.

Once the fourth specimen was ready, Jack picked up the sword and got in position. He raised the sword above his head and struck. The blade got stuck.

"Oh damn!"

Jack pulled it out and used his full strength. The pig's head fell to the floor.

"Sorry!"

"Don't worry about it," said William.

William took pictures of the severed head. He then loaded all the images into the computer and observed them.

Tom waited for him to speak but then lost patience, "What do you see?"

"I was right. A different person beheaded each wolf. Someone of smaller stature or strength cut two of the heads," he said.

Tom rolled his eyes. "Oh, that really narrows it down."

"So, we need to ask why seven people would kill seven different wolves?" said William, clearly not listening to Tom.

"Maybe it's a group of people and beheading the animals is a declaration of power or a beginning of something," answered Jack.

"Explain," Tom said.

"Animal sacrifices are common offerings to the gods. In some cultures, they ate the edible parts in the feast and burned the rest. In ancient times, Kings used to sacrifice animals before heading to war to please the gods."

"It doesn't please me," Tom muttered.

"You are not a god," Jack replied.

William chuckled.

"That's not funny," Tom said.

"But it is…" Johnathan added, laughing.

Jack continued, "We might have discovered the heads this time. Maybe this wasn't the first time the ritual was performed. Maybe it's a warning. Remember, we found Neville's body after discovering the heads."

"Looks like someone has been busy," William remarked.

Jack looked proud. "Since Norris told us about the heads, I got interested and read as many articles as possible. It is

possible this is a cult. A group of people following a particular practice," he said.

"Let's not jump to conclusions," Tom said. "Are we done
here?"

"Yes, thank you," William said. "I'll email you the details
of the sword."

"Thanks. I will check it out. What is this place?" Tom
asked, looking around.

"It used to be an office space. But when the pandemic
struck, they cleared this floor to make space for the victims
before cremation. They vacated it four weeks ago."

Tom eyed the hall uncomfortably.

"Now it mostly remains empty."

Tom nodded absentmindedly and was about to leave. This
was the first time William had conducted such an experiment
at the morgue. A question popped into his mind, "Does your
boss know what you are doing here?"

William straightened. "No. He is working from home."

7th April 2020
City Morgue, New York

William felt very tired. He had reached home around 4:00
am after cleaning up the fourth floor. Last night was good,
and he felt an excitement he had lost a long time ago. Tom
was right. Computer models could have given him the
answers, but William was eager to do something different.
He wanted to do something exciting to feel alive. Conducting
experiments or something out of his normal routine always
lifted his spirit. Last night helped. The truth was, he missed
Joan too much. Again, this morning, he had thought about

calling her. Instead of listening to his heart, he showered, ate breakfast, and got to work.

It was a long day. William had to use his lunch break to manage his workload. He had too much to do, and bodies were flooding the morgue. His assistant was busy with other cases. Thankfully, they were now once again focused on crimes related to deaths rather than managing victims of the pandemic. William hustled the trolley with Neville's body down the narrow passageway. He turned and entered the radiology department. Henry, the technician, was waiting for him.

"Hey, William, how are you?" he said.

"I am good."

Henry was a stalky African American of William's age. His cheeks were bombarded with acne scars. His bald head shined underneath the tube light.

"Do you mind if I start now? I am leaving early today."

William pushed the gurney into position. "It's all yours."

As he waited outside, William spent his time scrolling through social media. The door opened, and Henry appeared with the X-rays.

"Here you go."

"Thanks."

Henry nodded, removed his apron, and hurried down the corridor.

William placed the X-rays on the body and pushed the

trolley to the lift. He returned the corpse to the freezer. He had two autopsies before he could start on this one.

"A headless man. Norris, you surely pick them," he muttered.

He wondered why the head was missing. Was it a piece of evidence? Or perhaps it was a part of a ritual?

He put up the chest X-rays against the ceiling light and observed it. Then he studied the films of the legs and arms. Nothing popped up. He shifted his attention to the pelvic region. To his delight, it was normal.

It was late in the evening, and the morgue was quiet. Johnathan had left for the day. Neville's body was out of the freezer and lay on the cold autopsy table. William was not used to having headless corpses. And he tried not to let it bother him. Armed with his camera, he began with the base of the neck. It was a clean cut with a sharp object. He took a few images and then concentrated on other parts of the body. Systematically, he took photos of bruises and bites on the leg. The superficial exam revealed nothing significant. He picked up the scalpel and began.

Two hours passed, and William had to stretch. He was exhausted, but he had to finish. He stared at the vast collection of tissue and blood samples.

I hope I can get Juliet to process these. God knows how busy she is.

Dr. Juliet Wave was a hardworking pathologist at the morgue. They had been friends for years and worked together on several cases.

He held the left lung in his hand, weighed it, and made a note. Then he detached the next lung. It almost weighed the same. He cut open the organ, and the bottom of the lung was patchy black. Neville was a chain smoker, and it showed. But it was not the cause of death. Surely, the decapitation had killed him, but why did he have to die? The heart seemed healthy and weighed within normal limits. Leaving the chest cavity, he focused on the abdomen. The stomach was distended and dark purple. He cut it open and identified the contents. He estimated Neville had eaten about eight hours before his death. Edgar found the body around midday. That meant Neville must have been killed around 6.00 am. Making a note of the time, he continued with his work. He gently pulled out the intestine. He sliced each segment, then separated them and prepared the contents for testing. There were no obstructions or signs of inflammation.

Once he was done, he shifted his attention to the liver. It was distended, dark, and with significant scarring. The after-effects of heavy alcohol drinking were clear. Regardless, he carved it and took samples. He knew his request for extensive tests would not make people happy. But he would rather do this once. The spleen spiked his interest. It was enlarged.

Maybe he had an infection.

He separated its muscle attachments and lifted the spleen. William froze.

"What the hell is that?" he said, leaning forward.

It was attached to the cisterna chyli, a cluster of lymph nodes linked to other nodes all over the body. It looked like a pouch about five centimeters long and reminded him of the gallbladder. The unknown organ was deep brown. He did not disconnect it but slowly squeezed it. It felt real. Just like real tissue. But it was not.

11

DOWN UNDER

17th April 2020 (Present Day)
Willow's Heart

Norris was still at the old, abandoned house, and he was glad to get a bit of a break. The pain in his knee was settling. Not knowing what to do next, Norris stepped out to get some fresh air. The sky was clear, the wind dry and crisp. There was not a soul in sight. Part of him wished to sleep, but he knew they would track him down if he stayed here. He had to keep moving.

Five minutes later, he returned inside and went through the small study. He found a map and spread it on the table. There were only two ways of getting out of the valley. Hiking was out of the question. The wolves would hunt him down. He had his truck, but he knew those two exits would be guarded.

They know I have escaped. I must find another way to get help.

He kept staring at the map, trying to find an answer. Suddenly, something dawned on him. His first priority was to call for help, the second to save his friends. Two distinct possibilities lingered in his mind.

Once outside, he slightly limped toward the stable. Getting behind the wheel, he started the engine. He tried the radio again; it was no use. He was probably out of range and peered out to observe the moon's position. He calculated that the sun would rise in eight hours. Norris had time, and he wanted to use it well. He pushed the pedal and drove into the wilderness.

17th April 2020 (Present Day)
Willow's Heart

Tom waited for his chance. After making sure their captors would not return, he reached for his shoe.

"What are you doing?" Kyle asked.

He said nothing and pushed a section of his shoe's sole. It opened. With his fingers, he felt a small hole. Using his index finger and thumb, he pulled out a smooth circular object approximately four centimeters long. With both hands, he twisted it. A sharp, thin pin popped out. He turned it toward the handcuffs and got to work.

It was hard, but once Tom was free, he stretched his legs and stood up.

Oh, that felt good.

"What's happening?" asked Kyle.

"Shush… stay quiet. I have a plan. Stay here. I'll be back."

"Don't leave me here!"

"Kyle, I will be back."

Blinded by the darkness, he reached for the surrounding walls. It was cold, uneven, and filthy. Tom took one step after another, gradually making his way down the tunnel. The ground was full of pebbles and rocks. His left foot landed on something soft. It shrieked and slipped away.

"Oh, good lord!" Tom cried out but quickly covered his mouth, hoping his voice had reached no one. He placed his hand on his chest and felt his beating heart.

"Are you okay?" asked Kyle.

"Yes, yes. Stay quiet."

He kept walking along the wall of the tunnel. Soon he came to a dead end. He grumbled. Maybe there was no way out of here.

"Ah-huh…" he muttered when his fingers sensed a cold, smooth surface. It was metallic.

This could be a hatch.

He found the latch. Reaching for the handle, he pushed it sideways. Then he gripped the handle and pulled it with full force. It opened with a loud clang. Tom froze. The noise resonated and then died out. He shut his eyes, expecting the kidnappers to show up. Nothing happened. He took a deep breath in and focused on the opened panel and felt mud. He frowned. They were trapped. Then something occurred to him. With both hands, he started digging. The mud splattered near his feet. The process was long and tedious. But he dug through the layers of rocks and mud. Soon, Tom's upper body was inside the opening. He was wary, but he didn't stop until he felt a hard surface. The remaining mud crumbled away. His eyes lit up, and his mouth curved into a smile. At a distance, he saw a dim light.

12

ORDEAL OF THE INNOCENT

7th April 2020
New York

Tom returned home after watching William's weird experiments. It was fun and exciting, but he was tired and fell asleep immediately.

Hours later, a bright light illuminated the room. The alarm buzzed. Tom shut it down and pulled the blankets over his head. A sweet smell crept in from a nearby bakery, and the neighbor's TV droned on. Covering his ears with a pillow, Tom groaned.

Soon he got ready for the day. The TV blared in the background as he prepared breakfast. The egg poacher chimed, and the toast popped out of the toaster. With his black coffee ready, he carried his food to the couch. He began watching the news.

The news reporter said, "After discovering the heads of seven wolves, the police found the body of Mr. Neville Easton in Willow's Heart."

Tom gulped down the piece of bread.

"Oh, no," he muttered.

"According to the report, Mr. Easton died approximately two days ago. The sheriff has refused to comment further on the matter."

Tom scowled and called Norris.

"Morning," said Norris.

"Morning. How did the press find out about the murder?"

"What?"

"It's on the news,"

"It wasn't me."

Tom hated himself for being the bad guy. "You should ask Edgar to keep this quiet. It might hinder our investigation."

"It is hard to keep the press away."

"I'm aware. But let's try to stay in control. Otherwise, all hell will break loose."

"Agreed."

Tom tried to stay calm. Norris was trying to help, and it was Edgar who had to be more careful. As he sipped his coffee, the news reporter continued with another story. Tom was not interested in watching anymore. He flipped through Gail Clegg and Neville Easton's case files. Gail was a criminal, and in Tom's eyes, he deserved to die. But Neville was a different story.

7th April 2020
New Jersey

The city was lively but still appeared barren compared to eight months ago. Tom despised it. He drove silently while his partner John sat in the passenger seat. The Ford drove into the well-lit Holland Tunnel. There were barely any cars, and Tom accelerated. His heart skipped a beat as lights zoomed past them. He hated tunnels. The concrete walls, the narrow lanes, seemed like a playground for accidents. He glanced at the speed-o-meter. They were traveling a hundred miles per hour. Gripping the steering wheel and kept his foot on the gas pedal. The car emerged on the other side. Tom relaxed his shoulders and glanced at Angela Vince's address. There was nothing about Angela's current life in the police file, which was normal. Cases once closed were forgotten. Very quickly.

They drove down Montgomery Street and neared the flyover. The Ford came to a halt near a lamppost. They both exited the car and walked toward the three-floored brick building with unpainted windows. Tom caught a whiff of roasted chicken as they entered the well-lit corridor. He'd only had egg and toast for breakfast but was hungry again. The cops knocked on the second door to the left and waited. An elderly African American woman with large glasses and curly hair opened the door. She crossed her arms and regarded them suspiciously. They duly showed her their badges. Tom touched his face to make sure his mask was covering his nose and mouth.

"What do you want?" she demanded.

"We want to speak with Angela Vince."

Blood drained from her face, but she quickly composed herself and said, "She is not here, go away."

She was about to close the door when Tom caught it with his hand.

"I am sorry. We need to ask you questions regarding a murder investigation."

"Oh?"

"Mr. Neville Easton was murdered a couple of days ago."

The woman huffed. "Justice has been served. But it's too late."

"What do you mean?" John asked.

"I don't care if that man died. Leave me alone," she argued.

"And you are?" Tom asked.

"Mrs. Usher, Angela's nana."

"Where is she?" asked Tom.

Tears filled her eyes. "You really don't know, do you? Oh! Your justice system is useless! After all those interviews and the courtroom drama... you really do not care what happens to us!"

Tom clenched his jaw. "Where is she?"

"She is dead! She killed herself!" screamed Mrs. Usher.

Tom felt as if a slab of cement fell on him. He stared at her openmouthed and then turned to John, who was equally shocked.

"What? When?" asked John.

"A year after that horrible trial! After all the testimonies, the witnesses, the drama, and the media. After everything we went through... you let that scumbag go!"

Mrs. Usher started sobbing and turned away from the door.

The detectives entered the apartment and waited for her to calm down.

"I am very sorry," Tom said.

She huffed. "All the policemen are the same. I am sure the detective screwed up her case. It was all his fault!"

Tom did not agree. The evidence showed otherwise, but he chose not to say anything.

"How did it happen?" John asked.

"The trial was horrible. Angela regretted it. She regretted all of it! She hated telling the police about what had happened. But her mother pushed her. She wanted to sue Neville and collect money." Mrs. Usher wiped her face with the tissue, trying to hide her feelings. She took a sharp breath and continued. "After that man degraded her, and she lost the battle in court, it was hard. She was depressed. Angela felt exposed and started drinking. She stopped talking or going out with her friends. It became hard for her to live. To move on."

The detectives nodded.

"I am so sorry," Tom said again.

"She was afraid to step out of the house. People talked about her, mocked her, and called her a liar!"

"What about her mother?" Tom asked, referring to his notes. "Mrs. Tamira Vince."

"What mother? That woman... she was no mother. She was a monster! She is the reason Angela is dead!"

Tom hung his head.

"She kept pressuring her to sue. Angela preferred not to. She did not want to go to trial. She wanted to seek help from a counselor. But after they lost the case, Tamira began harassing Angela. Blaming her for everything! She told her she was a burden and what happened to her was her fault!"

"She blamed her own daughter?" asked Tom, surprised.

"She was horrible, worse than Neville."

"Where is Tamira now?" asked John

"I hope she goes to hell!"

The detectives exchanged worried glances.

"Mrs. Usher, where is Tamira?" Tom asked again.

Tears flowed down her face, and Tom quickly reached for a pack of tissues from his pocket.

"I threw her out," she said, accepting a tissue.

Tom raised his eyebrows.

"This apartment is mine. Tamira was worthless. A drug addict, smoker who couldn't hold a proper job or even take care of herself. Nothing except getting her next fix mattered to her. I would have thrown her out earlier, but I let her stay for Angela... she is... was my grandchild. But after Angela's death... it became unbearable to have her around. And I hated her for what she did!"

Mrs. Usher resumed sobbing. Tom shook his head, hating himself. Regardless of the outcome of the trial, Angela did not deserve to die.

Mrs. Usher wiped her tears. "I hope Neville goes to hell for what he did to my child!"

"Do you have any idea where Tamira is?" John asked, sticking with the subject.

"I don't care. And as I said, she can go to hell!"

After making sure Mrs. Usher was all right, they left. It was all they could do. Tom did not have the power to turn back time and bring Angela to life. The detectives returned to the car and sat quietly for a moment.

"There are too many loose ends in this case," remarked Tom.

"I know. We are still looking for the nurse who treated Gail," John said.

"Ella Morgan is not in the system?"

"Her slate is clean, but she is off the grid. And now we have to find Tamira."

Tom let out a long breath. "Well, let's keep looking. There must be a trail."

John nodded. "Where to next?"

"Well, we spoke to the victim's family. Time to speak with the suspect's family."

"A suspect who is now a victim," remarked John.

7th April 2020
Queens, New York

The drive to Queens was not too difficult. Traffic was bearable, and the weather was behaving. The wind was cool, with a mix of smells of garbage and pollution. The sunlight sparkled over the Ford as the vehicle propelled down Tudor Road. After Tom found a good parking spot under the tree, the cops made their way toward a six-floor white building.

Mrs. Claire Easton tried to smile when she opened the door. Her husband had been missing, and two days ago, she had been informed that they had found his body. Blinking her swollen eyes, Claire pressed her dry lips and welcomed the detectives into her house.

"How are you?" asked Tom, sitting in a corner chair in the sparsely decorated living room. John stood leaning on the door with his hands in his pockets.

"I-I am fine. Thank you."

"We are sorry for your loss," said Tom.

Claire hung her head.

"How did he die?" she asked.

Tom knew the question would pop up, but he didn't

know how to answer it. He liked to be sensitive about these things, but they couldn't lie to Claire about her husband's missing head. She was going to eventually find out.

John spoke up, "He was decapitated."

Tom was shocked. How could his partner be so insensitive?

She glared at John in disbelief. "What? No! No!" she said, getting on her feet.

"We are sorry," Tom said.

"It's not possible... how do you know its him?"

"His fingerprints were on the system," explained Tom.

Claire covered her mouth and sobbed. Tom had never felt so helpless. But they had to be patient and give her time.

Claire asked in a choked voice, "Who killed him?"

"We don't know yet," replied John.

"We are following several leads... it could be something related to his past," Tom mentioned.

Claire frowned and closed her eyes. "That damn case."

"Anything except that?" Tom asked.

"It was enough! It was enough to ruin our lives. That incident... it just... broke us. It destroyed us!" Claire cried out, getting on her feet. Her hands trembled as she wiped the tears rolling down her face. Tom got on his feet to help her, but then stopped himself. Maybe she needed the space.

"Even after all these years... it haunts us like a curse!" She paused and realized she was losing her temper. "I'm sorry...I..."

"It's okay. You have been through a lot," John said.

Claire smiled weakly and sat down.

"You believe your husband was innocent?" asked John.

"I don't believe. I know."

Tom eyed her.

"I... I was furious when we were dragged into it. The police investigation, the trial, the media, and then the public exposure was too much." She paused. "You see, no one understands. My husband was telling the truth... they did not listen to him! They did not believe him."

Tom remained silent.

"I feel for Angela. What happened to her was not right! Not fair! She was so young... only sixteen. I guess now... much older. But it was not Neville. It was not him."

"How did you come to that conclusion?" Tom asked.

"I know it's a cliché, and people have told me I am stupid for believing him! But he didn't do it. I love... loved him. I am convinced he didn't hurt her. He was a hardworking, simple man with simple needs, and he had an alibi!"

"What happened after the trial?" Tom asked, opening his notepad.

"The ordeal took a toll on us. On him. He changed. Neville never drank. He started drinking, smoking, gambling, and getting into fights. Even though the court cleared his name, he was 'labeled' a rapist, and they fired him."

Tom shut his eyes momentarily.

"He had to work in a bar and sweep floors in a hospital. I had to get a job to pay the bills. As the years passed, we grew apart, and he continued to drink."

The detectives remained silent.

"Then it became tougher."

Tom wondered what else could have happened.

"He started staying out and wouldn't come home for days."

Tom sulked.

"I asked where he had been. At first, he did not respond. When I pressed him for a response, he said he was trying to figure out how to pay for his sins."

Tom's heart melted.

"He thought he was responsible?" asked John.

"I think he blamed himself for what had happened to us... to his family. I tried to console him. I-I did my best... but it was no use."

Tom rubbed his jaw.

"He started talking about being a servant of Satan, and he had to fix what he had done wrong."

"Satan?" asked Tom, surprised.

"Satan...devil...whatever you want to call it."

"That's unusual," said John in a slow deliberate tone.

"It was very unusual. All his life he never invested a second in these things. But recently he thought he had to be a martyr. He had to pay for what he had done, so that others would learn from his mistake."

Tom rubbed his forehead. He was trying to understand why Neville would say that.

"Detective, we are not religious and don't go to church. But suddenly, I felt he had become a slave to these beliefs, and they had turned him into something he wasn't."

"What do you mean?"

"He thought there were superior and inferior beings... and those who won't follow the right beliefs would burn in hell."

Tom ran his hand through his hair. "Where was he learning all these things?"

"He did not tell me."

"What else did he do?"

"He just vanished for most days. Returned home and then gave no explanation."

"I am sorry to ask this... did he mistreat you?" Tom said.

"No. But he was no longer the man I married. It's... almost a relief he is dead," she murmured.

"Excuse me?" said Tom.

She blanched. "All these years, I felt he was suffering. He felt guilty about what happened to Angela. For what he had become. For what the case had done to us. He was miserable, and I felt his soul was gradually withering away... although he was innocent."

Tom felt a knot in his stomach.

After thanking Claire and promising her they would keep her updated, both detectives marched down the corridor. Once they were out of the building, they returned to the car. Tom was deep in thought when John spoke.

"Satan?"

Tom eyed him. "Maybe he just lost it."

"Or someone used his vulnerability to lower him into a... group of people who believed in such things."

13

NIGHT HUNT

17th April 2020 (Present Day)
Willow's Heart

Norris had left the house he had been hiding in. With no phone or computer, it was no use staying there. The expanse of trees ahead was never-ending. It was like he was driving through a natural dark tunnel. He hoped the engine wasn't too noisy. The truck exited the canopy and drove on an uneven, muddy terrain. The valley was eerily quiet, and a thick fog settled over the treetops.

The truck rocked on the bumpy road, full of potholes and he could not see beyond the headlights. He felt as if he was driving through a void. Norris tried to stay alert as he scanned both sides. Still, there was no sign of the hunters. Maybe they left him alone. Spared his life. He almost laughed at himself. No, they would not. They would kill him and the others in an instant. Before he knew it, he reached his destination and pressed the brakes. The vehicle came to a halt.

Switching off the engine, Norris wondered if this was a good idea.

What choice do I have?

He craned his neck and saw a spot to conceal his vehicle. Restarting the truck, he drove over rough terrain into a cluster of trees. Making sure his truck was out of sight, he stepped out. Checking his surroundings, he began walking.

Afraid that someone might see him, he remained low and cautious. He winced as the twigs crashed under his foot and cautiously made his way through the bushes towering over his head. When he saw the clearing, he paused. He felt he wasn't alone. If the wolves were nearby, they would have ripped him apart. But the hunters. They were worse. They liked to watch, hunt, and, most of all, make their victims suffer. It was a game for them. Minutes passed. The forest remained still as if waiting for him to make a move. Norris rushed across the clearing. He jumped over the low fence and cringed.

"Ah," he muttered, grabbing his leg.

Limping slightly, he made his way to the structure. The windows were covered with layers of dust and cobwebs. Looking behind, he checked the window. It was locked. Grabbing a stone beside his foot, he broke the glass, unlocked it, and vanished inside.

The old Willow's Heart sheriff's office was a rectangular hall with furniture covered in white cloth. The moonlight crept through the windows, beaming an inch of light over the torn and tattered carpet. Glancing at the ceiling, he wondered if there was electricity. He flipped the switch, and the fan groaned to life. Norris shut it down.

Edgar had told him the old sheriff's office was now a

storage space. The new office was in the main village. Norris hoped to find something useful. He pulled off the white sheet draping a desk and saw multiple files and an old land-line. Hurriedly, he connected it to the socket and waited. The line was dead.

"What the hell?" he muttered.

The second desk was stacked with paper tied in bundles. There was no phone. He searched the entire office and found nothing.

This can't be possible!

At a distance, a loud howl echoed. The sensation left his body, and he went as still as a stone.

17th April 2020 (Present Day)
Fortress, Willow's Heart

Standing in the cold, dark cave with his hands full of dirt, Tom looked at the light with hope. His heart leaped with joy. They might be able to escape. He cleared the dirt and bent forward to observe the old cracked concrete square tunnel. It was not wide enough for them to walk, but they could crawl their way to freedom.

Tom dusted his clothes and found his way back to Kyle.

"Let's go," Tom said.

He freed the deputy, and both cops headed into the tunnel. Together, they scurried through the pitch-black tunnel. Stumbling on the uneven surface, they reached the opening.

"How did you find this tunnel?" Kyle asked.

"We got lucky. Come on. We must keep moving," Tom crawled through the hole and entered the square passageway.

Kyle was right behind him. Tom's knees rubbed against the hard surface as he hurried toward the light. Finally, they reached the end of the tunnel. Tom lifted his head. The moonlight was creeping through the small ventilation covered by a mesh. Balancing himself on his knees, he pushed it upwards, and after a few attempts, it gave up.

Though it was tough, he squeezed through the opening and got on his feet. It was easier for Kyle because he was leaner. The cops found themselves in an old hall with large columns, a dome-shaped roof, and an aged, hefty door. They were in the main hall of the fortress. The air carried the smell of blood. His heart leaped to his throat, and his eyes widened. At the far end of the hall, a wheel made up of bones with human heads attached to the ends dangled above a platform held by heavy chains. In the middle, supported by bony spikes, was a huge mask with big daunting eyes. Four curved horns emerged from its head.

"What the hell is that thing?" Tom whispered.

Just above it was a window in the shape of a pentacle. Above him, he saw another pentacle-shaped window in the center of the dome. He gulped and glared at the third pentacle, opposite the first one.

"That thing is... scary," Kyle remarked, still staring at the wheel.

"We need to get out of here," Tom said, placing the mesh over the opening. They rushed to the door, and Tom unlocked the latch and pulled. The door opened with a heavy dragging noise. He saw a clearing beyond which was a pitch-black forest. A loud clang echoed behind them. A chill ran through his spine and sweat tickled his brow.

"Run!" he yelled.

14

ANOMALIES

7th April 2020
City Morgue, New York

William stood with his hands clamped together. He had hit a wall during Neville's autopsy. The anomaly daunted him. Neville had something implanted in his body, and he wished he would have picked it up sooner. It would have shown up on an MRI scan. But it's not customary to MRI dead bodies.

"Maybe I should MRI the bodies found by Norris," he told himself.

He turned to the laptop and searched the morgue's database for anomalies uncovered by medical examiners. They were common. Not everyone was the same. There were reports of the medical examiner finding extra organs during autopsy. Deaths because of undiagnosed diseases, which were flagged as suspicious deaths, were common. In such cases, mostly, the cause of death was an undetected cardio-vascular condition. He glanced at the body. There were some structural changes in the heart, but not enough to cause a cardiac arrest.

But he was decapitated.

He concentrated again on the reports. When a body is brought to the morgue, the cause of death may not always be apparent. Hidden tumors in fatty tissue and undetected abscesses in the liver were just a few examples. Although these cases had been solved, several remained unsolved. In the records room, thirty cases sat in a folder where the victim's organs had been removed and disposed of. The 'empty bodies' case was still waiting for answers. After satisfying himself that no one else had reported such an anomaly, he focused on the body.

"How did you get in there?" he said to the anomaly.

He turned over the skin of the abdomen and noticed a faint mark. It looked like a surgical scar. How did he miss that? William turned to the cabinet and found his portable UV lamp. He switched it on and checked the skin. There were no other scars.

"One fading scar," he muttered.

He studied the pattern of muscle arrangements in the area. The muscles had been split apart and then stitched together. He estimated the surgery might have taken place a year ago, but the scar should have been darker. He turned his attention to the pear-shaped anomaly.

Maybe it's a tumor. But that doesn't explain the scar.

He palpated the anomaly's attachment to the cluster of lymph nodes. If it was surgically implanted, there should be evidence of sutures. Using forceps, he examined it. Then it occurred to him. Biodegradable sutures might have been used. If the surgery were about a year ago, the sutures might have dissolved, and the body would have flushed out any residues.

"So, losing your head was the least of your problems," he muttered.

William separated it from the lymph nodes. His hands trembled. A few months ago, he had gone to Nightridge to investigate a case. While conducting an autopsy, he had found nanoprobes inside the victim's brain. What was it? A tumor? A cluster of mass? But it looked like a well-shaped human organ that he had never seen before.

He placed it on a sterile tray and slowly sliced it open. It felt less soft than other organs, and he had to apply more pressure. He cut it in half and studied the interior. The tissue was irregular and reminded him of the alveoli of the lungs. In each half was a main branch. From it emerged several small branches to which clusters of tissue were attached. What was this thing? Was it linked to the incident at Nightridge? There was only one way to find out.

His heart raced as he carefully sliced a part of the tissue and deposited it in a container with formaldehyde. Leaving the dissected unidentified organ on the bench, he plucked out the sample with tweezers and bent over to separate a tiny piece. Putting the rest of it back into the container, he reached for a sterilized slide. He placed the sample on the slide and then used hematoxylin and eosin stain. Placing another slide on the first one, he waited a few minutes for the sample to set.

Once he thought it was ready, he positioned it under the microscope. William breathed sharply and peered into the eyepiece. It was completely blurry. He adjusted the focus and the position of the illuminator. In seconds, he saw hundreds of pink-colored cells lumped over each other. He knew they were human cells, but then something caught his eye. Floating within the cells were black objects with multiple spikes. A wave of irritation rushed through his veins. Shutting his eyes, he looked away.

"Fuck!"

15

MESSAGE

17th April 2020 (Present Day)
Old Sheriff's Office, Willow's Heart

Trying to stay out of sight, Norris leaned against the wall and quickly glanced out the window. There was not a soul in sight. He took out the bottle of painkillers and popped a pill. A wolf's howl caught his attention. He rushed to the other end of the room and peered through the dusty window. The piercing howl resonated again.

"Shit!"

He dashed down the hall and tried the door. It was locked. He kicked it, breaking it open to reveal a small office with two cabinets and a desk. Walking to the old oak desk, he hurriedly searched for the drawers. Finding nothing, he turned to the next door. It was locked too. He broke the lock, and a sign of hope flashed on his face. It was the evidence and storage room.

"This could work," he mumbled, looking at the shelves of boxes.

He rushed toward the first shelf and grabbed a box. Inside were packets of heroin, a set of knives, some keys, old notebooks, cracked laptops, packs of narcotics, and broken watches. Grumbling, he tossed the contents of the next box onto the floor and started going through it. Under the beam of the flashlight, he saw two laptops, a pair of eyeglasses, and two brass vases. But then he noticed an old Nokia phone in an evidence bag.

"Yes!" he cheered.

He removed it from the packet and attempted to turn it on. The screen didn't come to life. He pushed the little buttons again. Nothing happened. He kept looking, and after going through several more packets from different boxes, he found three phone chargers. One by one, he tried to connect them to the mobile, and the last one fitted perfectly. He quickly plugged it in and waited.

"Come on...come on," he said, glancing at the door.

Norris jumped when he heard a low growl. The wolf was nearby. The device vibrated in his hand, and the mobile began charging. Leaving it on the floor, he rushed back into the evidence room and searched inside the last two boxes. One after another, he tossed their contents onto the floor. He was losing hope when in the heap of paper and plastic; he saw something. A gun. It was a 38-caliber Colt. Smiling, he grabbed it and checked the cylinder. It was empty. He scowled.

Norris glared at the door, his heart beating fast. He was not ready to face his nemesis, and he felt he was close. Frantically, he searched, and in the dim light, he found three bullets in a small evidence bag.

"It will have to do," he said and loaded the three bullets.

Norris checked the phone. It was still starting up.

"Damn, this thing is slow," he whispered.

When the phone finally booted, Norris waited for it to connect to a network. He dialed a number and waited, no one answered. He tried again, but the call dropped. Bringing the device close to his face, he typed. But the alphanumeric keypad made the task difficult. It had limited capabilities, and he could not type long text messages. He missed his smartphone. After a few minutes of struggle, he finished typing the message.

He read it once more: *Get help fast. I am in Willow's Heart. You were right. Norris.*

"Oh, she is going to love this," he muttered and pushed the send button. He frowned as a small bar appeared, showing the message was still being sent.

A growling noise resonated. Norris got on his feet and leaned against the wall. The phone made a beeping noise, indicating the text had been sent. With the gun in his right hand, he waited. Sweat trickled down his spine. The creature would not be alone. The masters always accompanied them.

Three bullets.

Norris frowned. He had to use them wisely. The howls stopped, and he wished the wolves had left. But he knew they were still out there, waiting, watching. He didn't want to take a risk. The phone beeped and glowed. In the screen's corner, a small bar appeared. It was charging. Norris dragged a chair and sat down, patiently waiting for the phone to finish charging. It was better for him to stay indoors, for now.

He kept a watch. The moonlight flooded the sky, and the clouds floated along with the swift wind. The trees swayed and leaves rustled as they rolled over the ground. He saw nothing beyond the clearing. Just black forest.

Time passed slowly, and Norris thought about the past couple of weeks. The ruthless beheading of the wolves and the death of several innocent people had led him here. If he thought he could stop the killer, he was utterly wrong. He didn't know if he would make it. Death was near. Martha's face flashed in front of his eyes, followed by his daughter. He had to live for her. He had to go on.

The phone beeped. It was forty percent charged. Norris hadn't heard the wolf, and he thought it was safe to leave. Picking up the phone, he unlocked a window and crawled out noiselessly. Looking in all directions, Norris dashed toward his truck. His leg still hurt, and he could not move as fast as he would like. Terror seized him. He stopped dead on his feet. In the bushes were two shiny eyes. A growl resonated.

"Shit," he muttered, arming himself.

The creature leaped at him at full speed. Norris pulled the trigger. But it was too late.

17th April 2020 (Present Day)
Willow's Heart

Tom was breathless. He could run faster, but the unfamiliar territory and the rocky terrain made it hard. He glanced over his shoulder. There was no sign of the hunters. At least not yet. Kyle jumped over a log, and Tom followed.

Tom calculated they had been running south for over twenty minutes. According to Kyle, there was a house nearby where they might have been able to get some help. If they were lucky, they might make it. They stopped to take a breath.

"We are doing good. We should keep going," Kyle said.

"Agreed. But don't forget, they have wolves who can track us. We need to confuse them."

Kyle nodded in agreement. "How?"

They stood trying to come up with an idea. Tom heard water running.

"Is there a river around here?"

"Yeah."

"Come on," he said, running toward the stream.

The ground was mushy, and he tried to keep his balance. The bottom of his trousers was soaked, and his face was covered with sweat. If they swam across the river, the wolves might lose their scent. He glanced up the hill.

Maybe it was too high.

He stopped abruptly, not wanting to jump off a cliff. It would be madness. He wondered if there was another way to the stream.

Kyle halted a few paces away. "What?" he asked breathlessly.

Tom was about to speak when they heard rustling and then a howl. Fear crept through his bones. He slowly turned. A figure with horns emerged from the mist. With him was a black wolf, its fiery red eyes fixated on the cops.

"Shit!" Tom muttered.

Both men bolted toward the stream. Tom skidded and fell on his face. Kyle raced ahead. Tom got up and ran for his life. The burning in his calves was unbearable, and he hated running up the hill. They did not know what was on the other side. How deep was the river? Would they make it alive? They reached the top of the hill and stopped. They were at the edge of a waterfall. The water gushed down into a pool of mist. Tom glanced behind. They had no time to think. The wolf raged toward them, baring its fangs.

"Kyle… don't think… just…" Tom's voice turned into a scream as they jumped over the cliff and into oblivion.

16

SHADOW CIRCLES

8th April 2020
NYPD Precinct

Tracking Neville's activities before his head was a headache, and now Tom had to investigate Angela's life. Her case was never solved, and the perpetrator remained at large. She was dead, and her mother had disappeared from the face of the Earth. Tom had been on the phone all morning. The mother's paper trail led them to a small, unkept shared room in a filthy Queen's neighborhood. But their trip got them nowhere. She couldn't pay the rent and left without a word. The landlord had got rid of her belonging. They had interviewed the neighbors and traced her to a bar where she worked for some time. The bartender did not remember her, nor did the owner. It was a dead end. He left his details and urged the bartender to call him if he remembered anything.

8th April 2020

Nightridge

Norris drove at a slow pace to soak in the beautiful day. After everything that had happened in his life, he desired to leave all the dreadful events of his life behind. The windows were open, and the fresh air was welcoming. Relaxation flooded his body. He had been struggling to sleep lately. The murder in Willow's Heart bothered him. He kept seeing Neville's dismembered body every time he closed his eyes.

No one deserves to die like that.

Nightridge was peaceful. The houses stood silent, and as he drove, he noticed the supermarket and the pharmacy were opening for the day. The construction work on two houses that had burned down during the Shadow Pandemic was half complete.

Norris ran his hand through his hair. He would give everything to forget that night. It was a traumatizing and horrific experience. The counseling worked and keeping himself busy was good for his mental health. But there was no denying it. He would have to live with the aftermath for the rest of his life. The loss to the community was unbelievable, with the death toll rising to two hundred people. He could help rebuild the village, but he could not bring the dead back.

He parked his truck on the roadside and stepped out. A cluster of trees welcoming the start of fall encircled the graveyard. It was serene. So heavenly. His heart swelled, and he swallowed the lump in his throat. On that fatal night, many villagers had died. They deserved to live and should have been here with him.

Walking past several tombstones, he came to stand in

front of Ethan Lark's grave. He bowed and controlled his tears. Remorse took over. He had lost his son and grandson to the pandemic. But when Ethan died, Norris felt he had failed everyone. He was like a son to him, and he was powerless to save him. He stayed with Ethan for a while and then left. There was very little he could do for him now.

Putting his feelings aside, he drove to the sheriff's office. Once inside, he found his deputies busy at their desks. The hall was full of coffee aroma. Kyle was in his chair reading a book on forensics.

"That looks interesting," Norris said.

"I was curious about the death in Willow's Heart and how the CSI unit operated. I figured it would be a good idea to educate myself."

"Excellent," Norris said, patting him on his shoulder. "Have you found something on Willow's Heart?"

"I should have something soon. I am waiting for a call."

Norris nodded and marched to his office. Mrs. Flores was on the phone. She waved toward him, and he waved back.

Norris poured himself a cup of coffee and settled in his seat. He noticed his screen was different. Before he could ask, Mrs. Flores stepped in with several messages in her hands.

"Hello there."

"Morning...what's wrong with my computer?" said Norris.

She raised her eyebrows. "Did you forget? The new computers came in yesterday. Kyle spent all evening setting up yours."

"Oh...I see."

"Don't forget to thank him."

He smiled.

"Of course, I will. Now, who needs my attention?" he asked, sipping his coffee.

"Well, Chief, I and the deputies can deal with lost cats and puppies and homes being invaded by possums," she said, smiling wickedly. "Detective Tom Nash called wanted you to call him back as soon as possible. And please ask Edgar to stop calling here."

Norris was stunned. "Why did Edgar call?"

"Maybe he wanted an update about the autopsy."

"William is not done yet," replied Norris.

"Hmm… Let Dr. Death take his time. I don't know what the hurry is. Edgar has called thrice since yesterday."

Norris clamped his hands together and leaned forward. "Why?"

"He wanted to speak to you."

Norris bit his lips.

"I wonder, why did he drag you into this?"

"I am happy to help," replied Norris lifting his shoulders for a second.

"I don't want you to get involved in this."

"Terresa…"

"And I don't want him to step foot in Nightridge!"

"He came here?"

"Yeah, just an hour ago."

Norris found that odd and leaned back on his chair. "I see."

"With his hands in his pockets, he stepped through that door and walked around the office as if he was the boss! It was appalling. I stood by watching as he poked his nose into everyone's business."

"I see."

"I asked him to leave or wait in your office."

"What did he say?"

"He refused to answer me and started asking Kyle and the other officer's questions."

Norris clenched his jaw, "About what?" he asked coldly.

Terresa placed her right hand on her waist, "Well…at first, it was the usual stuff. He asked them about their personal lives. Like if they had families and how long they had worked for you. Things got a bit interesting when he began asking about the Shadow Pandemic. The fire in the village, the bridge, and the deaths."

"It's all in the case files. He should have access to them. It's no secret," he replied, feeling a bit defensive.

"Correct. Everyone knows that. God knows what his problem was. Then he began asking me questions about you, your family, the ex-mayor, and especially your friends from New York."

"What did you tell him?"

"I told him nothing! He can kiss my flabby old ass!"

"Now…look, Terresa…" Norris said, trying to control his smile.

"I don't care what you say, Chief. I don't like that man snooping around this village. Not here. Not on my watch! I shall not have it. I would prefer possums or killer rabbits!" she exclaimed and left, banging the door shut.

Norris sat glaring at the door.

By afternoon, Norris had completed all the administrative tasks. Mrs. Flores had calmed down, changing back to a lovely small-town lady. Norris was a bit surprised. Edgar had got on her nerves, which was very rare. As he finished his work, the phone rang. It was William. He answered the video call immediately. They wished each other a good afternoon. Norris noted that William's French beard had lost its shape, and the circles under his eyes were darker than usual. He thought he appeared a bit jaded.

"Any luck with the swords?" William asked.

"Not yet. I had a chat with Tom this morning. He is still looking."

William ran his hand through his beard, "Did you find Neville's head?"

"No, that's Edgar's job," replied Norris.

It was true. He did not have jurisdiction.

"Well, the time of death was around 6.00 am. I got the reports from the lab. His blood had no traces of drugs, or toxins. The crime scene was clear of blood spatter, tissue residue, or any other forensic evidence."

"That is unusual."

"Almost feels like someone knew how to clean up after themselves."

"Or he was killed somewhere else and then brought to the barn," Norris said. "We need to find the actual crime scene."

"I know."

Norris shook his head in disbelief.

"Any idea what he was doing in Willow's Heart?"

"No. According to Detective Tom Nash, his wife was visiting her mother and wasn't aware he was missing until the next day. She called the bar where Neville worked, and they told her he finished around 11.00 pm and went home. No one has seen him since."

"What about the neighbors?" William inquired.

"They didn't hear or see anything, and I don't think he made it home."

"What do you mean?"

"Tom found his car still parked near the pub," explained Norris.

"So, he was kidnapped?"

"Possibly."

"What about the motive?" William asked.

"Well, I thought he was killed because the killer thought he got away with a crime," Norris said.

William studied his face. "What changed your mind?"

"The evidence was circumstantial, and he had a solid alibi,"

"Sheriff, you and I both know people lie."

"Agreed. But if he really were a sexual predator, he wouldn't have stopped."

"You think Angela might have misidentified him?"

"It is possible. She went through a traumatic event, or someone pressured her."

William leaned back in his chair, folded his arms, and said, "So, Neville may or may not have committed the crime. He goes to court, gets acquitted…"

"It destroys his life," Norris added.

"And then he is brutally murdered."

"Yes. One year after Angela committed suicide," said Norris.

William hung his head, "Oh, God… what a tragedy!"

"The system is not perfect."

Their eyes locked each other.

"What about Angela's family?" asked William.

"Tom is trying to find her mother, Tamira. So far, there is no trace of her."

William massaged the back of his neck.

"Anything else on your mind?" Norris asked.

"One thing. There were traces of peculiar black powder at the crime scene."

"Yes. I noticed the half wiped out circular markings on the floor."

"The chemical analyzes for the power are complete," William said, reaching for a piece of paper. "It mainly comprises of forty-seven percent phosphate, twenty-five-point-three percent calcium, and eleven percent sulfate. Traces of additional nineteen minerals were detected, including potassium, sodium, magnesium, and iron oxide."

Norris was confused.

William took a deep breath. "It's ash. Human remains after a body is cremated."

Blood drained from Norris' face.

"Traces of sodium and chlorine were mixed with the ashes. That is salt. The murderer mixed ashes with salt, A similar black powder was found in the ritualistic killing of three children in which Gail was one of the prime suspects."

Norris froze. "What?"

"The killer used it to create shadow circles. Generally, black powder used in witchcraft doesn't contain human ashes. I think that the murders that halted with Gail's disappearance have begun again. It could be him or a copy-cat. I searched the internet, and the tourists and villagers have posted several pictures of these symbols all over the country. I have identified a few locations in Willow's Heart."

"Really?"

"Yeah."

"Let us assume this is Gail. Cremating a human body is not a simple process. I would check the funeral homes in Willow's Heart. But I doubt he would resort to those. It has to be a hidden chamber."

"If someone were to burn a body, wouldn't it smell bad?" Norris asked.

"Very bad, and I wouldn't be surprised if the villagers told you of an obnoxious smell coming from the valley."

Norris sulked and started making notes.

"The beheading, cremation, mixing of salt with human ashes and the shadow circles indicate that this could be a radical group."

"You mean a cult?"

William managed to smile. "Are there any cults in Willow's Heart?"

"I have no idea. I'll look into it," Norris said, writing it down.

"It might be worthwhile to check if relatives of Angela and Neville are linked to any religious groups."

Norris nodded. They were finally getting somewhere. He paused as a question popped into his mind. "Is it easy to find a cult?"

William rubbed his chin. "Maybe we should Google it."

17

LOVE ME DEAD

18th April 2020 (Present Day)
Old Sheriff's Office, Willow's Heart

I t was a fight of life and death. Outside the old sheriff's office in the dead of night, a shot rang. But it could not stop the wolf. Norris fell hard on his back. The beast's jaw clutched just inches from his face. He pulled the trigger again, and the bullet ripped through its heart. The wolf wailed loudly and collapsed on him. Norris tried to catch his breath, but the weight of the dead wolf was crushing his chest. With all his might, he pushed it off him. But it wasn't over. Then appeared its master. As cruel as the creature itself, or even worse.

"How dare you?" said a hoarse voice. "You will die for your sins!"

Screaming at the top of his lungs, the horned head man charged at him. Norris grabbed the blood-soaked gun and pulled the trigger. The bullet ripped through the hunter's chest, passing straight through his heart before disappearing into the wilderness. Even though the hunter wore a mask, Norris sensed the hunter's shock at the unbelievable turn of events.

A sense of tranquility returned to the valley as he sat at a distance staring at the dead wolf and its master. He rose to his feet and stared at his arms and clothes drenched in blood. Still recovering from the shock, he limped to the hunter and unmasked him. He didn't recognize the man, but he knew who was behind all this.

"You are not invincible, you fucking idiot! You are just a creep and a murderer," Norris shouted angrily.

18th April 2020 (Present Day)
Willow's Heart

Tom and Kyle jumped into the water. The wolf stumbled to a stop and peered into the void. It howled loudly. Tom felt the powerful pull of the water. He forced himself to swim upwards as he struggled against the strong current. The waves pulled him under, pinning him down. Not ready to give up, he kicked his legs and pushed himself above the water. He gasped for air and coughed.

"Kyle! Kyle!" he shouted.

There was no response. Tom saw a figure floating.

"Kyle!" he yelled, swimming toward him.

He swam with the current to get closer to Kyle. Before he could drift away, Tom caught his leg and pulled him closer. The deputy was unconscious.

"Kyle! Wake up!" he shouted, shaking him.

Kyle did not respond.

Tom was out of breath, but he swam to the shore and

shoved Kyle to the bank. Pulling himself out of the water, Tom fell on the mucky ground, soaking wet. He felt dizzy. He remained still and took deep breaths. A sudden movement in the corner of his eye drew his attention. Kyle woke up and coughed uncontrollably.

"Are you okay?" he asked, clearing his throat.

Kyle shook his head and continued coughing, "I am fine. Thanks. Thanks for getting me out of there."

"Don't mention it."

Tom checked their surroundings. The forest was dense, with enormous trees. The ground was uneven, full of bushes and huge roots sprouting from the earth. Several logs lay between the trees, and a thick layer of moss and fallen leaves covered the ground. He wished to leave Willow's Heart, but he knew better. They were in the middle of the forest, and it was a long way home. He wished to jump into the water and let it carry them away. But it was not an option. The river flowed west, away from their destination. The sound of coughing distracted him from his thoughts. Tom approached Kyle. He was on his feet, but his face was pale and his eyes red.

"We have lost them for now, but they will find us. We need to keep moving," Tom said.

But Kyle was not listening to him. He stood still like a statue, mesmerized. Tom followed his gaze. Dominated by the thick forest was a cave. Above it stood an ominous structure.

"What's that?" asked Kyle.

"I have no fucking idea," said Tom.

AN EYE FOR AN EYE

9th April 2020
Nightridge

The aroma of the eggs and toasted Turkish bread delighted Norris. He sipped coffee and ate in peace while relishing this moment of calmness before starting his hectic day.

Soon he was on his way to the office and was the first to arrive. After entering his office, he opened the window and settled down. Norris thought about the seven heads story. The media loved it and kept playing it over and over. He guessed it was something different from the pandemic and piqued the interest of journalists. Edgar had been interviewed twice, but to Norris's delight, he had kept the conversation light and didn't reveal vital information about the case. The NYPD detectives denied the interviews and left the journalist speculating.

Norris had discussed shadow circles with Tom. While he thought they were important and could be a symbol used by the cult behind the murders, Tom was skeptical. It was understandable. But there was more. The killer drew the shadow circles using a black powder, which was a mix of human ashes and salt. Over a decade ago, similar symbols were found at the crime scenes of the ritualistic killing of the three children in which Gail was involved. And now they had found them at the house where Neville's dead body was found.

Norris wanted Tom to follow this lead, but he was busy. He was still trying to trace Angela's mother and gather information about the swords. Norris took it upon himself to find out if these symbols meant anything. His search showed they could be linked with witchcraft. But he did not know. The world had changed. Hardly anyone believed in curses or demons and witchcraft was considered a work of fiction. People didn't care about this stuff. Other matters horrified them. Like unfiltered pictures on social media. Regardless, there was a killer out there who believed, and he had to find him.

The internet provided him with a wealth of information. Magic and rituals had been a part of every society for decades. He discovered most rituals involved shadow circles. Although, they were mostly used for peaceful purposes. The subject mystified people but also led to wild ideas about possession and black arts. According to the literature, given the propaganda by the media, many people had misguided notions about magic and occults and directly associated them with demons, death, and chaos. But there was some truth behind the stories.

Unfortunately, rituals related to cult murders had been reported throughout the centuries. Cults were common, and their practices were dark. Each used different symbols—like pentacles. Some created special symbols for their cult. He glared at the list of incidents just in the state of New York. It was hard to track cult members, and of course, their meetings were kept secret.

At first, Norris thought everyone could be a part of a cult. But he was wrong. He soon discovered cults were groups of people following a particular belief system and could be a danger to society and themselves. Several journalists believed that cult leaders controlled the members by psychological manipulation. He was searching for a group using shadow circles and beheading men and wolves. Until now, he had found nothing. Obviously, the members would not blog about it, but from his experience, he knew the internet was a wonderful resource. He kept looking.

His first target was Willow's Heart. The list was short, and most of the websites were old, with no recent comments or activity. Then he checked Nightridge. His jaw dropped. Fifty years ago, there was a powerful cult in his own village. It was called Noble Lives. They aimed to bring peace and pleasure to the soul. From what he gathered, it had over sixty members and many visitors who chose this lifestyle for a limited time. He thought that was odd. Usually, members of a cult could not leave easily. He searched a bit more but found no more details. Once the group's leader, Oliver Alter, left the organization, the cult dissipated, and the members vanished.

Norris felt tired. He got to his feet and made himself a cup of coffee. He returned to his desk after a few minutes and continued reading.

New York was a completely different story. The list of

cults and violence committed in the name of religion, gods, and justice was long. He felt he could spend his entire life reading on this subject. Horror filled Norris as he read one article after another. He had not realized the power they held, and the destruction caused by cults in human history. More or less, all cults followed a pattern. First, the birth. The cult was mostly created or taken over by a delusional man or woman. Then came the growth period—where the cult grew in numbers and prospered. After that came the fall, leading to death, mayhem, and chaos.

Norris enjoyed the last drops of his coffee and thought about what he had read. Most leaders thought they were avatars to the spiritual world or descendants of gods. They believed they had the power to heal, guide, and predict Armageddon. People followed them because these cult leaders promised to save them or help them find a place in heaven. It was believed that those who didn't follow the cult, or its beliefs, would burn in hell. Norris wasn't surprised. Fear led to submission. These leaders were like con artists who used the fear and insecurities of vulnerable people to control them.

He continued reading. Some groups were small and inconsequential, but certain groups started by cunning leaders grew and spread all over the world. The cult leaders had a history of abuse and delusions of superiority. In order to compensate for their own insecurities, they preyed on vulnerable people. Their grasp was so powerful that the members not only donated several million dollars to the organization but also served under the cult leader. It surprised Norris that the followers worked day and night, while their leaders lived like kings. But with all the money they got, they did not use it to improve the lives of their followers or to develop the community. These cult leaders bought weapons and deadly gases to prepare for Armageddon or to destroy the inferior beings or people who did not share their beliefs. The result—the cult ended in violence and death, leaving several people scarred for life.

Norris picked up the image of the shadow circles. *What kind of group am I dealing with, and what do they want?*

10th April 2020
Tom's Apartment, New York

Tom preferred to stay in bed and get some rest. He had spent an hour talking with Jenny the previous night, and it was exhausting. It was good to have a girlfriend, but it would have been great if she were here with him. The door to his bedroom was closed, yet he could hear the neighbors fighting. The bickering never stopped. Outside his apartment door, the women were screaming at each other. Dogs barked at the other end of the street. A loud drill echoed from a construction site two blocks down the road. He frowned.

Rubbing his eyes, he dragged his feet to the bathroom.

"Shut the fuck up! Can't a man have some peace?" he shouted.

No one heard him. The scream, the horns, and the barking continued.

"I need to move," he told himself.

Tom's foul mood was not entirely due to the neighborhood he lived in. The case was getting on his nerves.

10th April 2020

NYPD Precinct

Tom headed for work. As soon as he parked, two news reporters approached him. They began asking him questions about Neville's murder. He waved his left hand and rushed towards the Precinct. He tried not to get frustrated and quickly entered the building. They didn't follow him.

The precinct was no different. Cops were on the edge. Riots were still on and were becoming unpredictable. The captain was irritated and running the precinct during the shadow of the pandemic was becoming harder. Tom shut the office door, and for a moment, he felt like he had shut away all the problems.

He had just begun working when the door opened, and John stepped in.

"Hey," Tom said, noticing his partner looked tired.

John rubbed his eyes. "Hey. Did you get any sleep?"

"Not much. You?" Tom said.

"Not really."

The detectives got to work. Tom reviewed the list of people who owned curved swords. The tech department has identified several collectors located all over the country. Until midday, Tom was on the phone trying to contact them. But they were not helpful. The collectors lived in different states and beyond his jurisdiction, and they refused to answer his questions. Frustrated, Tom and John contacted law enforcement offices. They spent hours calling and emailing the collector's details. So far, their emails were received with polite autoresponders.

In the afternoon, Tom sat in the passenger seat and read the list of the sword collectors in New York. He studied the ten names and addresses of collectors and swordsmiths. Finding the first two swords was easy. They were at the museum.

10th April 2020
Metropolitan Museum of Art, New York

The Ford moved slowly down Fifth Avenue. Traffic had picked up, and horns blared from every direction. Tom sipped his fifth coffee, hoping it would keep him going. John parked behind a white van. Tom got out and straightened his jacket. The guard let them inside the museum, and Tom almost felt as if he had traveled to another world. The ambiance was completely different—the dim lights and smooth surfaces enhanced the tranquility. He smiled for the first time during the day.

"Mr. Edward Mitchell is on his way. Please wait here," said the guard.

Tom nodded. John stood beside him, chewing gum. He wore a face mask, and it looked awkward. Tom recognized the man who approached them. The skinny, experienced African American curator did not look happy. Since the last time he had seen him, Tom thought Ed had turned grayer.

"Good afternoon, detectives," said Mr. Mitchell.

"Morning. How are you today, Ed?"

"Good. You?"

"I am well," Tom said.

John yawned. Tom tried not to roll his eyes.

They followed the curator as Tom admired the décor. They entered the Great Hall, turned right, and climbed a few stairs. The floor was quiet, and their footsteps echoed as they walked past several artifacts. They stopped at the entrance of the Arms and Armor section. Tom saw hundreds of swords, knives, blades, and armors on display. Ed stopped, and Tom regarded the display holding ten swords.

"See, they are right here," said Ed.

Tom bent forward to study the last two swords.

"These were found in Bohemia, believed to be forged in the fifteenth century. Pure steel, and you can see the rust in the edges, and the part of the hilt is broken."

"These are beautiful," Tom said.

"They are called scimitar swords."

"Have they been used recently?"

Ed laughed. "These? They have been here for ages."

"Who has access to them?"

"The staff. But the museum has been closed due to the pandemic."

Tom knew it was a stretch, but he said, "I need to test them."

Ed let out an exaggerated sigh. "I am telling you, Tom, they haven't left the museum. Their edges are blunt. I don't think they would even cut a tomato."

"Ed, a man has been murdered. I want to make sure," Tom said, showing him a warrant.

Without reading, Ed shoved the document into his coat pocket.

"Sorry, I have to be thorough," Tom urged.

Ed said nothing and reached for the keys.

Tom tapped his fingers on the steering. He felt edgy. Two of the most expensive swords lay in the trunk of his car. They might not cut a tomato, but if he lost them, the captain would certainly cut him loose. He decided it was best to drop them for testing at the precinct.

10th April 2020
Hudson Street, Lower Manhattan

Mrs. Loren Stallard's apartment was spectacular and decorated with unique furniture and artifacts. The middle-aged woman in a blue dress looked curiously at the two detectives. Tom explained the reason for their presence.

"Do you own a sword like this one?" John asked, showing her a picture.

"Yes."

"If you don't mind, can we look at it?" asked Tom.

Mrs. Hawkins narrowed her eyes. "Why?"

"A man was murdered with a similar sword. We want to make sure it wasn't taken from your home."

"Murder?"

"Yes," Tom replied.

"Oh, my Lord!"

"And you still have yours, right?" asked John

Mrs. Stallard didn't look enthusiastic and led them to a display in the lavish living room.

"Here it is. I wish someone had stolen it. It was the ugliest twentieth-anniversary gift a husband could give his wife!"

Tom controlled his laughter, but John didn't.

Mrs. Stallard looked amused. "Don't get me wrong. I loved my husband. God bless his soul, but I hate swords."

Tom grinned. "And no one has touched it."

"I don't believe so."

"Then you don't mind if we take it for testing," Tom said, handing her over the warrant.

She swayed her hand and said, "Go ahead. I won't mind if you lose it."

Tom laughed. He wore gloves, opened the cabinet, and carefully lifted the sword. It was lighter than he thought. The hilt had lost its glow, and he noticed the blade was blunt, and the steel had rusted at some spots. Tom already knew it was not the murder weapon. And something told him the murderer would not leave it on a display for everyone to see. They thanked Mrs. Stallard and left. He placed the sword in the trunk and drove to their next destination.

10th April 2020
Midtown West, New York

Tom was losing hope. They had nine out of the ten swords, but he knew none of them was a murder weapon. When John pulled over, Tom studied the old building. They climbed a few steps and turned the knob. The door opened with a loud creak. Tom covered his nose from the foul stench hovering over the dim corridor. Dingy, muddy footprints covered the torn carpet and shouting echoed from one of the apartments.

They glanced at each other and climbed the creaking spiral staircase. Tom knocked on door number 5. Loud music blared from the other side. John banged his fist on the door, and a second later, the tenant, Earl Pitts, came out of his cave.

As soon as the door opened, the detectives were hit by

the pungent smell of cigarettes, pot, and alcohol. If Tom knew, he would have used two masks. A young man with long hair and tattoos on his chest looked at them with sleepy eyes.

"What's up?" he said.

Without a word, both detectives showed him their badges.

"What's up?" he asked again.

"Do you, by any chance, own a sword like this?" John said, showing him the photo.

"Oh, this baby... Yeah, I sold it!"

"Sold it?" Tom said.

"To whom?" asked John, stepping forward.

"None of your business."

"Say that again," said Tom glaring into his eyes.

"Back off! I needed the cash, man."

"To whom?" John repeated sternly.

"To some dude online," Earl replied and turned to take a seat on the couch.

The detectives carefully tip-toed over the littered floor, trying not to step on empty cans, wrappers, and food packets.

"When?" Tom asked.

"Ah... many months ago."

Earl drank the can of beer with a single gulp, crushed it, and threw it away.

"What was the name of this buyer?" John asked.

"I don't know... it could be a dude... could be a chick."

If the situation were different, Tom would have laughed. But today, he felt like breaking Earl's nose, "How did you get the sword?" he demanded.

"It belonged to my father," said Earl loudly.

"How did you send it to the buyer? By post? By courier?" John inquired.

"No, man, it was an exchange. Face to face."

"Right. Where? Where did the exchange take place?" Tom asked.

"At a club. Angel Wings."

"When?" Tom pushed.

"I don't know, dude…"

"When?" said Tom firmly.

"Just before Christmas… and all this pandemic shit!"

"Fine. Can you describe this man?"

"Tall, beard, drowsy eyes, no hair, and a lousy tipper," replied Earl.

John was making notes.

"How old was he?" Tom asked.

"He was an old dude, like you."

Tom raised his eyebrows. "Did he say anything to you?"

"No. We just talked."

"About what?"

"Girls and drugs, man!"

Tom stepped forward, grabbed Earl's collar, and made him stand. Earl's foul breath blasted in his face. "What did you talk about?"

"Nothing, man! Nothing!"

Tom shook him. "Tell me!"

"I told you. I told you… just girls and drugs."

Tom glanced at his partner, who stood with his hands folded.

"You better try harder," Tom said.

"I'm telling you, man… nothing! He bought the sword. We talked about stuff." Earl paused.

"And what else?"

"Nothing else!"

"Think, or you are going to spend the rest of the night in jail!" John pressured.

Earl's face turned pale, and he stared into John's eyes. The detective didn't flinch and glared back at him.

"Okay! Okay! He asked where he could get more swords of the same design. I told him about the swordsmith!"

Tom's eyes became fixed on him. "What swordsmith?"

"The shop from where my father got it custom made."

"What shop? Where is this swordsmith? Tell us where he is!"

"It's a she!" Earl yelled.

10th April 2020
Brooklyn, New York

Getting from Midtown West to Brooklyn was a long drive. Although Tom was not driving, he felt fatigued. He was almost ready to go home. After parking, the detectives entered the small mall. It was full of little shops selling various products. It was close to 6.00 pm, and most of the shopkeepers were preparing to finish for the day. Riddle Markson's shop was at the far end. Tom pulled on the handle, but the door was locked. He knocked and waited. There was no answer.

"Maybe she went home early," said John.

The door opened, and a young woman with short, highlighted red hair, wearing a crop top and funky jeans, stood in front of them.

"Sorry, I was changing," she said, letting them in.

She stepped behind the counter and waited.

The detectives entered the beautiful shop adorned with an assortment of designer knives and swords. They studied the blades in the display. They were not a match.

Tom and John identified themselves.

"Oh, cops…did someone get stabbed?"

They gazed at her.

"There was a stabbing six months ago. The owner caught a young guy stealing from him. The burglar got his hands on the knife and stabbed the owner. It was unfortunate, but I am glad no one died," Riddle explained.

"Did anyone lose their heads?" John asked sarcastically.

Tom turned to glare at him.

"What?" Riddle asked.

"Ignore him," Tom said and showed her the picture of the sword. "All we need is information on this sword."

"Sorry. I can't give you client details."

"It's a homicide, and we can get a warrant," said Tom.

She hung her head and reached for the register.

"Those are customized swords."

"How many of these have you sold?" he said, pointing at the picture of the sword.

She looked through the register. "Too many."

Tom looked at John. As if he was reading Tom's mind, John popped the question.

"What about in the last six months?"

She eyed him. "I am sure there were a few sales."

"Has someone ordered more than one?" John asked.

Riddle nodded. She went through the list of her customers and gave them a name.

"Ivy Hawkins. She ordered over two dozen swords five months ago."

"Two dozen? It didn't bother you?"

"It did. She said she was a sword trainer, and it was for her sessions. Trust me. I didn't believe her, but it was good money."

"Anyone else?" asked John.

"No. Only Ivy Hawkins ordered these customized swords in the last six months."

"Do you have her contact details?" Tom asked, reaching for his pocketbook.

"Yeah. A phone number and an address."

"How did she pay?" John asked.

"She paid in cash."

Tom took down the address.

10th April 2020
Brooklyn, New York

A thick blanket of night fell over the city. The bright city lights shimmered. Their car carried a mixed smell of coffee and snacks. Tom's back was stiff, and he wished he had some painkillers. Thankfully, this was their last stop of the day. After this, he headed home. He turned into Brunswick Avenue and slowed down the car. Tom was a bit surprised. It was a quiet neighborhood and reminded him of retirement homes. Bells rang, and the subway whooshed over the tracks.

Leaving the car behind, the cops entered the building. Ivy lived on the first floor. Tom banged his fist on the door and waited. It was answered by a lady, perhaps in her late eighties. She was frail with a mask on her face. An oxygen cylinder sat on the trolley behind her.

Tom smiled and showed her his badge. "Good evening, ma'am."

She nodded.

"Are you Ivy Hawkins?"

"Who?" she said loudly.

"We are looking for Ivy Hawkins," Tom said.

"Who the hell is that?"

Tom and John stared at each other with rising frustration.

10th April 2021
Nightridge

Norris shoved the paperwork aside. Today it had been only him and Mrs. Flores. The deputies were helping Edgar's team. He wondered if he should call them back. What if he needed them in Nightridge? A knock on the door drove him out of his thoughts. Kyle stepped in with his usual stride and dropped into the chair.

"How was your day?" Norris asked.

Kyle frowned. "We have been working with Edgar's men to find Neville's head. So far, we have found nothing. There is too much ground to cover and unfortunately the dogs have not picked up the scent."

Norris wasn't surprised. Finding a human head in that valley was like finding a needle in a haystack.

"You asked me to check out what is happening in Willow's Heart. I began with the villagers who stay on the outer edge of the valley. Most of them had heard about the murder but did not recognize Neville or noticed any strange occurrences on the night of the murder. But I must tell you, that place is creepy."

"The village?"

"Nah...the valley."

Norris raised his eyebrows. "Why?"

"First, the villagers despise going there. It has a grim history. Most of the land is owned by twelve families. They built homes, grew their own crops, and lived around an ancient fortress. In the last three decades, the descendants took over the ancestral land. Several moved out of the old houses and built new ones. The villagers who live on the outskirts of the valley don't like them. They describe them as strange, unconventional, superstitious, and dangerous."

"Dangerous? Why?"

"They are violent. There have been complaints of attacks on the villagers, and people tend to go missing in that valley."

"Really?"

"Seven men and six women were reported missing in Willow's Heart in the last nine months."

"That is a lot."

"They were tourists planning to hike in the mountains."

"Was there an investigation?" he asked.

"The state police arranged for a search and combed the entire valley. But found no traces of the missing people."

"This is not good."

"I agree. But there is very little we can do about it. I went to the sheriff's office and asked for the report. All I got was a death stare and skinny files with hardly any notes. I made photocopies."

Kyle put the thin stack of papers on the desk.

"What is the search status?" Norris asked.

"The search has been called off."

"Why?"

"Due to lack of evidence. It's assumed that these people might have vanished from somewhere else."

"But they were last seen in Willow's Heart," argued Norris.

"True. But the trail is cold. No one has heard or seen them since. The cops didn't even find a bag or shoe. It's like they vanished into thin air."

"When was the last disappearance?"

"Three weeks before the discovery of the wolves' heads."

Norris remembered the shadow circles. Was this killer murdering people, burning their bodies, mixing their ashes with salts, and using them in rituals?

"What else did you see?"

"Grass. Homes. More grass…," Kyle replied sarcastically

Norris regarded him. "What about the call you were waiting for?"

"It was a local shopkeeper. He was sure he had seen the last woman who had been reported missing."

"Who?"

"A Ms. Darla Reed," Kyle said, opening a file and showing him a picture of a woman in her thirties with long blonde hair and deep green eyes.

"And?"

"His shop was closed when I visited the village the last time. I had written my number on a card and left it in his letterbox. He called and told me he had seen her the day she was hiking in the valley."

"She visited his shop?"

"Yes. She had bought some supplies. After that, no one saw her."

Norris gritted his teeth. "And no one is looking for her?"

Kyle shook his head.

"What about their families?"

"The families have put in several complaints, but without evidence, nothing can be done."

Norris touched his head. "Good work, Kyle. I think we are done for the day. Keep searching. Contact the families of the missing people and find out the circumstances under which they disappeared."

11th April 2020
Meadow Cottage, Nightridge

Norris's bedroom was still cold when he woke up the next day. It was a Saturday, a day Norris liked to catch up on his sleep. The clock struck nine, and he stretched on the bed. His mobile chimed, but he ignored it and covered his face with a blanket. The phone rang again, and this time, he picked it up.

"Sorry to disturb you, Chief."

"Morning, Kyle. What is it?"

"Edgar called."

Norris sulked. "Again? Why?"

"He tried to reach you. I guess you are having network problems."

"Maybe," Norris replied not caring.

"He said we should come to Willow's Heart."

"Why?"

"He didn't tell me. He just said we should come right away."

Norris held his head.

He drank coffee as he drove. Kyle sat in the passenger seat, yawning. He stretched over the seat and then frowned.

"What could be so important?" Kyle grumbled.

"We will find out," Norris replied.

The truck raced on the road leading to the village. The truck shook, and he gripped the steering wheel firmly. During their one-hour journey, neither of them spoke. Norris was grumpy. He wished to return to Nightridge and enjoy his weekend. This was not his case or his county. The reason for Edgar's call remained a mystery until they reached their destination. Norris pushed on the brakes and jumped out of the truck. He marched towards a small house facing the mountain. Two cops stood near the entrance of the house. One of them was Edgar.

"Hey," Edgar said grimly.

"Hey," Norris replied. "So, what do we have here?"

Edgar frowned. They entered the house, and Norris noticed a middle-aged woman sitting on the couch sobbing.

"What happened?" Norris asked, feeling his heartbeat accelerate.

They came onto a large deck at the back of the house. A pool of blood grabbed his attention. A dead body sat against the fence with two large holes drilled through its eyes.

19

DEATH RUN

18th April 2020 (Present Day)
Old Sheriff Office, Willow's Heart

Norris stared openmouthed at the lifeless wolf. He felt terrible. The creature was innocent. His eyes shifted to the hunter. He felt no remorse for him. Not knowing what to do, he returned indoors. His knee ached. In the evidence room of the old sheriff's office, he found a pair of trousers and a white shirt.

He changed and dropped his blood-soaked clothes on the floor. Exhausted, he wanted to doze off and give up. But it was not an option. He retraced his steps to the dead hunter and found the gun where he had left it. He checked the cylinder. It was empty. Frustrated, he threw the weapon away. Finding his way back to the dead animal, he searched for the phone.

"Oh damn," he muttered, picking up the broken device covered with blood. Its screen was cracked. He pressed a few buttons, but it was useless. He tossed it away and retreated to his truck.

In the dead of night, he drove through the valley. Norris forced himself to stay awake. He needed to find a way. Two hunters were dead. He wished they would stop following them, but they were nuts and had lost all sense of reality. He glanced back. All he saw was a trail of dust. Suddenly, he pressed on the brakes. The vehicle stopped. He thought he heard an engine. A sharp beam of light cut through the void.

"Shit!" he shouted. He changed the gear with trembling fingers and pressed the accelerator. The truck reversed.

The hunters had found him again. The four-wheeler charged ahead, tailing the sheriff's truck. Norris pushed the pedal, attempting to maintain distance. But the four-wheeler was more powerful, and it rammed into the sheriff's car. Norris lost control. The truck spun and came to a sudden halt. Norris shook his head. The hunter's truck stopped and began turning. Taking his chance, Norris swung the wheel and floored the pedal heading straight for it. The tip of the truck hit the four-wheel drive. Sparks flew, and loud screeching echoed. The glass to his left shattered; Norris ducked but didn't slow down. The momentum pushed the hunter's truck to the side of the road. Norris increased speed. He glanced over his shoulder and saw beams of yellow light in the distance.

"Damn it! It didn't work!"

He pushed the accelerator, jolting the truck over the uneven surface.

He pushed the vehicle to its limit. It sprung over the rocky road. In the dim light, he noticed something—a narrow dirt road. He slammed the brakes. His hand dangled on the gear, and the vehicle reversed. It was perfect. He drove into the rough path and swayed the wheel, entering the bushes. When he thought he had gone far enough, he stopped the truck and shut off the engine. The vehicle sat in the middle of the bushes. Norris waited. He heard the roar of an engine as the hunter's vehicle passed by. In a few minutes, silence returned. Resting his head on the steering wheel, he wished he had never stepped foot in this valley.

Half an hour passed, and he continued to wait. The clock struck 1:00 am, and he didn't know what to do next. He could go back and save Tom and Kyle, but that was a bad plan. He was unarmed, injured, tired, and alone. Peering out of the window, he gazed at the moon. They still had time. He hoped his message had gone through.

18th April 2020 (Present Day)
Willow's Heart

The sound of water filled the silence in the forest. Tom shivered. He was soaked from top to bottom. He glared at the cave and then looked at Kyle.

"What do you think?" Kyle asked.

"We should check it out," said Tom.

"Technically, it should not exist. It was not on the map."

"Well… it does exist," said Tom.

He wiped his face. Cold crept through his body. He rubbed his hands to keep himself warm as they made their way toward the cave.

The sound of the flowing water subsided as they entered the cave. Tom welcomed the quietness. But then he heard something else. The humming noise was unmistakable. Tom reached for his gun and realized he was unarmed. He cursed under his breath. Watching their step, they moved to the deep end of the cave. Tom paused a few minutes later, letting his eyes adjust. He thought he saw a glimmer of light.

"Do you see that?" he whispered.

"Yes."

Together, they made their way to the source of the light, which was a small window near the roof of the cave. Kyle gave Tom a boost. Gripping the rocks, Tom peered in. His jaw dropped. Plastic curtains divided the hall into four parts. Moonlight crept from the narrow windows near the ceiling. Tom strained his eyes but could hardly see anything. He jumped down.

"What did you see?"

"A room divided into sections with plastic sheets. Could be a lab. We have to find the entrance."

"Good idea," said Kyle, "and there might be a phone or computer we can use."

Tom nodded.

They emerged from the cave and walked around the structure. Tom pushed the branches of the trees to clear their path. He took a step forward, his foot landed on a rock. He slipped but caught a tree branch to break his fall.

"You, okay?" Kyle asked.

"This is nuts!" Tom muttered, missing the clean and flat roads of the city.

They searched the woods and soon found another opening.

"Wow…," said Kyle

"They have hidden it well," Tom remarked and entered. As soon as he did, he knew it was manmade. The stone walls were smooth, and the ground was flat with layers of tar. He believed it would be extremely hard to find this place. It was in the middle of the forest, enclosed by trees and its openings were well camouflaged. They came to a halt and gazed at the door. Tom took a deep breath and extended his hand. It opened with a creaking noise.

"They left it open?" Kyle remarked.

"Maybe they don't expect anyone to turn up," replied Tom.

Wishing he was armed, he entered the narrow, short passage. A pungent odor caught him by surprise. As if something had died. Then there were hints of a disinfectant. It reminded him of the hospital. Cautiously, the cops entered the hall. Tom pulled the sheet aside with his fingers and saw three large tubes that emerged from the roof, with several lights at the end. Below the lights, sat a shiny, cold steel table. No one needed to tell him what it was. He had seen it too many times in hospitals and at the morgue. Next to the operating table were three cabinets attached to the wall. An empty trolley, an oxygen tank, a ventilator, and a defibrillator were placed in a corner. Tom headed straight for the cabinets. He flung it open to find several surgical instruments. Tom left the operating theater and entered another section of the hall. Kyle stood glaring at a stack of red boxes with the words "human organs" imprinted on them. Tom gulped and opened a red box. It was empty. Kyle checked the rest of the boxes. There was nothing in them as well.

"Where did these come from?" Tom asked out loud.

Kyle ran his fingers through his soaked hair.

Tom scanned the boxes for any details. There were none.

"Any idea what was in there?" Kyle asked.

Tom had a guess, but he was not sure. The origins of the artificially created organ remained unknown. "I can't say. Let's find a phone."

Tom was getting desperate. He wanted this night to end, to go home, and forget about the case. He wished he had killed Gail when he had the chance. A cold draft hit him in the face when he opened the refrigerator. It was empty. He spun around, noticing two long benches covered with plastic sheets. He pulled the sheets off and found two microscopes and dingy test tubes stored in a tube rack. Tweezers and beakers of several sizes sat in a corner, collecting dust. In a box, Tom saw petri dishes, boxes of slides, goggles, and masks. But there was no phone. He turned to Kyle, who looked apprehensive.

"Let's get the hell out of here," Kyle said.

Tom was exasperated. They had not found the phone. But now he knew where the victims had undergone had the organ transplants.

20

THE FIELD OF ASHES

12th April 2020
Willow's Heart

Norris could not believe it, but it was true. Another victim. He removed his hat and kneeled to look into the hollow sockets. All he saw was blood and tissue. Bile rose to his throat. The blood had drained over the victim's face and neck and spread on the floor. The long deep scars on the victim's legs were horrible. He had been attacked by wolves. Splattered on the floor was a substance mixed with blood. It was black powder. As he stood up, he saw a half-wiped-out shadow circle on the floor.

The gruesome scene made Norris lightheaded. He returned to the living room, where Edgar was talking with the owner of the house. This case worried Norris. Gail's death remained a mystery. Neville's murder was still a mystery, and now another man was dead.

The house owner, Mrs. Gina Feyrer, was a short woman with snow-white curly hair. She regarded Edgar through her thick glasses. "I was away for two days, and when I returned... oh my god. Oh, my god... it's horrible. Horrible! Please take him away. Take him away!"

"You saw no one... saw nothing?" asked Edgar.

"No. No. It was just another day. I had gone to visit my son and his family, and when I returned...he...was there."

Edgar frowned.

"Have you seen him before?" Norris asked.

"I don't know! I didn't see his face... I cannot!" she cried.

Norris nodded.

"Does anyone fitting his description live in Willow's Heart?" Norris asked Edgar.

"Stop asking questions and get him out of here!" Gina yelled.

"Gina," said Edgar, "it is going to take a while. We need to search the house for evidence that could lead us to the murderer."

"What? No! No..."

"Gina...it will be best if you stay somewhere else for a few days," said Edgar.

"It is not fair! This is my home! Why would anyone do this? Oh, my god! What am I going to do?"

Edgar tried to smile to show his sympathy. Norris didn't say anything. He didn't know these people; not like he knew the villagers of Nightridge. He felt like an outsider. Norris gave them space and left the house. The sunshine warmed his skin. Birds were singing in the trees and the wind played with the crops that swayed back and forth on its tunes. Horses galloped in a large wood enclosure, and pigs snorted as if complaining of the muddy ground. The cool wind blew as he strolled over thick, dried grass. He saw Kyle glaring at something through his binoculars.

"What is it?" he asked.

"I am not sure… take a look," Kyle said.

Norris glimpsed through the binoculars. Adjusting the focus, he blinked twice. It was unbelievable.

"A tower?" he muttered, eying Kyle.

"It's odd, isn't it? What is it doing here?"

He observed the structure once again and said, "Let's go check it out."

Together they approached Edgar who was still talking with Mrs. Feyrer. When their conversation finished, Norris said. "I am heading off. Could you send the body to Dr. Sterling?"

Edgar appeared uncertain. Norris wondered if it was a problem. On the other hand, Edgar had asked for his help.

"Shouldn't you stay until the CSI unit finishes?" said Edgar.

"I don't think I can contribute anything at the moment. I am needed back at Nightridge. But you can call me anytime."

Edgar looked unconvinced. Norris didn't care and left with Kyle on his side.

"Chief, you just lied to the sheriff," Kyle whispered.

Norris glanced at Edgar's officers. They had begun searching the premises.

"I know. Let's go."

Kyle raised his eyebrows. "If you say so, Chief."

Norris marched toward his truck, and Kyle followed.

12th April 2020
Field of Ashes, Willow's Heart

The drive was beautiful. Bulky trees stood on both sides of the road. The ground was full of a mixture of soil and layers of leaves. From within the trees, he saw the massive mountains. The road became steep, and he reduced his speed.

As Norris drove, he noticed a billboard: *Ancient Lands. Private Property*.

Norris saw the tower and knew he was close. According to the map, it was called the Field of Ashes. He thought the name was a bit unusual. When he thought he was close enough, he stopped the truck on the side of the road. Flabbergasted, he stepped out and stared at the large clearing.

"What is it?" asked Kyle, marching ahead, almost stumbling on a rock. Norris grabbed his arm.

The cops stood in awe. The Field of Ashes was nothing like they had seen before. It was big; and Norris imagined it would take him at least 10 minutes to run from one point to another. The twelve pillars stood in a circular fashion and were almost two meters tall.

"This is beautiful," muttered Norris, stepping nearer to a stone pillar.

Deep indentations divided the surface of the pillar into four parts. Norris kneeled and observed the strange carving in the lower section of the pillar. It reminded him of incarnations and carvings on stones he had seen in museums. He lifted his head. A few of the symbols looked similar. Like the pentacle. It had been drawn in several locations all over the village and around the victims. The next one was a pentacle with two crescent moons. The symbol above it attracted his attention—a triangle was carved over a pentacle. He wondered what it meant. He glowered at the third section with an array of strange symbols. Faces with horns and a snake eating its own tail. Inverted crosses and a creature with a wolf's head and wings. Then his eyes set on the last symbol. It was a daunting mask drawn in the middle of a wheel. Four hours emerged from its crown shaped head and its eyes were wide, and horrifying. Norris gulped nervously.

His eyes roamed to the top, and he wondered out loud, "How do we get up there?"

"I have an idea," said Kyle and rushed to the truck.

Norris waited as Kyle maneuvered the truck closer to the pillar. He climbed on the hood and stood on the roof. Standing on his toes, he observed a structure which was about forty inches tall with a triangular roof and four pillars. It sheltered an old rusting mirror on a stand. Norris studied the position of the sun. He jumped off the truck and marched to the furthermost pillar toward the east. Kyle repositioned the truck, and Norris stood on the truck's roof observing. This pillar was higher. His eyes turned toward the west, and he noted another pillar exactly opposite to this one. Stepping down, he wondered why these pillars existed. Kyle drove the truck back to the roadside and parked it.

Norris wandered to the middle of the field and, for the first time, noticed the smooth sand. A mixture of black powder with a hint of gray covered the surface. His blood ran cold. He bent over and touched it. It was smoky and devoid of any smells. It was a mixture of ashes and salt. He froze.

Kyle came to stand beside him. "Chief is this..." his words trailed away.

The cops stiffened. They were standing in the center of a

field full of ashes. He thought it was a metaphor. But he was wrong.

"This is unbelievable!" Kyle muttered.

Norris kneeled, running his hand through the mixture of mud and ash. He felt something hard. Out of the smoky dust, he picked a long, thick white object. To the naked eye, it looked like a bone. It was over five inches long, thin, and white. He stood up, and his heart was drumming hard. Placing the bone in an evidence bag, he put it in his pocket. Kyle collected a sample of the ashes and sealed the bag. They slowly retraced their steps back to the truck. Once out of the field, Norris felt a bit better.

"Where did all this ash come from?" Kyle asked.

Norris was tongue-tied. He didn't have the answers. His eyes settled on another tower at a distance. It was the fortress.

"Kyle, take pictures of the pillars and let's see what we can find out."

Kyle nodded.

12th April 2020
NYPD Precinct

Tom was furious. He cursed under his breath as he reviewed the thin file. Ivy Hawkins, who had ordered the swords, did not exist. The culprit had stolen the identity and the social security number of the real Ivy Hawkins, who was eighty years old and could barely walk without a cane. The swords that he had collected had no traces of blood.

Tom rubbed his temples and shut his eyes. He was determined not to let Gail get away again. He was sure fake Ivy was working with him. But right now, it was all in his head. He needed evidence. Tom was getting edgy. He flipped through the files as John sat munching on his third donut. The phone rang, and Tom answered it quickly. It was Officer Jake Karamen. Since Neville's murder, Tom had Gail's wife under surveillance. Jake had been on the job for the last couple of days and Tom had been waiting for an update.

"Morning, Detective," said the officer.

Tom heard a commotion in the background. "Morning. What have you found?"

"I have interviewed Mrs. Clegg."

"Any luck?"

"She didn't say a lot. According to her, her husband is dead, and the NYPD is responsible for his death. Did you know she planned to sue the department?"

Tom grunted. "No. I didn't."

"Her lawyer persuaded her to leave it alone. But she was annoyed at me for asking questions about Gail and told me to let him rest in peace."

"I hope for the same," Tom said sarcastically.

"I have been watching her house for the last four days. Nothing odd about her routine. She is in her forties, works in the post office, goes to church every week, and has no criminal record."

"Any kids?"

"Nope," replied Jake.

"And she didn't remarry?"

"Nope, and there is no boyfriend in the picture."

"Okay."

"I spoke with her neighbors. They think she is lovely. Most of them pity her because she is alone, with no kids, no one to support her and an ex-husband who was a criminal. Mrs. Kathon, a retired lady living in the apartment next to Mrs. Clegg, says she has a lot of visitors."

"Visitors?" Tom said.

John came to stand beside him.

"Yeah. Around four to six people every few days."

"A different group or the same?"

"Usually different, except for one lady."

"Who?"

"She doesn't know her name. But yesterday, Mrs. Clegg had visitors, and I took a few pictures. Mrs. Kathon has just identified her, and I am emailing the picture to you."

"Sure," Tom said, opening his email.

Jake sent the pictures, and Tom placed all the images next to each other on the screen. The woman had sharp blue eyes, and a long nose with a broad forehead. She had tied her thin blonde hair up in a neat pony. Physically, she looked fit. Like someone who did rigorous exercises. She was taller than the others and carried a sense of authority.

"Does she look familiar?" he asked John.

He shook his head.

"Could she be the woman who ordered the swords?" John asked.

"Maybe."

Tom hit the print button.

"Good work, Jake."

"I will keep you updated."

The call ended.

The printer came to life, and a piece of paper with the suspect's image popped out.

"John. Would you pay a visit to the swordsmith and ask if this was the woman who had ordered the swords?"

John thoughtfully studied the photos and picked up his jacket and left the office.

The clock struck 1.00 pm, and Tom rubbed his eyes. He stretched and got ready to go for lunch when his phone rang. It was Norris. Tom answered quickly.

As soon as they finished their pleasantries, Norris got to the point, "Did Edgar call you?"

"Nope. Why?"

"We found another one."

Tom's heart sank. "Oh no! Another victim? Who? Where?"

"Peter Elsher. In Willow's Heart. His body was found in Mrs. Feyrer's house. He has a criminal record."

Tom did not think Peter was linked to Gail.

"What's his story?" he asked.

"Married, has a son, and lived in Queens. He was a cashier working in a café. Here is the thing. Seven years ago, he was arrested for a hit-and-run."

"I see," Tom said, leaning forward in his chair and searching for the name in the system.

"A black sedan hit Luke Taylor. Luke was taken to the hospital but did not survive the accident and died within an hour. The police arrested Peter Elsher because he had a similar car and was in the vicinity. In his first statement, Peter denied his involvement in the accident. But the cops found traces of Luke's blood on Peter's car. When he was questioned again, Peter changed his story and confessed."

"So, he did it," Tom said.

Peter's record popped up on the monitor.

"He did. But he claimed the kid came out of nowhere. The cameras supported his statement. Luke was jaywalking. There were no streetlights, and it was foggy and dark. Hell, even I would not have seen him," said Norris.

"What happened?"

"Peter was charged with Class D Felony, an accident resulting in death. He spent seven years in jail and was released last year. Five months before the pandemic hit."

"Poor guy. It looks like it was an honest mistake," Tom said.

"I agree. But to kill him in such a way…"

Tom shivered. "How did he die?"

Norris became silent. "Oh, sorry. I didn't tell you?"

"Nope…" Tom replied, not sure if he wanted to know.

"His eyes were drilled with a…"

"What?"

"Yes. The body has been sent to William."

Tom held his head. "Someone thought his sentence was not enough?"

Norris said nothing.

"Did he live in Willow's Heart?" Tom asked.

"No."

Tom sulked. The call finished, and Tom shut his eyes. He glared into nothingness, wondering how he was going to handle this case. Another murder. A man who had already paid a high price for his mistake. Seven years in prison is grueling, not to mention the aftermath. Tom wondered about Peter's family. It was a tragedy, and he was powerless to do anything about it. Shoving his feelings aside, he called John.

"Hey, where are you?" he said.

"Huh! Stuck in traffic!" John replied unhappily.

"There has been another one," Tom said.

"Another murder? Oh, no…"

"This one is worse…" Tom muttered.

12th April 2020
City Morgue, New York

One glance at Peter's body, and William's plans to relax this evening melted away. This was an extra case, and he had just finished paperwork for six recent cases. However, he could not hand over Peter's autopsy to someone else. The second body they had discovered in Willow's Heart had a head, but the eyes were gone. He wondered why the killer was targeting specific parts of the body. Neville was beheaded, and Peter was blinded. Why? William frowned. He was still working on Neville's autopsy, and another body had turned up. He wondered if Peter also had an artificial organ.

He ran his hands through his head and remembered his boss's protests. He was not happy and wanted William to wrap up the case quickly. William was glad he stood his ground and bought himself time. He hadn't shared his unexpected findings with anyone and thought it was best not to reveal anything for the time being. He had taken precautions and asked Juliet to keep the samples separate and away from prying eyes. The pathologist was skeptical but promised to keep things quiet.

He sat down and went through his schedule for tomorrow. He had a lot of paperwork and two autopsies. Johnathan's primary examination suggested the two people had drowned. Police officers had found the bodies in the Hudson River near George Washington Bridge. They were unidentified, and as medical examiners, their first job was to find out who these people were.

"It could be accidental drowning or a murder," he said to himself.

Checking the time, he realized he had to start now if he wanted to get home and get a little sleep.

"Maybe I should just sleep here," he murmured. But as soon as he said it out loud, he hated the idea.

He rushed to the radiology lab. A little after 6:00 pm, the technician began taking and developing the X-rays. William returned to his office with a cup of coffee. He went through the crime scene photos. Peter was forty-five, with straight light brown hair and a narrow face. He was barely ninety-nine pounds. A wolf had clearly made the long, deep lacerations on his limbs. He had seen similar ones on Neville's lower limbs. Except for the bite marks, there was a long scar on his left leg. It was an old injury. He found multiple blue bruises on his arms, legs, back, and chest. Peter had been beaten with a blunt object maybe a week ago. Did Peter get into a fight? Similar injuries were found on Neville's body.

That's interesting.

The crime scene was clean. They only found the prints of the house owner, Mrs. Feyrer, and two more unidentified prints. The owner claimed those prints might belong to her children, who often visited her. It was a possibility. He guessed Edgar would be trying to get hold of the children. William studied the blood on the floor. The drenched clothes and neck were enough to tell him the blood belonged to the victim. William could not imagine the pain Peter would have felt. Did he die because of his injuries? William did not know. The technician dropped Peter's X-rays, and they spoke for a while. Once he was gone, William got to work.

Back in the autopsy room, William secured the gully. Everyone else had left, and he was glad. It was the best time to get some work done. He mounted the X-rays on the view box and went through them one by one. All of them were normal except the head. The eye sockets were larger than normal and gave the skull an unusual appearance. At first glance, it gave the impression that the head belonged to a genetically mutated human or an alien. But he knew it was neither. It was an unfortunate man who had been tortured and killed by a psychopath. He read Norris's notes and realized Neville and Peter: both had criminal records.

Now that looks like a pattern.

He turned to the body. Before he began the autopsy, he inspected the skin. William thought it was better to do this methodologically. He began from the toes. He studied the feet, cut the toenails, and bagged them. Then he focused on the ankles. The bones were intact, and there were no recent injuries. The legs were a different story. They were full of bruises made by a blunt object. Maybe a baseball bat. The deep lacerations on both legs were no surprise. He had been attacked by wolves.

Once he was done with the left leg, he shifted his attention to the right. He paused at the mid-thigh. Between the bluish patch of skin, he saw a scar. Picking up a marker, he circled it, then took pictures. Afterward, he flipped the body. There were multiple lacerations, and from their angles, he assumed they were from two different blunt objects. There had to be two assailants. He checked the skin for scars.

Nothing caught his attention. Content with his evaluation, he repositioned the body, and now it was facing upwards. Like Neville, Peter had no surgical scar on his abdomen.

Next William focused on the head. The hair on both sides was drenched with blood. It meant when he was killed; he fell back, and the blood drained from his eyes, spreading over the skull, and dripping to the ground. He made a note to search for soil and chemical residues. After preparing the samples to send to pathology, he turned to the body and made a Y-shaped cut.

It took him no time to cut through the chest cavity to expose the heart and the lungs. There were no signs of enlargement or scarring of the heart. There were also no visible lesions. He weighed the organ and placed it on a tray. Then he autopsied the lungs.

Once he had disconnected the left lung, he sliced open the organ. Unlike Neville, who was a chain smoker, Peter's lungs looked healthy, with no fluid or unidentified masses. The alveoli appeared normal, and there was no evidence of pneumonitis or other infections. The major pulmonary vessels and airways were free of any blood clots or emboli. Satisfied, he checked the right lung. The findings were no different. The lungs weighed around seven hundred grams each. He made notes and continued his work.

Peter died approximately eight hours after his last meal. The stomach contents were minimal. Finding nothing more to report, he checked the colon. It was healthy. The liver was normal for a forty-five-year-old. He did a quick biopsy and then turned to the spleen. He paused. It was enlarged. Fear gripped him.

"Oh, please don't tell me," He muttered.

He quickly sliced the muscle's attachments and partially disconnected the spleen from the body. There it was. The unidentified organ. It was attached to the cluster of lymph nodes also known as cisterna chyli. While conducting Neville's autopsy, he had discovered the unknown organ at the same spot.

"I don't believe this," he said.

He examined the abdominal muscles. They had been sliced through and then stitched together. The muscles had healed, that meant the surgery had taken place over three months ago. But without more information he couldn't determine the surgery date. He closely reexamined the superficial skin of the left side of the stomach. There was no scar. There were methods of getting rid of unwanted scars, and Peter might have used them to hide the surgery.

"Okay…now there are two!" he shouted.

William focused on the organ. After disconnecting the unidentified organ from the lymph nodes and spleen, he stared at the two artificial organs in the jars suspended in liquid. The pear-shaped organs were about three centimeters long and two centimeters wide. Each weighed around eleven grams. They appeared identical. Maybe this was a good thing. Juliet would have two samples, and she could use them to confirm her findings. William was eager to find out what Juliet would come up with. He noticed the clock. It was 1:00 am. His eyelids drooped, and he thought it was best to complete his work and head home.

13th April 2020
NYPD Precinct, New York

Tom had a sleepless night. He turned up at the precinct in the morning feeling dreadful. Peter's death bothered him. He wished no one else would die and they would catch this killer soon. He had barely eaten anything since last night, and now his head was sore due to all the caffeine he had consumed. Taking an aspirin had helped little. He glanced over his shoulder. John was away. His last message said he was with Jake, trying to find more information. To kill time, he checked his email. There were too many of them. He frowned.

After a few minutes of answering emails, the door opened. Tom smiled at his partner.

"Morning…" John said.

"Good morning. How did it go?"

John took a seat. "Better than I expected. The people who visited Mrs. Cleggs this week were Mr. Jon Turner, Mr. Walt Hackett, Mrs. Ria Potter, and Mrs. Julia Lloyd. Their stories check out. Mrs. Clegg volunteers as a social worker and offers support to people who have lost their family. These people have lost a family member to cancer, old age, or suicide. None of these people are involved in any current or past court cases."

"So, she organizes group sessions for coping with family loss… like the AA," Tom concluded.

"Yep."

Tom sulked. "It's a dead end."

"Not really. Remember Ivy Hawkins?"

"The woman who bought the swords. Is she one of them?"

John stepped forward and showed him the picture of a

woman. It was the same one who had visited Mrs. Clegg several times.

"I showed her the picture to the swordsmith. She said she looked like the woman who had ordered the sword but was not sure. We ran her through the system."

"What's her real name?"

"Mrs. Ella Morgan," John said with a smile, "She is a nurse who joined this group after she lost her daughter."

The detectives matched Ella's old photo as a nurse with the one Jake had taken a few days ago.

"The nurse who operated on Gail when I shot him!" Tom added, feeling excited.

"The same."

"It could be possible she saved Gail and faked the records."

"But why? Why would she save him?" Tom asked.

"I don't know. She didn't have any priors and just vanished after her daughter's death. As far as we know Gail and Ella didn't know each other."

"Hmm... find out everything we can about her. Tell Jake to follow her the next time she comes to visit Mrs. Clegg."

John texted Jake.

Tom sat with his arms folded, wondering about their next steps.

"But why? Why would she help him?" he said.

"We don't know."

Tom slid down in his chair and crossed his feet.

"The second victim is Peter?" asked John.

"Yep."

"Has William completed the autopsy?"

"He has begun."

Both cops sat thoughtfully.

"It makes no sense. When Neville was set free and murdered after one year of trial, I thought someone wanted revenge. But with Peter's death, that theory does not make sense anymore. And none of the victims have the slightest connection with Gail."

"I agree. There is something else going on," John said.

21

TOO CLOSE TO DEATH

18th April 2020 (Present Day)
Garsow Radio Station, Willow's Heart

Norris's heart was still beating fast. He could see the dead hunter and his wolf in front of the old sheriff's office. Hiding in the bushes had worked. The hunters had lost his trail. As soon as the coast was clear, he reversed the truck returning to the main road.

Norris mindlessly drove the truck through the dense forest. Norris felt lifeless and couldn't think straight. What had he done? What had he become? How was he better than these hunters? Tears rolled down his face. He thought he had left the war behind, but he was wrong. Putting his feelings aside, he focused on what needed to be done. In order to survive, he had to kill them. Or it would have been his dead body lying in the dirt.

You did what you had to do. You had no choice.

But it felt like he was lying to himself.

Shaking his head, he tried to focus on his destination.

Choosing a vantage point, Norris parked the truck. He came to the edge of the cliff. The view was not great. He climbed a tree, set himself on a branch, and looked through the binoculars. He watched the woods. The old fortress was shrouded in darkness. He then turned his attention to the Field of Ashes. It was vacant. Dust rolled along with the soft wind. The road leading out of the valley was quiet. He was all alone. He had killed two huntsmen and wolves, but there were more, and they were dangerous. So far, he had been lucky. But he knew he would need help soon. If his message had gone through, he knew Mrs. Flores would leave no stone unturned. She would find him. Get the help they needed. The moon would vanish in a couple of hours, which meant game over.

Do I just sit here and wait until help comes?

If help didn't come on time, he would lose his friends. Then Norris thought of why he came here. His eyes set on the dwelling. The Garsow Radio Station was abandoned a long time ago. A broken satellite dish atop the station's roof was as big as the sheriff's office in Nightridge. He tried to talk himself out of it.

But I can do more.

"Damn,"

Making up his mind, he climbed down the tree, dusted his clothes, and was about to head for his truck. He paused. It would attract too much attention. He walked instead.

18th April 2020 (Present Day)
The Temple, Willow's Heart

Tom felt his legs ache and his muscles tearing apart. But

they were running out of time. The moonlight brightened the cloudless sky, and a sweet scent of jasmine lingered through the forest. Surrounded by trees that touched the sky, Tom wondered when they would reach their destination. The nearest house was too far away. They had been on the run for over two hours. He watched his step as he treaded over a log and jumped to the other side. Kyle followed. The young man was about to walk ahead when Tom pulled him behind a tree.

"What is it?" Kyle asked.

Tom put his index finger on his lips. The men peeped from the shadows. Six figures wearing unusual masks with horns walked in pairs. A tall figure wearing a mask led them. It reminded him of the dragons in the Chinese festival. It was not big, but equally fierce looking.

"Where are they going at night?" Kyle whispered.

"That is an excellent question," he replied and signaled for him to follow. "Let's see where they are heading."

Kyle looked uncertain. "That is not a good idea."

Taking cover behind the trees, Tom followed the group. To his surprise, they were heading away from the fortress.

Where are they going?

Tom felt the temperature rise, and his heart was beating faster by the minute. Soon, they neared the foot of the mountains. He hid behind a tree and watched the group vanish into a small opening.

"Exactly how many caves are there in this valley?" Tom muttered.

Despite their situation, a smile crept across Kyle's face.

"Okay. Let's check it out."

"I don't think we should follow them. It could be a trap," said Kyle.

"True. But don't you want to know what they are doing out here?"

Kyle gaped at him. "We just escaped one death trap. Are you sure we want to step into another one?"

"Let's go."

Tom knew it was crazy, but he was curious to find out what else the hunters were hiding. Making sure they were not being watched, Tom swiftly ran into the cave. Kyle was right behind him. Fastening himself to the uneven wall, Tom checked to ensure the tunnel was empty. Using the wall as a guide, they slowly made their way to the end of the tunnel.

Tom paused when they heard murmurs. The tunnel opened into the heart of the mountain, which was dimly illuminated with candles along the wall. Staying out of sight, they hid behind a big box.

Tom checked their surroundings. The temple was as wide as his living room. Three large rocks of different shapes stood close to the entrance. Candles decorated the wall of the temple. It was around seven feet high. Smoke rose from several incenses displayed upright on a table. Two vases holding fresh flowers sat beside an image of a naked woman with wolves. Two pentacles were painted in red on the wall. The hunters got on their knees and began praying. Tom assumed these were traditions their predecessors followed. He had no issues with customs. What bothered him was the murders, kidnapping, and experimentations.

The hunters began to chant, their voices echoing throughout the temple. The prayers finished, and the figures bowed. They got on their feet, bowed once more, and left the temple as peacefully as they came. Tom thought it was best not to disturb anything. He studied the walls and did not see a surveillance camera.

"Let's have a quick look...and leave."

Kyle nodded.

Tom peered into the tunnel to make sure the hunters were not returning. He approached the image of the woman. A scent of rose and lavender dominated the air. He checked and found no other exits. Satisfied this was a dead end, Tom got ready to leave. A low mourning echoed.

The men froze.

22

MYSTERIES OF THE PAST

13th April 2020
Meadow Cottage, Nightridge

Nightridge was peaceful, but Norris was restless. Lying in his bed, he felt like a sword was hanging over his head. It was past midnight, and he hadn't slept a wink. There was something more going on, and he kept thinking about Edgar. A sheriff? He could not believe it. Had he changed? He remembered how Edgar had treated him when he left the military. Every bone in his body told him he was not trustworthy. He had an ulterior motive. He forced himself to think positively.

People change, and I should give him the benefit of the doubt.

But no matter how hard he tried, it bothered him. Edgar's sudden return to his life was unusual. The case of seven slaughtered wolves, followed by two brutal murders.

Why did he call me?

Mrs. Flores was right to doubt Edgar, and Norris shared her concerns. He turned to his side and imagined Martha's smiling face. He didn't know how much time he had left, and it was best not to waste time worrying about things out of his control. Leaving his comfortable bed, he came downstairs and poured himself a drink.

Yellow lamps stood along the village streets. Norris drank whiskey in a rocking chair on the porch. He had to wait for things to unravel. William was on the case, and Tom was dependable. He would not give up and most of all he had Kyle on his side. They were a good team. If there was a problem with Edgar, they could handle it. The drink and cool breeze helped, and Norris soon returned to bed.

13th April 2020
NYPD Precinct

Tom read William's preliminary report on the second murder. Peter had been restrained. His neck, hands, and legs showed ligature marks. The crime scene photos revealed the killer had destroyed his eyes using a powerful drill with a seven-millimeter drill bit. The murderer had destroyed the left eye first. Tom held his head. It was a terrible way of killing someone, and he couldn't comprehend the pain Peter must have endured. The drill had destroyed the eyeballs, fractured the sockets, and entered the skull, causing severe hemorrhage in the brain. The cause of death was excessive blood loss. According to William, Peter would have survived if he had been taken to a hospital immediately.

It was unbelievable that people were capable of such horror. Why torture and kill him? What did they want? Was he a part of a gang? Maybe this was justice. In the killer's eyes, Peter got away with a crime, and he was destined to die.

But the motive didn't make sense to Tom. Peter had spent seven years in jail for his crime, and Tom thought people deserved a second chance. William thought it would be hard to track the drill because it was a common tool. The killer did not behead Peter like Neville. He wondered why? Maybe it was symbolic. Neville was accused of sexual assault. The killer chopped off his head. Peter was charged with manslaughter, and he kept saying he had not seen the victim on the road. It was an accident. The killer destroyed his eyes. Was there a connection?

13th April 2020
Lindenwood, Queens, New York

Tom was glad to be out of the office but weary of being on the road. A part of him was happy to see the lively city again. However, he dreaded traffic jams. The pandemic was not over yet, but with the lift of the lockdown, people had begun emerging out of their homes. But danger still lingered, and just like everyone else, they followed the rules. Tom felt like screaming. The truth was, he was angry about the case. In the middle of it all was Gail, who had vanished without a trace. John remained quiet since he returned to the office. But it was his style, and Tom understood.

The suburb had changed little. Lindenwood was part of Howard Beach in southwest Queens. Most of the red brick buildings had six floors and were constructed in the 1950s. Tom's rundown Ford turned into 153rd Avenue. On both sides were apartments, broad pavements, and tall trees. It was warmer than yesterday, and pedestrians crowded the pavement.

After parking the car, they walked to 88th street and found Peter Elsher's home. They climbed the stairs and knocked on the door of apartment 1. Tom didn't like this part of his job. Talking with the victim's families was always hard. As expected, Mrs. Elisa Elsher opened the door. She was a petite woman with short brown hair, and hazel eyes.

"Yes?"

"I am Detective Tom Nash, and this is Detective John White."

Elisa's face turned pale. "What happened?"

"You had reported your husband was missing…"

"Yes. I went to the nearest NYPD Precinct two days ago. They took my statement and filed a missing person's report. They said they would call. But they never did. He hasn't come home yet. What happened? Is he all right? Tell me he is all right… please."

Tom gulped.

"I am sorry, Mrs. Elsher… we found Peter," said John.

Elisa gasped, and her body shivered. She wrapped her hands around herself.

"I am sorry…" Tom said.

Tears flowed down her face as she sobbed into a corner.

Tom knew it was best to give her time to accept the news. He focused on the one-bedroom apartment. A couple of family pictures decorated the walls. The small kitchen had a homely flair with antique furnishings.

In a few minutes, Elisa settled down. Her face was red and wet, and she wiped it repeatedly.

"How did he die?" she finally asked.

The detectives glanced at each other.

Tom couldn't find the words but told her what had happened to Peter. Her eyes widened, and she stared at him. Dead silence hit the room until she covered her face with her hands and cried.

"No. No. You are lying!"

Tom said nothing and let her vent.

"Who would do that? And why?"

"We do not have all the answers, but I promise you we are doing our best," Tom said earnestly.

"It's not fair...he had suffered enough!" she cried out.

Tom looked at his shoes, trying to hide his grief.

"We understand," John said.

"One mistake destroyed his life!" she shouted.

Tom felt his insides twist. Gathering his courage, he asked, "Can you tell us anything about your husband after he was released from prison?"

Elisa took a deep breath. "When he returned, he wasn't himself. Peter had changed. He was a stranger to his own son. It felt as if prison had stolen his soul. I think he blamed himself for taking a life, although it was an accident. I have spent seven years raising my son on my own. It has been hard." Elisa stopped to wipe her tears away. "He started drinking a lot and turned to drugs for a while," she continued. "We tried everything. The counseling helped a little, and once he got a job as a clerk in an insurance firm, he began recovering. Actually, in the last year, he was doing very well. I think he found someone to help him."

"Who?" John asked.

"A group of people he met up with every week. I noticed

the change in him in the last six months. He wasn't completely reconciled, but he was getting there."

"What did he tell you about this group?" Tom asked.

"Not much. He told me they showed him the way."

"The way?" Tom said as his pulse picked up. He remembered Neville's wife mentioning he had joined a group that believed in Satanism. Was this the same group?

Elisa clamped her hands together. "After the accident, the trial, and prison... Peter was lost. He felt miserable. Life was a sentence for him. I think this group helped him heal."

"Have you ever met them?" John asked.

"No."

"Did Peter talk about them?" Tom asked.

"No."

"What kind of group was this? Was it like Alcoholics Anonymous?" questioned John.

She shook her head.

"Did they have any practices? Where did this group meet?" Tom asked.

"I-I don't know. Peter never said anything. He said he had found something that gave his life meaning," replied Elisa.

Tom slipped John a curious look.

13th April 2020
Sheriff's Office, Nightridge

As the day made way for the night, the sky turned deep blue. The moon rose from the east, spreading its whitish glow. Norris had forgotten the time. A knock on the door jolted him back to reality. It was Kyle.

"Evening, Sheriff," Kyle said.

"Hey! How was your day?"

"Productive…"

"Good."

Kyle had been looking into the ancient pillars and the missing people in the valley.

"Yep. I think we might be on to something."

Norris quickly stood up and cleared the table. Kyle put close-up pictures of the pillars in the Field of Ashes one after another.

"On each pillar, a pentacle is carved on four sides: east, west, north, and south. The circled five-point star was carved with a blade. Maybe a knife. Now, the pentacle is a tool, and it depends on its use. It is generally used for protection or casting a spell."

Norris eyed him. "And you believe that?"

"It doesn't matter what I believe. What matters is what these people and the killer believe."

Norris agreed. People had a right to have their personal views.

"I think the natives probably drew pentacles on the pillar to protect their land and their people. It makes sense. The five points of the pentagram represent five basic elements: earth, air, fire, water, and spirit. In witchcraft, it is used to grab the energy of the spell and release it in a controlled manner. Shadow circles are pentacles drawn on the ground during rituals using black powder—usually not made up of human ashes."

"I see."

Norris picked up an image and studied it. The cravings on the pillars looked fresh.

"I think the villagers are taking care of these pillars."

"I have no issues if they are preserving their ancestral monuments."

"I agree."

They turned to the next image. This symbol had a pentacle in the middle and two crescent moons on each side.

"Witchcraft again?"

"I believe the natives of the valley might have been practitioners of witchcraft."

Norris observed the pentacle above which a triangle was carved into the stone.

"That is the symbol of the third-degree witch," said Jack.

Norris scrunched his forehead.

"In many traditions of Wicca, the study of witchcraft is marked by degrees. A third-degree witch means someone with considerable knowledge and experience and can lead their own covens."

"Is this still applicable?"

"Probably yes."

"Are they any third-degree witches in Willow's Heart?" Norris asked.

"Well…I found three shops that sell this stuff. There are pentagrams drawn on people's doors and other symbols. No witches, though."

Norris nodded. The next image intimidated him. It was a pentacle with a goat's head. It had fierce eyes and long curved horns.

"Yeah. That one is freaky," said Kyle.

"Is it on all the pillars?"

"Yes."

"What does it mean?" Norris asked.

"It's the sign of Satan."

Norris was confused. "This makes no sense. A single pentacle may represent protection, and you believe the natives drew these to bless their land and people. But on the same pillar, there is another symbol that represents Satanism. Why?"

"I think as time passed, the latter generations changed their views," said Kyle.

"You believe they started using their skills for something else?"

"Maybe. Look at this."

"This was buried near a pillar."

Norris had to focus and notice the tip of a jar. "Someone buried a jar?" he asked.

"Yeah. I made inquiries. They said it could be a curse jar."

Norris frowned. "Any blood, DNA on the pillars?" He wanted tangible evidence to convict the murderer.

"Nothing. But the villagers were not happy about my visits. As you know, I have been asking a lot of questions this week."

Norris turned to him. "That is your job."

"Yes. But I think the investigation is bothering some villagers."

"Really?"

"A group approached me and demanded that I leave the village. They found out I had taken pictures of the pillars and wanted me to delete them from my camera. When I explained why I was there, they became more furious. They didn't want to know about the missing people or the two men that had been murdered. Then Edgar came to the scene, calmed things down, and asked me to leave to avoid further issues."

Norris was a bit surprised. But Willow's Heart was not Nightridge. He or his deputies didn't have any influence.

"I have sent the images to Dr. Sterling and Jack."

"Good. I think they might get us more answers."

Kyle nodded. "I asked Edgar about the Field of Ashes. He said it had been there for a long time. I asked the same question to the folks living in the new village. They were unaware of its existence."

"They didn't know?" Norris asked, astonished.

"No."

"They never went there?"

"It's the location. It's deep in the valley, surrounded by miles of thick forest. Also, the villagers fear it," replied Kyle.

"Fear it? Why?"

"Remember, I told you about the fifteen tourists who have gone missing. The villagers on the outer edge of the valley believe it's cursed. And no one wants to go there."

Norris's face turned grave.

"I contacted the families of the missing people. There is no sign of them, and the families haven't given up. When I called, most of them thought we were restarting the search," Kyle said, looking at his feet.

"It's okay. We might find them. But we have to focus on solving these murders first."

"Agreed. If they were murdered, the bodies could be buried anywhere."

"People just don't disappear," Norris muttered.

"There is more. The villagers living on the outer edge of the valley report hearing screams and mourning coming from the valley. As if someone is dying or crying."

Norris recalled his conversation with William. "Did they mention smells?"

"Smells?"

"Yeah. Strong smell of burning flesh."

Kyle eyed him and referred to his notes. "No. Why do you ask?"

"The black powder found on the crime scene contains human ashes and salt. The killer used it to draw the shadow circles. We are guessing in order to get the ashes the killer is burning bodies. If that is the case burning flesh gives out a specific smell."

"If it's deep in the valley, the villagers would not know."

"What about the screams? How often did they hear them?"

"It's not frequent, but it's loud and scary. The villagers believe the natives are involved in sinister rituals."

Norris controlled his amusement. "Tell me about the residents of the valley."

"Nothing terribly wrong with them, except they are strange and a bit old-fashioned."

"I am old-fashioned."

Kyle laughed. "Let me explain. It's the twenty-first century, and they don't have a proper internet. They don't use smartphones or computers. Their homes are old, and they still use outdated farm equipment. They would rather go to a healer than a doctor. There is no medical center or a pharmacy, can you believe it? It is as if the entire valley is against technology and is disconnected from the world."

"But the houses on the outer edge of the valley are well developed."

"Yes."

Norris studied his face. "What about the valley itself?"

Kyle picked up the map of Willow's Heart and spread it on the table.

"There are only two ways to enter the valley. One is from the west. This is where the new village and Sheriff Edgar's office are located. This road connects to Route 9, which links it to the city, Nightridge, and other counties," Kyle explained. "The second way to leave the valley is through the East Road. It takes you through a dense forest. It's about an hour's drive. In the valley's heart is the Field of Ashes. There are power lines running through the valley, and it has two telephone towers."

Norris nodded.

"The fortress is located to the south of this field. It is said to have been built by the Drakos and Walsh families. Later, the others contributed. But with time, it was forgotten."

"Did they finish it? What was it for?"

Kyle eyed him. "It's complete. But its purpose remains a mystery. According to the villagers, no one ever lived in the fortress."

Norris agreed. When he had visited the fortress, it looked abandoned. "Why build it?" he wondered.

"They thought it could be a sanctuary or a temple..."

"Has anyone gone inside?"

"No. It's always locked... and it's creepy."

"And no one has the keys?"

Kyle spread his hands. "Do you think they will tell me?"

Norris shook his head emphatically. No one was going to just give them the information they wanted. It was a close-knit society.

"Tell me about the families," he said.

"I got as much information as I could. The county we know as Willow's Heart was first occupied and developed by twelve families. It is said the Drakos family was the first to settle. Demitri Drakos was a wealthy man who bought the land and began farming, keeping horses, and growing trees which are still standing long after his death. In a few years, others joined," Kyle said and referred to his notebook. "I found references to eleven more families—Walsh, Floding, Brackin, Melgren, Stolly, Feyrer, Cador, Carpenter, Garsow, Pesano, and Mastaw."

Norris bit his lips. "When was this?"

"Early nineteen hundreds."

Norris whistled.

"They built the fortress and were called centurions because all of them lived for over a hundred years."

"That cannot be possible," Norris said, feeling a bit envious.

"Oh, trust me. They did. These were some tough folks," Kyle replied with a wide smile.

Norris wished to know their secret. "Well, good for them."

"I spoke to a few elders," said Kyle. "The twelve families that owned the inner valley were a bit of an enigma. They had weird practices and were religious, God-fearing. They were known for sacrificing animals and holding bizarre rituals."

"That explains the symbols on the pillars."

Kyle nodded.

"Are any of the ancient families still there?"

"Yes. Most of them. Originally, the twelve houses were spread across the valley, about half an hour's drive from each other. Each had their own farms, animals, and wells. Every household was self-sufficient. With time, they built more houses. The twelve families in between themselves had forty-three kids."

"That's a lot," Norris said, surprised.

"People had big families back then. Over time, the children married, and the community grew. But then four couples with their kids left in search of greener pastures. This was during the seventies—the time of drugs, music, and hippies. But the grandparents refuse to leave the village."

Norris smiled.

"Descendants of the families—Drakos, Walsh, Brackin, Garsow, Pesano, Mastaw, Feyrer, and Melgren now own the land. They continue to farm, own several horses and cattle, and are mostly independent. With only eight families living in the valley, the rest of the houses are abandoned." Kyle paused and cleared his throat.

"Do any of the families own wolves?"

Kyle smiled. "I asked. People don't think wolves make good pets, but they confirmed that they have seen several in the wild and around the fortress. I checked, and none of the families are animal breeders. But they are hunters. They have animal heads mounted in their living rooms."

"Okay, but that doesn't make them murderers," Norris said a little dissatisfied, "So, we have no suspects."

Kyle looked amused, "All of them look like suspects to me."

13th April 2020
City Morgue, New York

William signed off the last report. He was relieved his work was done. The door flung open, and Juliet entered. She closed the door and stood with her hands on her waist. She looked much better these days and prettier. Her blonde hair was longer, her blue eyes sparkled, and she had applied her usual makeup. The smell of rotten food was now mixed with perfume. She removed her glasses and took a seat.

"You always do this to me, don't you?" she said taunting him.

"How was your day?" he said, trying to lift the mood.

"You always do this to me!" she complained.

"Because I trust you."

She rolled her eyes.

She is calmer than I thought she would be.

"What have you got?" he asked, encouraging her to get it off her chest.

"Well. Neville's toxicology report is clear. No toxins and drugs. The liver showed heavy fat deposits. There were signs of swelling and inflammation due to the heavy drinking. He had a few drinks before his death, and his alcohol level was 0.10. His lungs showed early signs of damage. The airways had grown and blocked with mucus. There was damage to the lung tissue. Clear aftereffects of long-term smoking."

William expected all this.

"Now. The number of T cells and white blood cells was really high."

William gave it a thought. "He had an infection?"

"Looks like it. But I didn't find a virus or bacteria in his blood. I don't understand the elevated levels of the white blood cell count."

"What about the unidentified organ?"

She gave a subtle smile. "That is very interesting. Believe it or not it has been bio printed."

"Bio printed?" William said, shocked.

"Yes,"

"Are you sure?"

"Yes."

William grabbed his head.

"It is made up of stem cells extracted from the bone marrow of the victims. I cannot track its origin. But here is something very interesting."

William's pulse rose. He knew what she was going to say.

"Millions of these," she said, handing him a picture.

William studied it. He wished he was wrong. A newer version of nanoprobes had emerged. It had several spikes and was round in the middle. It could be easily mistaken for a virus. He had thought this had ended in Nightridge.

"What the hell is this?" she asked.

"Excellent question. I only have one theory at the moment, and I will not share it with you."

She studied his face.

"It's not organic," she said.

He eyed her. "You are right. It's manmade."

"And it was discovered close to Nightridge?" she asked, biting her lips.

"Yep."

As if still not trying to accept the truth, she asked, "What is it doing in the organ?"

"I have no idea. Do you know what this artificial organ does?" William asked.

"God knows!" Juliet said, with her hands running over her face.

23

INTO THE LION'S DEN

18ᵗʰ April 2020 (Present Day)
Garsow Radio Station, Willow's Heart

Thousands of trees stood in the windless night. Mosquitoes and flies buzzed around his head. Pigs squealed in the wilderness. Hidden behind a tree, Norris waited. Several minutes passed, but nothing moved. Norris had expected the hunters to appear. Unarmed and alone, he was not much of a threat. But if he played his cards right, they might make it through the night.

His leg ached, and the pain was escalating. He reached for the bottle and popped a pill. The painkiller was not effective anymore. He was weary and rattled. How long could he keep this up? He was running out of energy and time. Norris thought about his daughter. She was the only family he had left. It he died tonight; she would lose everyone. He could not let that happen.

The moon descended west, and it was going to be daylight soon. He turned east and hunched his shoulders, looking at where the slopes of two mountains met. The coast was clear. His destination was about twenty yards away. Getting on his feet, he dashed toward the Garsow Radio Station. Huge barks of trees and thick bushes dominated the terrain. The brick building with a broken chimney and multiple holes in its roof was a sad sight. The skeleton of the dish seemed as if it had been bombarded with rocks.

Norris heard a rattle. He hid, vanishing into the dense bushes and waited. The forest became quiet again. He surveyed the region. No one appeared from the woods, nor did he hear a roar. His eyes remained fixed on the forest. It was dense, and even the moonlight could not penetrate the canopy. The pounding in his chest slowed when he felt he was safe.

Taking cover, he plodded ahead. He paused momentarily, and a strong sense of fear engulfed him. It was not the woods. It was the radio station. The doors and windows were shut. The large rolling door bore several cracks. But his instincts told him there was more.

Jumping over the wired fence, he crossed the meadow surrounding the building. His knee ached, but he ignored it. He checked the door, but it was bolted. He struck the lock with a stone and opened the latch. Closing the door behind him, he waited. The air inside was stale, cold, and the walls icy.

Norris waited for his eyes to adjust to the gloom. There were four desks and a few chairs, all coated with dirt. In a corner were six cabinets standing next to each other. He hurriedly pulled open a cabinet. It was vacant. He tried the next one, and a flurry of cockroaches rushed out.

"Whoa," he muttered.

The filing cabinets and desk drawers were bare. It was all in vain. He spun and checked the other side of the hall. The radio console with multiple knobs and buttons sat under years of dirt. He cleared the dashboard and turned the knobs one by one. It was dead.

"Damn it!"

Dusting his palms with his pants, he wondered if he should give up. There was nothing here but dust and cold. A peculiar smell caught his attention - a faint whiff of rotting meat. His footprints were clearly visible on the floor. He cleared the sand underneath his shoe and saw cement. Norris pushed the desk to a corner. Kneeling, he smelled the floor.

Nothing.

He checked under the next bureau. The cement was hard, and it had not been tampered with. A large army of red ants crawled through the gaps between two cabinets. He followed the insects and pulled the cabinet to the side. The ants were creeping into the wall through a crack.

He pulled out all the cabinets.

"What do we have here?" he muttered.

A section of the wall was sealed with cement. Pulling out a knife, he began breaking the cement. He let out a long breath when he was done. Tracing the stone that was separate from the wall, Norris dragged it out. It took all his strength. Pain shot through his leg.

"Ah," he muttered.

But he did not stop and kept pulling. A strong pungent smell hit him. It felt like a million rats had died. He hesitated, covered his mouth, and then crawled through the opening and emerged in a chamber. The air was foul, almost unbreathable. His eyes widened as he stared at the pile of bones. He gasped and leaned against the wall. In a corner sat a body covered with maggots, and beside it was Neville's head.

18th April 2020 (Present Day)
Temple, Willow's Heart

Tom and Kyle stood in the temple, waiting to hear the moan again.

"What was that?" Kyle asked.

"Sounded like a cry. There might be someone here," Tom replied, reaching for the wall.

The cry echoed again. The cops looked at each other. Tom tapped the wall in front of him. It was solid rock. He walked ahead as he continued tapping. Kyle was checking the ground. He displaced the sand with his foot. Tom halted. The surface to the left of the altar felt different. Near the floor were two-inch-wide meshed windows. He moved all the candles to the table. When he picked up the last candle, a part of the heavy rock slid automatically and vanished into the mountain.

"Okay...," said Kyle.

The men glared at the gloomy staircase, which vanished into a void. Cautiously, they came down the steps. When they reached the last step, Tom estimated they were at least two feet below the surface. They stood in front of a glass door. On one side, they saw a dimly lit nursery. Babies who might be around five weeks slept peacefully in incubators. The other section was full of computers.

"What in god's name?" Tom said.

"And I thought these people didn't even have internet," Kyle remarked.

Kyle was about to step ahead, but Tom stopped him. He surveyed their surroundings for cameras or security systems. He saw nothing. One infant wiggled its hand and cried. Tom slowly opened the door and patted the baby. The baby smiled, with its eyes still closed. Tom looked at the second child, who was sleeping peacefully. Her lips turned into a small curve, and she wiggled her hands. The baby was dreaming.

What were they doing here? Where were their parents? Were they kidnapped? Taken by these hunters?

Kyle watched another child while Tom searched for a chart.

"What are these babies doing here?" Kyle whispered.

"I wish I knew," Tom replied, turning to a cabinet. He silently opened it and discovered several files. Randomly, he picked one. It belonged to Baby 3.

Baby 3. What kind of name was that?

Ms. Lilian Remer was his surrogate mother. There was no mention of the sperm donor. He read through the reports. Baby 3 was born on 15 March 2020. He read through the doctor's notes, which showed the baby was healthy. Its blood, physical, neurological, and genetic tests were within normal limits. He had been vaccinated for Hepatitis B, Diphtheria, tetanus, and several other diseases.

Tom wasn't a father, but he knew all newborns had to undergo mandatory vaccinations. He ignored the rest of the list and found surgery details on the next page. Cold fear rushed down his spine. He remembered the unidentified organ that William had found in Neville and Peter.

The surgeon's notes were hard to understand. It gave details about anesthesia, surgery time, and after-surgery care. He didn't find any diagnosis but read the concise description of the operation. The hair on his neck stood up. Tom turned to the baby, and slowly, without disturbing it, he unwrapped the cloth. He gulped when he saw a bandage on her abdomen.

"What the hell?" Kyle asked.

They were putting it in babies. What if this baby dies? Has a reaction?

He searched the file to find if the baby had any more tests after the operation. The reports were normal. He turned to the next file. This report said Baby 4's white blood cell count was dropping. He remembered William telling him it was not a good sign.

Tom came to stand near to Baby 4 crib and softly placed his hand on her forehead. He grimaced. She was warm. Uncontrolled fever could mean a lot of things, and if they had implanted the artificial organ in these babies, they could be in danger.

"We need to get these children out of here," Tom said.

"We can't even help ourselves. How can we help them?"

Tom searched for a phone, finding one hung pinned to the wall. He quickly picked up the receiver, but there was no dial tone.

"What's with this place?"

Kyle softly shook his head.

"Let's check the lab," Tom said.

Tom entered the cold compact room, which had one massive computer with three monitors. Along the wall were four rectangular boxes with glowing lights. To the far left was a refrigerator.

"I think that is a server," Kyle said.

It looked similar to the one Norris had found in Nightridge. Tom noticed a bench with a microscope on top. He peeked through the eyepieces and saw nothing. Besides, it was a 3D printer. He spun and saw Kyle standing in front of the refrigerator with his mouth open. Tom peered over his shoulder. Three light pinkish pear-shaped organs sat suspended in a liquid.

They were creating them here.

He turned to the 3D printer and the computer. They had probably used the computer to program and create the blueprint for the artificial organs. The setup was elaborate, and Tom did not have all the answers. The surgical lab they had found earlier was vacated. He doubted they planned to continue their work here. He focused on the computer and tapped the keyword. As expected, it was locked.

"We can't access it?" Kyle asked.

"No. We have to…" His voice trailed away when they heard a bang.

They looked at each other.

"Go! Go!" Tom said.

Glancing behind at the babies, Tom rushed up the stairs. He felt guilty about leaving innocent children behind, but he had no choice. For now, the children were at the mercy of the hunters. God knew what they had planned for them. They rushed up the stairs and returned to the temple. He placed the candles back on the rock, and the door closed. Tom saw light coming from the tunnel.

Quickly, they ducked behind the large rock. A figure

holding a torch appeared and stood in the middle of the temple, looking around. Tom glued himself to the rock. He shut his eyes trying not to imagine what the hunters would do to them if they were caught. The figure turned and left. Tom waited. When the silence returned, they rushed out.

In a few minutes, they were out in the open. They stopped for a moment to catch their breath. They had seen too much. Standing against the mountain, Tom surveyed the still forest. The wind had died out. A group of bats flew over the mountain.

"Now what?" Kyle asked.

"We need to get to the house and find a phone."

Kyle agreed and dashed to the left. Tom followed. He saw a shadow move amongst the trees forest. Suddenly, both men stopped. A hunter appeared from the darkness.

24

THE MOON AND THE SUN

15th April 2020
NYPD Precinct, New York

Two days passed without incident, and Tom was becoming restless. He had done everything in his power to speed up the process. But it was not to be. William had completed the autopsies but was awaiting more results. Kyle had extracted a lot of information about the valley and the twelve families. He wondered if it helped them. They had little on Ella Morgan. She was a suspect and the last person to see Gail alive.

Tom secretly wondered, was this personal? Should he make it personal? In his profession, they had to be careful. Making things personal clouded one's judgment. Tom knew Gail was trouble the first time he had set eyes on him. The file was thin, with limited information. Once declared dead, people lost interest, and that is what Gail wanted. To disappear.

Tom had turned every stone, but it was all in vain. Neville

and Peter's families had no history of mental disorders, drug abuse, traffic violations, debts, and no complaints registered by their employees. He had checked if Neville, Peter's, and Gail's paths had crossed over the years. He found no connection.

He sat back in his chair. Maybe the traumatic incident caused one of the family members to lose control and murder. But again, except for Angela's mother, everyone was accounted for and appeared to live their life peacefully. He didn't think Angela's mother would have beheaded Neville. But again, speculation would not get him anywhere.

He rose to his feet and picked up a file. It was labeled Ella Morgan. Another theory began to form in his mind. He paced the floor, trying to stretch his legs. From his point of view, Neville and Peter were murdered, but Ella might not agree. For her, maybe it was justice. Her daughter's death might have made her emotionally unstable and depressed and changed her perception of right and wrong. Did she kill them? A woman could easily commit these crimes.

Tom recalled Gail believed he was innocent, and the cops were to blame. The law, in Gail's eyes, was wrong. Neville and Peter had been charged with crimes, but Neville was acquitted, and Peter served his sentence. Tom believed the cops who worked on the cases were thorough, but Ella and Gail might have thought Peter and Neville deserved to die. Just like Gail thought he could sacrifice the little orphan girl for his benefit.

Suddenly, something occurred to Tom. He read all the files once more. Several thoughts ran through his mind. How did the killer know about Peter's release? Or details of Neville's case. Where did they live? How did the killer get the information about their families? There were a few possibilities. The perpetrator was keeping a tab on the activities of the accused. To do this, he must have power, money, and resources. He would need access to their records. He may have known the victims. Most crimes were committed within close circles. The next possibility was that the murderer had access to police and court records. The thought gave Tom no comfort. It could be someone in this building or employed at the sheriff's office. He picked up the phone and called the records office.

"Hello, Ian here," said a crisp male voice.

"Hi, Ian, this is Tom. How is everything going?"

"Fine. As much as it can be. I'm busy, Detective. What do you need?"

"I want to know if Neville Easton and Peter Elsher's police or court records were accessed in the last five years?"

"I'll look into it, but don't expect an answer soon."

"Why not?"

"Well, we are understaffed, and the paperwork is monumental."

"Oh? How long will it take?"

"Maybe two weeks."

"Two weeks?" said Tom, somewhat surprised. "Can I get access to the system?"

"Sorry, no. I can't grant you access without the captain's authorization."

"I'll get it."

"Then it shouldn't be an issue," said Ian.

Happy that he was making progress, Tom ended the call.

15th April 2020

Brooklyn, New York

Cold crept through the gap in Tom's trousers as he followed John to a filthy street. They soon came to an abandoned building.

"You have got to be kidding me," he muttered.

"No. This is the last known address of Tamira."

Mrs. Tamira Vince, Angela's mother was a hard woman to find. He had hoped that she could shed some light on Neville's murder. A year ago, she had been hospitalized because of a cocaine overdose. A man had brought her in. She had been treated, and she left this address when she was discharged. Tom was thinking she might help them, but that hope was fading.

Tom fumed as they entered the building with broken windows, a foul stench, and a gloomy interior. Numerous filthy tents became visible as they made their way down the broken stairs. The chaos of the street died out, and Tom felt like he was in a different world. Illegal immigrants and homeless people hid in the shadows as the cops made their way.

Tom gulped hard. A naked man lay in the gutter, and a group of flies hovered over him. Children played with broken toys in a corner. John approached a man, who quickly vanished into the tent. His partner glanced at him.

"We are not here to cause any trouble. We are looking for a woman," he spoke.

Blank eyes stared at them. An old man with a crooked stick neared them.

"Leave us alone."

"We will," said John. "We are looking for this woman," he said, showing him a picture.

"Go away."

"No. We won't," pressed Tom. "Tell us where she is."

"She died…"

Tom's heart sank.

"When?"

"Two months ago…we burned her body."

"How did she die?"

The old man huffed, "That man was kind to save her life, but there is nothing you can do for those who don't want to be saved."

"She took drugs…"

"She chose her fate," the old man replied. Coughing, he turned away from the detectives.

Tom contemplated what to do, but John had other ideas.

"Let's look around."

"What?"

"I don't believe what he says," he stated.

They searched the area and left the building empty-handed. Tom pulled out his notebook and scratched out Tamira's name from the list of suspects. As they approached the car, he said, "Let's hope that watching Mrs. Clegg's home leads us to Ella Morgan."

John just shook his head.

15th April 2020
Tom's Apartment, New York

Tom drove home, and surprisingly, the traffic was not too bad. He heated the frozen spaghetti and sat in front of the

TV. Avoiding watching anything concerning the murders or the pandemic, he focused on a classic old movie. His phone rang, and a smile spread across his face. It was Jenny.

"Hey, how are you?"

"I am good. You?" she asked.

Tom's heart sank. He wished to hold her, kiss her. But it wasn't possible yet.

"I'm fine."

"Oh, darling. Don't worry. Isn't it wonderful to have each other?"

Tom smiled. "You are right. I am sorry."

"Oh! You don't have to apologize. Tell me, what is going on?"

Tom gave her a quick update but kept the details of the case to himself. When they started dating, he had realized it was better not to discuss cases with his girlfriend.

Time flew by fast, and when the call finished, he was too tired. Tom crashed in the bed and dozed off.

The phone buzzed loudly on the side table. Tom grudgingly opened his eyes. Still half asleep, he answered.

"Who is this?"

"Tom, it's Jack."

"What do you want?"

The overexcited computer engineer spoke at a high pitch. "Can you come online?"

Tom forced his eyes open and glared at the clock. It was 3.00 am.

"Really, now?"

"Yes! Everyone is already here!"

So, it was just not him. Tom grunted and cursed under his breath. He slowly got up and turned on the laptop. He could hardly stay awake as the video call connected. On the screen, he saw the weary faces of Roumoult, William, and Norris. Jack was the only one who was wide awake and super excited.

"Morning," said Roumoult, yawning.

Tom just nodded.

"Oh great, everyone is here!" Jack said, rubbing his hands together.

"You found out more about the pillars," concluded Norris, smiling.

"Yes. Yes. It's exciting."

"Just get to the point and fast. I need to be at the morgue in three hours, and I want to get some sleep," complained William.

"The pillars are a tribute to the land, village, and the people they loved. There are symbols on it, one of them—the one pentacle with two crescent moons—represent Goddess."

Roumoult scrolled.

"Hear me out, boss. I found a blog by the descendants of one of the families. He relocated to Canada and has written a few blogs about his family history. I put together all the information, and this is what I have. They specifically prayed to the Goddess Laksa. She is the goddess of death, torture, revenge. She gives power, makes her followers fearless…"

"To kill innocent people," remarked Tom.

"In the killer's eyes, they might not be innocent," Norris commented.

Tom was too tired to even roll his eyes.

"The pillars are over a hundred years old. But someone has refurnished one of the sections in the last year."

"Do the pillars give information about a specific family?"

"No, not really."

"How does this help us?" Roumoult asked.

Jack shared a map of the valley. "You see these two points?"

Tom studied the slopes of the mountains.

"They are opposite to each other, and the pillars are in their path."

"The fortress is near the pillars," remarked Norris.

"You are right. Norris, I read your notes. Did you find mirrors on the top of the pillars?"

"Yes," Norris said looking a little surprised.

"I think they carry a significance. They might be reflectors."

"What do you mean?" asked Norris

"Well, when there was no electricity, men used mirrors at certain angles to reflect sunlight into temples."

"I did not see a temple," said Norris.

"Hm…"

"What else did the blog mention?" asked Roumoult bringing them back to the subject.

"According to the blog, there was a fight between the families."

"About what?"

"About their practices. Some wanted to move ahead and not follow the old ways. Others had different ideas."

"That is not unusual," Tom said.

"That was one reason. The other reason was… attempted murder."

Tom's sleep vanished. "Murder?"

"Well… actually sacrifice. It was around the time the pillars were built. Drako and three of the powerful families agreed to sacrifice a member of the community. It was a time when a lot of cattle died, and there was a drought, and the crop yield was poor. They thought sacrificing a child would solve their problems."

"Hold on, I thought they sacrificed only animals," Tom asked, feeling uneasy.

"Looks like we were wrong. When they decided to kill one of their own, the families split up, and there was a riot which resulted in three men getting killed, and two of the homes were set on fire. Feyrer brought the community back under control and reminded Drako and others of their peaceful ways."

"Did they?"

"Yeah. Things got back to normal."

"Why did his family move to Canada?" Tom asked.

"They didn't like it anymore. If I read between the lines, I think they didn't feel safe."

"They were becoming dangerous," said Norris.

"Drako didn't like anyone *interfering* with his beliefs and lifestyle."

Norris huffed. "Anything else?"

"No, that is all for now," Jack said. "But I am curious about the fortress. Have we checked it out?"

"I did. There is nothing there. It's locked and private property. It is out of my jurisdiction, and I need a very good reason to get a warrant," replied Norris.

Everyone became silent.

"And we couldn't talk about this tomorrow?" complained Roumoult.

"No! I was so excited. I couldn't sleep. So, what else did you guys find?"

Tom grumbled and ended the call.

16th April 2020
NYPD Precinct

Tom glared at the empty coffee cup in his hand. The elevator shuddered to a stop, and the doors opened with a creaking noise. The precinct was in the usual chaos, with cops on phones or doing paperwork. The holding cells were packed, mostly with protestors railing against the shutdown. Some believed the pandemic was a hoax. Tom used to get irritated listening to such crazy theories, but now he was indifferent. He wished everything returned to normal. But unfortunately, nothing would be normal again.

The aroma of the coffee spread throughout his office. His computer came to life, and Tom regarded the extensive list of emails. He ignored most of them, but one caught his attention. The captain's letter had expedited the process. He had requested access to all the details on the trials through the National Archives of New York City and the Division of Criminal Justice Services. He now had direct access to records and surveillance tapes.

"Yes!" he said excitedly.

Eagerly, he searched. A wide smile appeared on his face. One year ago, a woman named Ivy Hawkins had accessed Neville's and Peter's records. He noted the dates she had requested them. Cross-checking the dates, he pulled out the surveillance videotapes and started looking. It took time to go through the footage, but he found her. It was Ella Morgan, AKA. Ivy. Ella knew Peter and Neville's history and probably ordered the curved swords.

But there was more. Recently, Ella had also requested information on the cases of Mr. Charles Hutton, Miss Shu Leo, and Mr. Chi Yu Feng. He bit his lips. Details of past criminal cases are available to the public, but police files are confidential. He wondered if she had access to all of them. Tom turned to his computer and searched for Charles Hutton. The record popped up on his screen. Charles had served a two-year sentence for third-degree burglary. He had an extensive list of petty thefts and financial problems over-shadowing his entire life. He had left prison twelve months ago and was working in a department store in Newark.

He turned to the next one on the list. Miss Shu Leo was convicted of drug trafficking and finished her six-year sentence in February 2020. Tom's heart sank. She was twenty-five years old and had spent most of her life in jail. She had dropped out of school, and with no working skills, she had limited options. Currently, she was working as a cleaner. It wouldn't surprise him if she ended up back in prison in a couple of years. Tom wanted to dismiss such thoughts, but wishful thinking would not help. The system was not perfect.

The last one on the list was Mr. Chi Yu Feng. He was thrown behind bars eighteen months ago for assaulting his boss. Classified as assault of the third degree, Chi Yu spent one year in jail. When he was a teen, he had been to jail twice for shoplifting. Chi Yu currently worked in a dry-cleaning store in Melrose, Bronx. He had no wife or children and lived with his stepmother. Tom tapped his fingers on the desk. Like Neville, were these people wrongly accused? There was only one way to find out.

After hours of searching, he didn't find any proof of their

innocence. He had to believe the records. He could not help but wonder, were these three people the next targets?

16th April 2020
Meadow's Cottage, Nightridge

Norris did not have a very fruitful day. He spent his time bogged down by paperwork, administrative tasks, and replying to emails. His typing speed did not help. But there was a silver lining. No one else had died today. All day long, he dreaded a call from Edgar, expecting another murder. Shutting the door after him, he strolled out of the building, feeling glad the day was over.

Norris drove home. There were a handful of cars on the road. After parking the car in the driveway, he disappeared into the house. The shower was relaxing, and he then focused on cooking dinner. The stir-fry was almost done, and it looked delicious. After dinner, he sat in front of the TV. The phone rang, and Norris sulked. It was a message from William. He was asking him to come online.

Norris was no stranger to technology, but he preferred to speak with people face to face. He found his laptop and turned it on. As he waited, he thought about their upcoming conversation. William had finished the autopsies of Peter and Neville, and Norris was eager to hear the results. The video call started, and William's face appeared on the screen.

"Hey, good evening."

"Hi, Sheriff. How are you?"

"Not too bad."

William nodded.

The screen blinked, and Tom joined the video call. Norris noted William appeared exhausted. He was in scrubs. His overgrown beard and sunken eyes told tales of late-night and stressful shifts. The workload could explain it, but Norris knew William had personal issues. He and his girlfriend Joan were not together anymore, and it was taking its toll on William. Norris wanted to discuss it, but he felt it was none of his business.

"Evening, everyone," said Tom.

William waved, yawned, and reached for a cup of coffee.

"How are you, Detective?" asked Norris.

"Just plodding along," replied Tom.

The screen split in three, and Roumoult's face appeared.

What is he doing here?

"Ah, the man I was waiting for," William said. "Everyone, I have invited Roumoult. I think we might need him."

Norris raised his eyebrows. "Okay." He didn't mind Roumoult, but he wondered why? "What about Edgar?" he asked.

"Let's leave him out for now," pressed William.

Norris glared at him. "Why?"

"Let us keep this between us," William insisted.

Norris studied Tom and Roumoult's concerned faces.

"I have not completed the autopsy reports yet."

"You are slow… that is unusual," remarked Roumoult.

William's shoulder slumped, and he shifted in his chair. "I-I need time. I want to be thorough, and I am checking all organs… for tissue damage or any… anomalies."

Norris suspected something was off.

"What did you find?" Roumoult asked directly.

William ran his hand through his hair. "Do you know the

number of organs in a human body?" he asked out of the blue.

Norris searched his memory. He had never thought about it.

"Don't look at me," said Tom.

"Every human being has seventy-eight organs. Recently, two more have been discovered, but their inclusion is still debatable." William paused. "Neville and Peter had an extra organ."

All the men glared at him.

"What?" said Roumoult.

"They had an artificial organ that looks like a gallbladder but isn't."

Norris had never seen a gallbladder; he had no idea what William was talking about.

William shared an image of a black object which matched the dimensions of a small rotten pear. Norris blinked. This was unbelievable. Everyone equally looked disgusted.

"Maybe they had two gallbladders," concluded Tom, spreading his arms.

William smiled.

"There have been numerous reports of people having duplicate organs who lead normal lives. It's called the super-numerary. It is genetic, and it happens during the develop-mental stages of the embryo. As a result, a person might have an extra spleen or a kidney. But I don't think supernu-merary applies here. This organ has been surgically inserted into both victims."

"And it is not natural?" asked Tom, pointing toward the unidentified organ.

"No."

"Have you…dissected it?" Roumoult asked.

"Yes. I had to be very careful. I didn't want to destroy… or damage evidence."

Roumoult studied his face. "Are you thinking this is the murder weapon?"

"Oh, no. Neville died of decapitation and Peter of excessive blood loss. But this could be why they were murdered."

"So, what is it? Where did it come from?" Tom asked.

William smiled weakly. "I don't know. These organs have been 3D printed using the victim's stem cells."

Norris felt as if the roof fell on his head. He struggled with operating a normal printer, and he was aware of the existence of 3D printers. But could someone use them to print human organs? It was unbelievable.

"It's called bio printing," William explained.

"Okay. Hold on," said Norris, raising his hands. "What is the difference between 3D printing and bio printing?"

"Three-dimensional printing or printers are used for creating three-dimensional objects. Bio printing is something like that, but instead of ink, you use organic material and produce living tissue, bone, blood vessels, and organs."

Norris was shocked.

"It is a new technology. Human organs are complex, and creating a replica is hard. The first stage is the creation of the blueprint, then the bioink, and lastly, the production of the organ. But it is not a straightforward process, and hence this technology will take time to develop functioning organs that can be used for transplants. That being said, trials in which scientists developed artificial bladders have been successful."

"How would they create the blueprint for the organ?" asked Roumoult.

"A blueprint can be created by developing a computerized model using the patient's CT or MRI images."

"How is the bioink made?" inquired Roumoult.

"Every tissue in the body is made up of different cell types, and to develop the ink, stem cells are extracted from the patient and then cultivated," William replied.

"Why? Did he need a transplant?" Tom asked, leaning forward. Confusion filled his features.

"Organ transplants are very common and save lives. I don't think it was the case for Neville or Peter. They were healthy and had all the organs required to stay alive. That being said, we haven't found Neville's head. But I don't think the unidentified organ had anything to do with it," William answered.

"Have you spoken to the victim's families?" Tom asked.

"Yes. Neville's wife said he didn't have any medical issues. She found a two-year-old MRI scan when he had bumped his head. I checked it. The brain looked normal. During his lifetime, he had undergone several medical check-ups. They were all normal. Peter had never been sick in his life. He did a periodic annual health check with his wife. His last reports were normal. Overall, in both cases, I think the surgery was unnecessary."

"Could it be an experiment?" Roumoult asked.

"I asked the wives of both victims. They said no. If Neville or Peter had volunteered for a study, they would have known."

"What if it was illegal? And they didn't want anyone to find out?" Tom said.

Norris was thinking of the same thing.

William eyed him.

Tom spoke up, "They could have done it for money. I have checked their finances. Both victims had financial problems."

"It is a possibility," William admitted.

"We don't know what this organ does, but do we know what it contains?" asked Roumoult.

William's face turned pale.

Norris felt his pulse rise.

"Oh, please don't tell me," Roumoult muttered.

William shared an image. Norris leaned closer to the screen. It was full of small dark spots with spikes. He felt his throat clutch. The image reminded him of the nanoprobes they had discovered during the Shadow Pandemic. Was it something similar?

"Not again," Roumoult said, massaging his temples.

"Is this what I think it is?" said Tom loudly.

"They are called nanoparticles," explained William.

The group turned silent.

Tom froze. "Are they the same as the nanoprobes we found in Nightridge?"

"I cannot say. I need more information. But I don't think it's a coincidence that we found a similar technology in two men who died in a neighboring county."

Roumoult covered his face with his hands.

"What did the Feds find out about the nanoprobes?" Tom asked.

"I have no idea. The agent has not been responding to me," William answered looking disappointed.

"This just keeps getting better and better," Roumoult said clearly infuriated.

Each turned to their own thoughts and became silent.

"Guys. We need to keep this between us. Okay?" William said.

They nodded. Roumoult sat biting his nails. Tom massaged the back of his neck. William sat with a pale face. Everyone remembered that terrible night.

Norris shook his head, "We know what we are dealing with now," he said, "Let's focus on what we can do. Any idea who could create an artificial organ like this?"

All eyes became fixed on him.

25

DEATH IS INEVITABLE

18th April 2020 (Present Day)
Garsow Old Radio Station, Willow's Heart

Norris's hand stayed on his chest. He glared at the mutilated body of a woman. Neville's head sat in front of it. His eyes remained open, and his face had begun to rot. Insects and maggots were feasting on the body next to the decapitated head. Norris recognized the young woman's face. The tourist who had disappeared a couple of months ago, Darla Reed. Kyle had recently contacted her family. On one side, he noticed what looked like an oven door. Staying away from the remains, he opened it and found an incinerator. His heart dropped to his stomach.

This is where they were burning the bodies.

"Shadow circles," he muttered, looking at the pile of bones. This was the source of the ashes.

He moved along the wall, ready to leave, when he saw another door. Bending forward, he turned the knob and crawled through the narrow space. When he emerged on the other side, he froze. The underground hall was wide, lit with small candles, and full of soothing scents. It had twelve thin cement blocks rising from the ground. On each cement block sat two bones with a skull. He was not a medical examiner, but he knew these human remains were old. Above the skulls painted on the walls were the symbols he had seen around the village. The pentacle with two crescent moons. He gulped. Sweat trickled down his face.

At the end, of the hall stood six candle stands and a portrait on the wall. Norris wet his dry lips. The skulls were clean. Herbs and candles encircled the cement blocks. He paused halfway when he saw a slightly different pentagon. On it was a triangle. He remembered Kyle's research. It was the symbol of a third-degree witch. The status granted to highly proficient witches who had the authority to create their own covens. He was unaware if this was still in practice, but it was clearly an ancestor in this valley was a practitioner. Hollow eyes gawked at him, and he felt as if the witch would come to life. Norris shook his head. These were probably their ancestors, the centurions who had perished with time. It was a burial ground.

The fine gravel crushed under his feet as he walked to the other end. He observed the portrait of a naked woman standing with two wolves. Her eyes were full of terror, fearless, and raging fire. Darkness emerged from behind her. It was the Goddess Laska. Norris felt a sense of power and fear when he looked into her eyes. Suddenly, he wanted to leave.

He took a step back and studied the woman in the portrait once more. He surveyed the area. The ancestors of Willow's Heart had respected, cherished, and taken care of their land. Regardless of their superstitious beliefs and conservative nature, they had led a healthy, prosperous, peaceful life and cherished their children. They were smart and built a memorial to leave their mark on this world. Despite how he felt, Norris smiled.

He sneaked out of the shrine, returning to the small room with a pile of degenerating bodies. He left them untouched and returned to the hall with the radio station. A rattle resonated. Norris stopped dead on his feet. A wolf with red eyes glared at him. It groaned. Just outside the window, a tall shadow with horns appeared. Norris's heart skipped a beat. He noticed the door was ajar. Could he get out? Escape? The beast roared and charged at him.

18th April 2020 (Present Day)
Willow's Heart

Tom stood at the mouth of the cave dumbfounded. The hunter's stony eyes were fixed on them. If he had found them, others would follow. The hunter must have realized they had been inside the temple and found the secret lab with the children. Tom and Kyle might have just given them one more reason to kill them. Sweat trickled down his face as the man drew a sword. The cops looked at each other.

"Kyle, go. I will handle him."

"No. We have to stick together."

"You can…"

"I'm not leaving you."

Tom eyed him angrily. He wanted to save him. What the hell was he thinking? Screaming, the hunter stormed at them. Both men ducked. The sword whizzed over them. Tom hit him hard in the face. The hunter grunted and tossed him to the ground, catapulting Tom on his back. The detective swiftly got to his feet and swung his fist, punching his attacker in the stomach. Kyle tried to take the sword away. The hunter grabbed him by the neck and heaved him immense strength slamming him to the ground. The hunter threw his mask on the ground and screamed like a madman. His eyes fixed on Tom. He was his age, with oily gray hair and bulging, maniacal eyes. Grinding his teeth, he swung the sword. Tom stepped back as the blade cut through his shirt. Before he could think, the hunter struck again; the blade scraping Tom's arm. He cried out, moving away. Kyle struck the hunter with a stone. The hunter stumbled and fell on the muddy ground. Breathless, Tom looked at the fallen hunter. Blood dripped from his head.

"Come on! Let's get out of here!" Kyle said, tossing the stone to the ground.

Tom followed him.

They darted into the pathless forest and rushed up the hill. Kyle was ahead of him, and Tom was failing to catch up. His arm was painful, and his feet were killing him. They had to get help. Tom stopped for a moment, trying to catch his breath. Kyle stopped.

"Keep going. I'll catch up," Tom said.

A soft rustle echoed. A chill spread through Tom's spine. From behind a large tree, a dark figure appeared with swift movements.

"Kyle!" he yelled.

The figure attacked the young deputy with the curved sword. Kyle cried out as the blade cut through his flesh. Holding his arm, Kyle moved away. Tom ran and knocked the hunter to the ground. Mud splashed over his face, and his clothes were soaked. Tom heard footsteps. Shadows appeared; pale forms materialized into two hunters. They were trapped. Both men shared a glance and ran up the hill. At the top of the hill, Kyle came to a sudden stop. Tom almost bumped into him. Freezing wind hit Tom's face. The water pounded over the large rocks gushing down the deep white abyss. There was no way out.

"This is a dead-end," Kyle shouted over the noise of the water.

Tom saw the hunter was getting closer. At a distance, he saw three more hunters emerge.

"I will distract them. You should go," Tom said, standing between the hunter and Kyle.

The hunter attacked him. Tom blocked his punch and hit him in his abdomen. It had no effect. The hunter twisted his arm and grabbed him by his neck.

"You die tonight," he said.

Tom gritted his teeth and stomped on his feet. The hunter cried out. Tom hit the man with his elbow. The hunter stumbled back, holding his nose. He tossed away his mask. Anger raged in his protruding eyes. Their arms locked. Without warning, the hunter heaved him into the mud. Kyle threw himself at the hunter, only to get struck hard in the chest and pushed to the edge of the cliff.

"No!" Tom got up and ran to grasp Kyle's hand. Their fingers touched; he was about to grab his hand when the hunter pounced on him. They toppled on the edge of the cliff. Kyle slipped; his feet flew in the air. He screamed for help.

"No! Kyle!" Tom yelled.

Kyle vanished into the mist. Punching the hunter in his face, Tom ran to the edge. All he saw was mist and raging water. Kyle was gone.

"Kyle! Kyle!" he called out.

The hunter leaped at the detective. The men struggled. Tom's face reddened, and he yelled in anger. He struck the hunter, growled, and hurled him to the ground. But the hunter was strong. He rose. Tom threw a punch. The hunter blocked it in midair.

"Ah," Tom cried as his bones crackled.

The hunter knocked the wind out of him.

26

HUNTER'S TRAP

17ᵗʰ April 2020
City Morgue

It was late, and the city had gone quiet. But William was not sleepy at all. He continued to work on the computer in his office, completing the reports he planned to send out tomorrow. If he didn't finish, his boss would not be pleased. His boss tolerated him to a certain extent. William often wondered why he worked so hard, and he should go home and relax. But it was his nature, and he was curious as a cat.

The unidentified organ worried and excited William. For now, it was a secret. But he knew he would eventually have to report his findings. That meant trouble. He wasn't worried about his boss, but this was beyond his jurisdiction. The FBI was still trying to trace the nanoprobes he had uncovered during the Shadow Pandemic in Nightridge. But, until now, the Feds had little success tracing their origin.

There was a knock on the door, and Jack entered his

office. "Oh, you are worse than me," he remarked, looking at the floor.

William didn't care. He knew he was messy. Joan had made it very clear, and she had constantly complained about it. But she was gone. He felt sad. It was different with her. Joan was not some girl. Their short but steamy relationship was the best one he ever had. However, like everything in his life, their love faded away. The funny thing was, while he had given up hope, Roumoult didn't. He kept telling him she was the one. William refused to believe it.

"You are late," William said.

Jack strolled toward him with his hands in his pocket. "Yeah. I had to get something done for Mr. Cranston. Can't say no to the big boss."

William nodded. Roumoult's father, Fred, was quite demanding.

"What have you got?"

"We have made some progress. But let's wait for Juliet.

William nodded.

"Could I see the actual stuff?" asked Jack.

He turned on the microscope. After preparing a slide with nanoparticles, he stepped aside.

Jack peered in.

"Wow... these are not moving?"

"Yeah. They are probably inactive," William said.

"Hmm... these look different," Jack remarked, observing the specimen under the scope.

"Yes. Compared to the nanoprobes, these are smaller and harder to find. Have you seen anything like this?"

Jack gave him a worried look. "No. Not really."

"They previous nanoprobes released a toxin and had a different design. These look like a virus."

"Well, the men who developed the nanoprobes are dead," said Jack.

"Yes. But we didn't know who they worked for, did we?"

"That is true."

Juliet stepped in. "Are you ready?" she asked.

"Yes," said both men.

Jack and William waited as Juliet set up the microscope and connected it to the monitor.

"Now, it was an enormous task, but the samples are ready. I have to say, I had to pull a few strings," she said.

The men waited patiently.

"Okay," she said and placed a petri dish under the microscope. Suddenly, the monitor came to life, and they saw several nanoparticles. William stepped forward.

"The artificial organs found in Neville and Peter were full of them," said Juliet. "I think these are self-sufficient."

"Self-sufficient?"

"Watch."

She took a vial of blood and added two drops to the petri dish. The monitor turned red. They saw hundreds of cells. But the nanoparticles floated peacefully amid the blood cells.

"Now watch this," she said.

She replaced the petri dish with a fresh one. Then added the nanoparticles. She reached out for a different vial of blood and added it to the solution. Now, the screen was full of a mixture of green, red, and black spots. It was infected blood. Suddenly, the nanoparticles came to life and engulfed the green particles.

"Wow!" said William.

"What is that?" Jack asked.

"That blood was infected with H1N1. Commonly known as influenza."

"How did you get hold of the virus?" William asked, feeling a lump in his throat.

Juliet frowned. "You have no idea how many strings I had to pull."

"Thank you," William said, leaning forward, "I'd appreciate it if you keep this between us."

"Hold it... tell me... how does it do that?" Jack asked.

"I suspect it's the close proximity to the virus. These have been programmed to detect and destroy it."

"Wow. They are perfect," Jack said.

"No, not really."

William eyed her.

"Watch," she said.

After destroying the green particles, the nanoparticles were still active.

"Why aren't they powering down?" William asked worriedly.

The nanoparticles then turned to healthy cells and started destroying them.

"I think this is a glitch. The body takes a while to return to normal after an infection. However, it appears that the nanoparticle's programming failed and did not power down. They continue to destroy normal cells..."

"Damn. Is this why they were killed?" asked Jack.

William wished he had answers. "I don't know."

"Hold on. There is more. These nanoparticles are from Neville's blood," said Juliet.

William faced her.

"Peter's nanoparticles are more interesting."

She reached out for another glass jar. She prepared a third petri dish and placed it under the microscope. William didn't see any difference in the shape or structure of the nanoparticles. Repeating the same process, she added the infected blood. The nanoparticles activated and killed all the infected cells. Once they were done, William expected them to continue. But the nanoparticles powered down and became immobile.

"Incredible!" Jack said. "Why are they different?"

"These were extracted from Peter's body. He was operated three months after Neville," said William.

"So?" asked Jack.

"These could be an advanced version."

Everyone became thoughtful.

"What activates them?" William asked Juliet.

"I think the specific proteins on the virus."

William bit his lips.

"Now, let's test some other viruses."

They watched as the nanoparticles fought and destroyed the viruses, one after another. However, for each test, Juliet had to add a new batch of nanoparticles. Once used, they lost their power.

"Wow... this is amazing," Jack said.

"So, it works against viruses... can it also neutralizes bacteria?" William asked.

Juliet became thoughtful. "I haven't tested for bacteria."

"So, the artificial organs were designed to store the nanoparticles in the body," William concluded.

"Yes. It makes sense. They possibly didn't want to keep

injecting the nanoparticles. They figured this was a better way."

William nodded and looked at Jack.

"Okay. My turn," Jack said. "Now that I have had a look at them, I can give you a quick update. Juliet what do you know about nanoprobes we found in Nightridge?"

"Not much," Juliet admitted.

"Okay. Dr. Jason Walker created them, and his investor was Sanders. Now, Sanders is no longer a player as far as we know, and Dr. Walker was found dead in the lab hidden in the mountain close to the swamp."

William nodded. It was sad but true.

"But this is an advanced version? That means someone is still working on it," said Juliet.

"It appears so. But let's not jump ahead. Also, I think if we could get our hands on the nanoprobes we found in Nightridge, it would have been great. We could compare them."

"We don't have access to them," William said. He had handed them over to the FBI simply because he didn't want to deal with this problem. But now it had found its way back to him.

"Okay. These new versions—called nanoparticles—are thick as a strand of human hair but are smaller than the ones we had found. The nanoprobes had arms and carried a tube-like structure. These have been condensed."

"How could someone create them?" asked Juliet.

"To answer that we have to travel back in time," Jack said winking, "The idea of nanotechnology first originated in the nineteen-sixties, but it was in the nineteen-eighties that we actually had a chance to bring it to life. Nanotechnology was only possible due to the invention of tunneling microscopes that can take images of particles at an atomic level."

William scratched his beard, wondering where this was going.

"Think of it like a probe which allows you to capture what a normal microscope cannot and also manipulate atoms. In a nutshell, it allowed us to build atomic-scale circuitry and data-storage devices."

"Smartphones?" said William.

"Exactly. Now, paired with carbon nanotubes, the tunneling microscope can create smaller, lighter, and more durable materials. We are already using this technology in devices like cell phones, computers, and spacecrafts. The sizes of our devices are shrinking."

"And they plan to use it in medicine?" said William trying to think ahead.

"Not yet. It is in the very early stages, and of course, there are concerns. With the origins of new technology, there are always new challenges and dangers."

"Like what?"

"Developing nanotechnology takes a lot of energy and generates a lot of waste. Its effect on the human body still remains to be seen. Take nanoparticles, for example. Once inside the host, we might not control the nanoparticles. It could damage the normal cells or kill its host. The host's body might identify it as a foreign material and attack the nanoparticles."

"We have a long way to go," remarked Juliet.

"It has had success in the technology field, but the medical field is a completely different frontier. Nanotechnology's interactions with biomaterials remain a mystery.

However, if we are successful, it has several uses—it can deliver medicines or vaccines and reach where no doctor can ever go without surgery. Doctors have been rallying about its use in cancer treatment because it could enter the body and destroy tumor cells and preserve the normal cells. Nanotechnology can create vital durable artificial biomaterials, such as skin grafts or human cells."

William thought about the artificial organ. "Or it could kill a virus…"

"These nanoparticles have been designed to do just that. I have dissected one of them."

The image on the computer changed. William peered in to see minute circuits and two black squares. He was immediately reminded of the time he had to open and fix a USB drive.

"Can they be destroyed?" asked William.

"Easily. If they enter the host's digestive system, which breaks down food, they will be destroyed."

"Interesting. How many nanoparticles were there in the organ?"

"My estimate, a million," Jack said.

William gave it a thought. Their nano-size would make it possible.

"Did you see any reactions, or did the body show any signs of rejecting the organ?" William asked Juliet.

"No. But we only know of two cases. There could be others. These could be manufactured to mimic human cells, and the body might not see them as a threat. They are dormant most of the time, anyway."

"Will all the nanoparticles leave the artificial organ if there is a threat?" asked William.

Jack and Juliet looked at each other.

"No. With the help of Juliet, we found out a little more. From what we understand, they follow a hierarchy. The nanoparticles sit on a layered mesh made up of tissue. The location of the nanoparticles determines when they go into battle. We conducted a little experiment to support our theory."

William turned to the screen.

"These are six nanoparticles taken from the first six layers of tissue, and there is our little virus. Juliet tells me this medium imitates normal environment in the body," Jack said, leaning forward.

"It is not perfect, but it does the job," Juliet said as she crossed her legs.

William watched the nanoparticle kill the virus. It powered down and became still. Then a second nanoparticle was introduced into the medium. It bumped against the dead nanoprobe, and nothing happened. Then they introduced the virus. Then he saw a pen-like structure touch the nanoparticle.

"What was that?"

"We introduced an electrical charge and disabled the second nanoprobe before it could act. Remember, we used a high electrical charge to disable the nanoprobes in Nightridge," Jack explained.

William nodded, impressed.

"Now, see what happens." Juliet said smiling.

As Jack said, the third nanoprobes came to life and began attacking the virus. In seconds it destroyed it and then became silent."

"Impressive."

"I know."

"How does the next nanoparticle know when to activate?"

"I have to make a guess… if the job is not done, the dying nanoparticles tells the next one to take over," said Jack.

"Neuronet?"

"You guessed right. They probably work like a hive."

"Is it possible to control them?"

"I don't know. They look independent. Once in the body they appear to work on their own," Jack said.

William nodded. "Okay, tell me what they are made of?"

"It's outer shell is made up of silica. It covers the entire surface except for the sensors. I believe they were created using carbon tunneling to make them durable and survive in the body."

"Sensors?"

Jack leaned forward and said, "These tiny stick-like structures that give it an appearance of a virus. It works like when you tap your phone to pay for a coffee… it bumps into a cell in the body and decides if it is a normal cell or a virus."

"But a virus disguises itself and enters the cells and then multiplies," Juliet pointed out.

"I have read about that. I think that is why it might not catch the virus in the initial stages. But as soon as the body recognizes the virus, the nanoparticles become active. I am guessing these help the body destroy the virus," Jack said.

"Yes. When the body detects a virus, it uses the lymphatic system to defend itself," Juliet said.

"True. But the body is slow… and these guys are fast," Jack remarked.

"What about the nanoparticles in both the victims? We noticed that those in Neville's body started attacking the normal cells after it had destroyed the virus. But the nanoparticles in Peter's body did not," William asked.

"Structurally, both nanoparticles are the same. I guess... it's a programming issue, or it could be a glitch. Also, I am not an expert in this field."

"Can we talk to someone about it?" Juliet asked.

Jack eyed William. "That would mean involving other people. Do we want to do that at this stage?"

William sulked. "Can we trace the manufacturer?"

"We could," replied Jack. "The development of this kind of technology needs expertise and a lot of money. This might be an organization led by a scientist or a group of scientists with several investors."

William agreed.

"We are still keeping this amongst ourselves," Juliet asked.

"Until I find out the extent of the danger."

She looked thoughtful. "Danger might be closer to home than you think," she remarked coming to stand between both men. "I have got to get going. Let me know if you find out anything else."

"Sure," said William.

Juliet left and William turned to Jack.

"Be careful with those, okay? Don't share more than you must, not at this stage. Report to Roumoult but no one else."

Jack nodded. William turned to the screen and wondered how he was supposed to handle this.

17th April 2020
New York

Tom had been thorough. He had searched the database and asked the tech department to check records requested by Ella Morgan. He had identified three targets, and he had to ensure there were no more. Despite having a long day, Tom did not want to wait for tomorrow. They had been trying to reach the three likely victims. But it was all in vain. Their attempt to contact them failed. Lives were at stake, and they had to act.

Tom was driving toward Cliffside Park and hoped Charles was at home. John went to Queen to talk with Ms. Leo. Officer Jake was on his way to Secaucus, to see Mr. Fang. Neville and Peter had been murdered. If these three people were the next target, he wanted to make sure they had police protection.

The drive was long and boring. It was slightly chilly, and the wind had died out. The traffic was bearable because he had almost reached his destination without cursing anyone. He swung the wheel and drove down Edgewater Road. Despite the time, people were out and about. He picked up the piece of paper on the passenger seat to check the address. He threw the paper on the dashboard and turned toward Anderson Avenue.

The Ford cruised down the barren, quiet neighborhood. The houses were dark. It was as if everyone had already fallen asleep. Tom pushed the brakes, and the car came to a halt in front of a townhouse. Leaving his car with a mask in his hand, he headed for the gates. Suddenly, a dog barked somewhere in the neighborhood. He paused momentarily. Unlocking the small gate, he hurried to the door. He knocked and waited. When no one replied, he rang the bell and banged on the door.

"Mr. Charles Hutton, open the door. This is the NYPD!" he yelled and grabbed his ID from his pocket.

When no one answered, Tom's pulse rose. He peered through the side window and saw vague outlines of furniture, but there was no movement. Tom was about to bang on the door again when a tired voice called from the other side.

"I am coming…"

Tom waited. His heart was beating fast, and he was perspiring. Maybe he should have arranged for backup.

A bald man around fifty with sleepy eyes opened the door. He was clearly annoyed to be disturbed at this hour. "Who are you?" he demanded.

"Sorry to disturb you," Tom said, showing him his badge. "I am Detective Tom Nash from the NYPD."

Charles peered at his badge. Concern filled his features, and he studied Tom's face.

"Okay. Detective, if this is about my neighbor's cat, I did not kill it."

Tom arched his eyebrows. "I am a homicide detective."

"Doing the late shift, are we?" Charles said, opening the door wide and allowing Tom to enter.

"Just working a case. I need to ask you some questions."

Charles sulked. "Could you make this fast? I want to return to bed."

"Are you on your own?"

"Yes, my wife and children have gone to visit my mother-in-law. What is going on?"

"Mr. Hutton, this is going to sound odd."

The man folded his arms and waited.

"Do you remember your trial?"

His face turned grim. "Some things are hard to forget. Detective, I have served my sentence."

"This is not about the robbery."

"I see. I understand no one is interested in knowing I was innocent."

Tom tried to smile. Unfortunately, the evidence against Charles was extensive, including a surveillance tape, and he did not have an alibi. But today, more important things were at stake. "Did a woman called Ivy Hawkins or Ella Morgan recently approach you?"

"No."

"Are you sure?"

"Yes."

"What about Mr. Gail Clegg? Do you know him?"

Charles shook his head. "What is this about?"

"We think you might be in danger."

Charles eyed him. "Trust me, Detective, I am not."

Tom was flabbergasted. "What?"

"I am in no danger. In fact, I have never felt so safe. Nothing can touch me. Trust me, Detective. You don't have to worry about me or my family. We have been taken care off."

Tom blinked. He was taken aback. Charles showed no sign of fear or concern.

"Have you had surgery?" he asked involuntarily.

Charles chuckled. "That's an absurd question."

"Answer me."

"I think you should leave," Charles said coldly.

Tom studied his face. Something was off. "I need you to come with me."

"Am I being accused of something?" Charles asked casually.

"No. But I believe your life might be in danger."

In a very calm manner, Charles said, "You need to leave. I am not in any danger. If you don't, you might be."

A rattle distracted Tom. He spun. Out of the darkness stepped a menace figure. Tom could never forget the fierce, cold steel-gray eyes and the devilish smile. His black, greasy hair limped around his ears. He was older now but brawny.

"Well, you finally found me," said Gail with a devilish smile.

"What the hell?"

Tom reached for his gun. A blow to the head knocked him out.

17th April 2020
Nightridge

As Norris dealt with the last email on his list, the last rays of sunshine kissed the village good night.

"Thank goodness," he muttered.

He closed his eyes and massaged his temples. He logged out and turned away from the computer. Tom had updated him about his progress. Norris was concerned. Tom thought he had figured out the next three targets, and while Tom and John were tracking them, all he could do was wait.

This case disturbed him. The deaths were brutal, the murderer uncanny and smart. It all started when Edgar found the wolves' heads and William found the DNA of a man who should have been dead. Norris stepped out of his office and stood with his hands in his pocket. All the other officers had gone home. He had just said good night to Mrs. Flores.

After stretching his legs, he returned to his office and pulled out a file from a cabinet. The file was getting thicker. As he flipped through the pages, he thought about the events. The wolf heads, the swords which led to Ella Morgan, and the murder of Neville. The DNA traces of Gail had drawn Tom into the case. But so far, they had found no other traces of Gail. It was like he was a ghost. They still had not found Neville's head. This case was not linked with Angela's suicide or the trial which ruined Neville's life.

Peter was next to die because of excessive blood loss. The killer had used a drill to destroy his eyes. Why? He wondered. Did the torcher mean something? Things got very interesting when William found an extra organ surgically implanted in Neville's and Peter's bodies. It was surprising that the unidentified organ was 3D printed and integrated into the victims' lymphatic system. Their fears spiked when they discovered these organs were full of nanoparticles. The pathologist speculated the nanoparticles defended the host from biological factors like viruses. He would not have believed it, but he did. The nanoprobes found in the bloodstream of villagers of Nightridge had turned them into maniacs.

They were right to suspect a cult. Somehow, Gail and Ella could have influenced the villagers living in the valley. They were a group of people with deep religious beliefs whose ancestors' practiced witchcraft. He wondered how did they got access to illegal technology? Who created this nanotechnology and why? According to Jack, 3D printing of organs was possible, but integrating the unknown organ into human bodies required skill. Tom believed Ella could have performed the surgeries.

Everything appeared to be connected to Willow's Heart and the twelve families. On his computer, Norris searched for the information collected by Kyle. He printed out the entire family tree and began tracing the names. It appeared the last living descendent of the Pesano family had moved to Canada. The man who had written the blog that Jack had found. According to the records, the man had sold his share of the land to the others.

Norris focused on the next family. The Stolly's had also sold their land and left the country. A name caught his attention. Aura Maxine Drakos. The wife of the first man who had settled in the valley, Demitri Drakos. He sat back. He had read that name somewhere. Norris searched the police database. A record popped up. He felt his chest tighten.

"This can't be good."

He looked closer, making sure he had not made a mistake. It was Edgar. His great-grandmother's name was Aura Maxine Drakos.

"You son of a bitch," he muttered.

The door to his office opened, and Kyle rushed in.

Norris was shocked.

"You are still here? I thought you went home."

Kyle ignored his questions. "Chief! Look what I found…" he said, showing him a print of the family tree.

"Edgar is one of them…"

"Yeah! How could I have missed this?" said Kyle.

Norris wanted to scream. He cursed himself for being so stupid. Edgar had been playing him from the beginning. Had he planned it all? But why? Norris had never wronged him.

Why did he drag him into this? A realization dawned on him. Edgar did not give a damn about his beliefs or values. But Norris's self-righteousness might have threatened him and bruised his ego. Edgar wanted to control him, like he had controlled his wife's brother Richie. But Norris wasn't Richie.

For the first time, Norris looked at Edgar's background. He cursed himself for not thinking about it earlier. He realized jealousy might have played a role. Edgar had been divorced twice, and one of his wives had put a restraining order against him. Norris had found a woman who loved him till the end. Edgar had no children, while he had been lucky to have two healthy and loving kids.

"How can I be so blind," he muttered.

It was outrageous, but Edgar's motives didn't surprise him at all.

Norris rushed out of the office. Kyle followed him. A white blanket of soft moonlight had fallen on the village. Running his hands over his face, he got behind the wheel. To his surprise, Kyle got in the passenger seat.

"What are you doing?" Norris demanded.

"I know that look," Kyle said. "I'm coming with you."

Norris chuckled. It was good to have a reliable partner. He turned the key, and the truck came to life.

17th April 2020
Willow's Heart

They drove silently into the valley. The neighboring woods extended for miles. There was not a soul in sight. Norris wondered what to do. Should he report Edgar? But he needed solid evidence. He should warn his team. His deputies had been helping Edgar investigate these murders. He wouldn't be surprised if he found out that he had led them astray.

They reached the village on the outer edge of the valley. Norris turned and took the main road to the heart of the valley. Driving at night was hard. Not seeing any civilization around him made Norris uncomfortable. He parked at the spot where everything had started. The seven crosses were still standing in the open field. The wolf heads were kept frozen at the morgue.

"What do you think, Chief?" Kyle said as they stepped out of the vehicle.

"He drew us in," Norris said, feeling angry. "How could I be so blind?"

"Why?"

"Maybe because he has a vendetta against me."

"What did you do?"

"Nothing. I was just trying to live my life," Norris answered, walking around a wooden cross as he rubbed his neck. He didn't know what he was hoping to find here, but he needed time to clear his head. One option was to confront Edgar, but it could tip him off. Perhaps he could search his house. But evidence gathered during an illegal search would be useless. No, he had to play this right.

The fortress.

An idea sprung in his head. Edgar had a claim to the fortress. His great grandfather had built it. It linked him to the valley, probably to the missing people, and two murders. Maybe he granted Ella access to police records. Using this information, he could convince the judge to grant him a warrant to search the fortress and all the houses in the valley. It was a risk, but he had to take it.

"What do we do?" Kyle said.

"We take him down," said Norris, heading back to his truck.

The tires screeched as the truck turned and raced back toward Nightridge.

"Kyle, get Judge Lockwood on the phone."

Judge Lockwood was an old friend with whom Norris had worked on several cases. Other judges were on his list, but Lockwood had a particular distaste toward corrupt cops. He would not hesitate to help him.

"At this hour?"

Norris glanced at his watch. It was nearing 8 pm. "Call him anyway."

He regretted wasting time. He should have figured it out earlier.

"He is not picking up."

"Leave him a message."

Kyle did what he was told.

"Call Tom. He must know."

Kyle nodded and dialed the number.

Suddenly, a powerful stream of headlights blinded Norris. He glanced behind. A black four-wheel-drive raced toward them. He pressed the pedal, and the truck picked up speed. The vehicle bounced and vibrated.

"Chief, watch out!" Kyle yelled.

Another vehicle emerged from the wood and hit them. Norris lost control. The vehicles spun and the sheriff's truck came to stop at the edge of the road. The engine died out. Norris shook his head. When his vision cleared, he saw the cracked windshield. He heard a moan. Kyle was tucked in his seat belt. Blood oozed out of his forehead. Glass from the broken passenger window covered the deputy.

"Kyle? Are you okay?" he asked, shaking him.

The blue sedan that had hit them had run over a log and smashed into a tree. Smoke sneaked out of its hood. Norris tried to fight his dizziness. The driver of the four-wheel-drive didn't emerge. He started the truck but paused. Out of the woods appeared shadows which turned into figures of different sizes.

"What the hell?" muttered Norris.

He gasped as figures with large wooden masks came into view, each of them carrying a curved sword.

"Oh, my god."

The Shadow Fraction surrounded them. The faceless figures stood in silence. Norris put the truck in reverse. But something pinched his neck, then his arm. He touched his neck and found a small wooden dart. His hands slipped from the steering, and darkness fell.

27

THE TIME HAS COME

18th April 2020 (Present Day)
Garsow Radio Station, Willow's Heart

Norris knew this was the end. He had been running all night, but now he was done. He locked eyes with the wolf. The wolf snapped its jaws and pounced at him. Norris picked up the chair, blocking the creature's attack, but it shattered it into pieces. Norris lost balance and fell to the floor, still holding the chair's frame. The creature leaped on him, but he blocked it with the wooden frame. It growled inches away from his face. Norris tried to push the beast off him. From the corner of his eyes, he saw a large figure standing at the door. The wooden frame broke into two, and the wolf growled and bit him on the arm. He screamed. Norris grabbed the chair's broken leg and stabbed it with the sharp end. The wolf howled in pain. Holding his bleeding arm, Norris dragged himself away from the beast. The creature bared its teeth and limped toward him. It would not give up. Norris scanned the old station, and he saw his chance. Gathering all his strength, he got on his feet and broke out of the window.

His landing was not smooth. The fall on the rocks aggravated his injuries. He cried out. Without looking behind, he struggled to get on his feet and attempted to run, but his knee gave way. Norris yelled as he fell to his face. Dizziness took over. The hunter waited with the blade. Norris forced himself to get on his feet but fell to the ground. With his bare hands, he crawled through the dirt. Grabbing a tree, he pushed himself to stand. He gasped for air and stared back. The figure stood still, waiting patiently. He tried to walk, but the forest spun in front of him, and he toppled to the ground.

When Norris came about, he saw the hunter standing over him, waiting for him to wake up. Its black lifeless eyes and horns bulging out of its head were daunting. Norris could not run anymore. He was done. This was it. Norris thought he heard an engine, but he was delirious and could have imagined it.

"Why don't you just stop? Let me go!" he said.

The hunter didn't answer.

A rustling echoed in the region.

"Please don't do this," he said breathlessly.

The hunter laughed. "You poor little creature," he remarked and raised his sword.

Norris stared at him, his heart thudding in his chest. A gun clicked from afar. He saw a silhouette and blinked twice to make sure he was not dreaming.

"Step away from him," the man said.

Norris almost smiled. Even in his deranged state, he knew that voice.

18th April 2020 (Present Day)
Willow's Heart

Tom's head pounded. A jolt ravaged his body, and he opened his eyes. Once again, he was bound and gagged. He was in the back seat of the truck driven by the hunters. He slowly sat up. The truck drove over the bridge toward the fortress. Sorrow filled his heart as Kyle's face flashed in front of his eyes. Tom heard his screams as he vanished into the void. What was he going to tell Norris? Then another thought entered his mind. Norris could be dead, and now Kyle was gone. Tom hung his head and let the sorrow drown him.

The bright yellow headlights snaked through the rough roads. This was it. He had failed. No one could save him. Tom felt like sobbing. He had lost two of his friends. He wearily looked at the woods. Perhaps his partner might look for him. But how would he find him? The truck came to a halt, and Tom offered no resistance as the hunters dragged him out.

The fortress was bright, with fires burning in several parts. With his head bowed, Tom walked toward the door. It opened swiftly, and another masked hunter stood by the door.

"What happened to the other one?"

"He met his destiny," replied his captor.

"You killed him!" he said, unable to control his rage.

The hunter grabbed his neck and pushed him indoors. They hustled him through the vast hall which led to a broad stone passageway. Tom did not know where he was. He had never been to this part of the fortress. The hunter opened a door, revealing a staircase dimly lit by two torches. Tom sulked.

Another dungeon.

The masked men ushered him down the stairs. Tom felt like a slave with the chains bounding his hands and legs. The hunters left, shutting the door with a bang. Tom scrambled to a corner in the windowless room. He didn't know who to shed tears for. For himself, Norris, or Kyle? He buried his head in his hands and just wished to see Jenny one last time.

28

THE SHADOW FRACTION

17th April 2020
Willow's Heart

Tom tried to open his eyes, but the dizziness was overwhelming. He couldn't stay awake. A voice echoed in his mind.

Get up. You are in danger. Wake up. Gail. You saw Gail. He is here!

Tom's eyes flung open. He felt his head pounding and his heart beating like there was no tomorrow. He looked up. The roof was built from stone, and voices filled the air. He slowly sat up and saw that he was in a hall full of people. Charles Hutton was tied to a wooden pillar in the middle of the hall.

"What is happening? Where am I?" Tom murmured.

A cold shiver rushed down his spine. He tried to move, but his hands were bound. He recalled he had driven to Cliffside Park to speak with Charles Hutton. The killer's next target. But then he had seen Gail.

"He was there," he murmured.

Perched against the concrete floor of the hall in the old fortress, Tom fixated his eyes on the gigantic wheel of bones with the scary mask. He felt as if the mask held by bony spikes was glaring into his soul and would come alive and drink his blood. He looked away.

It was pitch-black outside. Icy wind swept indoors through the windows. Candles glowed in multiple stands along all four sides of the wall. He sat at the far end, away from the group of awkwardly dressed people. Several were wearing horned masks with wolf faces. These hunters wore golden loose sleeve shirts with black trousers. Each carried a sword. A few others wore masks with horns that split into two at the end. They painted their masks blue, and their eyes were large and stony. These figures wore long blue gowns which looked warm. Tom guessed these were women. Two figures stood out. One wore a blue mask with a crown-like structure near the forehead. Wings emerged out of the side and curved upwards. Her soft silk golden gown touched her feet. The second figure beside her wore a red mask with horns. Its appearance was fierce, with eyes bulging and a wide jaw with a wicked smile. Tom's heart dropped when he saw six small figures. The children wore white gowns, with blue masks covering their little faces. Three of them were looking at him.

What were they doing here?

Tom struggled to his feet. His heart sank as he caught sight of Charles bound to a pillar and surrounded by the Shadow Fraction. In a corner was an enormous platform. Tom's eyes rolled upwards to see a big, wide flat stone almost the same size as the platform. Six chains supported it and appeared heavy. Tom hoped it wouldn't fall on anyone.

The woman in a golden robe, a winged mask, and revealing lifeless eyes stepped forward. She raised her hands and began chanting. He leaned against the wall. What was happening? What were these people doing? Then she began speaking words that made no sense to him. Her voice was smooth, almost hypnotizing. Other voices joined her, and they chanted for several minutes. Tom looked to his left. Two hunters were guarding the exit. Charles's face showed no fear, only determination. He stood with his eyes closed, like a man who had accepted his fate.

"What the hell are you doing?" Tom murmured.

Charles neither resisted, wept, nor cried for help.

The chanting ended. The door opened with a loud bang, and the hunters pushed Norris and Kyle inside the hall.

"Stop this madness!" shouted Norris.

But his words fell on deaf ears. Tom was shocked and watched in disbelief as the hunters shoved them beside him. A part of him was relieved. At least he was not alone.

"What the hell are you two doing here?" Tom asked.

"Kneel!" ordered the hunter.

"Now look—" Norris said but lost his voice. The hunter punched him in the stomach and struck him on his head.

A second man pushed Kyle to the floor. Tom knew there was no point in resisting. He slowly got on his knees.

The chanting continued. Tom watched curiously. The hunters turned away from them, and Tom leaned toward Norris.

"Why did they take you?"

"Because we found out who they are. What are you doing here?"

"I went to save Charles," Tom said, "but found Gail."

Norris's eyes widened. "What? He is alive?"

"Yes, and he is behind all this."

The sun rose, and its first light fell on the valley. It penetrated the framed pentacle window and shrouded the mirror just above Charles. The room brightened, full of golden light.

Again, the chanting began.

The woman in the golden robe said, "It's time."

Time for what? Tom wondered. But then he realized and tried to free himself. He couldn't let a man die. Innocent or guilty, this was wrong. Kyle and Norris struggled to free themselves. The heavenly glow reduced. A door opened, and two enormous wolves appeared.

"No!" Tom tried to shout, but fear muffled his voice.

As if given a command by an invisible voice, the wolves charged toward Charles and ripped through his legs. Four more animals appeared and pounced on the victim. He screamed in agony as the beasts mangled through his body.

"Stop! Stop!" Norris screamed.

A hunter hit him in the face with the hilt of his sword. "Stay silent."

Blood splattered on the ground and the pillar. The cops watched in horror as the wolves ate the man alive. The spectators remained unaffected. They watched; their emotions hidden behind their masks. Tears flowed down Tom's face. His body turned numb. Every sound died out except Charles's screams. He wanted to break his restraints and run to help him, but he felt as if his feet were glued to the floor. It was unbelievable. Why would they do this? Why didn't he run or resist? Tom remembered Charles was with Gail. Did they know each other? Did Gail make him do this, or did Charles just accept his fate? Was this a sacrifice? It made little sense. Tom shut his eyes. He heard the growling of the wolves, but the cries had died out.

A bell rang, and the woman in the golden robe said, "It's done."

The crowd dispersed as if they had watched a show at the theater. The cops stared at the dismembered body. The wolves were still feeding on Charles.

Soon, they faced their nemesis. The hunters approached the cops and made them stand. The woman with the blue mask stood in front of the small group of hunters.

"What the hell do you think you are doing?" shouted Norris. "This is wrong! It's wrong!"

"Who the hell do you think you are? That's murder!" shouted Tom.

The figures in front of them remained speechless.

"Why the hell did you kill him?" demanded Kyle.

"Just answer!" shouted Norris.

There was no response.

"Why did you bring us here?!" yelled Tom.

The strangers remained indifferent. Their stony eyes fixed on the officers.

"You are cowards who hide behind your hideous masks. You have lost it! Edgar, I am sorry you have involved yourself in this shit!" Norris yelled.

Tom glared at him. "What?" he said, trying to determine who was the sheriff's friend.

"Answer me! Edgar... how can you justify feeding a man to the wolves?" demanded Norris.

There was no answer.

"Of course, you are a fucking coward and a damn show-off. Butchering the wolves and mounting them on crosses was not enough! You had to kill innocent people!" Norris shouted.

A figure stepped forward and removed his mask. Tom felt a shiver run through his body. It was true.

"Are you sure I am the coward? Or are you? A man who hides behind the law and lets the innocent die…"

"Coward? You are calling me a coward?" said Norris.

Tom looked from one man to another.

Edgar scowled. "People like you have let us down. You make this country weak. The enemy thrives on your weakness, your sympathy! You are done! Gone! Welcome to the New Age, where we will be the most powerful force that ever existed. People like you don't deserve to live! You are the reason the Shadow Pandemic prevailed, and hundreds died… how do you justify it?"

Tom was speechless.

"I don't. It happened. It was out of my control. I did my best," replied Norris.

"What you did wasn't good enough!"

"What do you recommend? I become a savage like you. And as far as I know, you are using the same technology that brought disaster to Nightridge. How do you justify yourself?" Norris said.

"I do not need to! We have done what no one has done before… we brought together the best of both worlds. Our powerful beliefs and technology. We will be better and more powerful than any human being. This is just the beginning."

Tom trembled. He thought about nanoparticles. What else were these people planning?

"But you are still a savage," Norris said.

Edgar smiled. "Aren't we all savage in the end? We are, after all, animals."

Tom stood in shock. His eyes shifted to the wolves who were feasting on the body.

"There are other ways. Better ways. End this madness. I beg of you... this is brutal. It is inhumane, and you are involving the children!" Norris pleaded.

Edgar smiled widely, and his eyes sparkled. "That is all it took for you to beg? To bring you to your knees. Wow. Norris, you are a disappointment." He stepped closer to Norris. Tom thought he was going to kill the sheriff. "Welcome to the dark world, where the superior should prevail, and the weak shall perish," he muttered, "You disgust me."

"Who do you think you are?" Tom said involuntarily.

As if it was pointless to even look at Tom, he kept staring at Norris.

"This world does not need you, weakling," Edgar said to Norris.

"Right. It needs maniacs like you who feed people to animals," remarked Kyle.

Stillness hit the hall. The figures remained motionless. Edgar took two steps back.

"Edgar, stop this. Let us go," Norris said somewhat calmly.

"Norris, the world is changing. To bring order, there must be chaos."

"Chaos?" Norris said. "This is murder!"

"I speak for all of us. We are tired of feeling powerless. The injustice, the state of the country, the pandemic... this shouldn't have happened. We have become lenient, ignorant... and weak. It's time we took control," said Edgar.

"So, you think it's wise to kill more people? As if the virus hasn't done enough already. You are not above the law," said Tom.

The lady in the golden robe stepped forward and removed her mask. Ella Morgan glared at Tom. "Your law is flawed… your methods ineffective. You punish the innocent and let the criminal lose. Look at the world. It's chaotic. Your law doesn't forgive mistakes. Peter made a mistake, and they condemned him for life. Neville never committed a crime… but your narrow-minded society and media powered by technology crucified him. Instead of helping him, your law and society destroyed his life. Those men were innocent. We had to do something."

"So, you chop off Neville's head and drill through Peter's eyes. And you have just fed Charles to the wolves. The law or society might not be fair, but it didn't kill them, you did!" Tom argued, feeling his blood boil.

"Change is inevitable. It's the dawn of the new world… where we, the superior, will prevail. We will be successful where your law and society failed," said Ella.

"Those are empty words. Nothing is perfect. It never will be," Tom spat.

"We are simply conduits. Our goddess demands blood… blood will bring stability and give us strength. We will bring back glory and power to the right people. To us. Everyone should be afraid of us. Everyone will be afraid of us," Ella said and smiled.

"I think you have lost it," muttered Tom.

"Edgar, stop this. Kill no one," Norris insisted.

Edgar looked at him blankly. "But it's their fate, and they have prepared themselves for this moment."

The cops became silent.

"What?" Norris asked.

"You call us savages, but we did not force anyone into this. Charles chose his way to the other side," said Ella.

Tom glared at her. A shiver ran through his body. "He chose to be eaten alive?" he shouted.

"Yes. The goddess picked him as the martyr. He was destined. So is the Shadow Fraction. We are destined to change the world."

Tom's head spun. It was unbelievable.

"We are martyrs of the new world and others have joined us..." added Ella rather proudly.

Her words rang a bell in his head. "Does that mean you have Ms. Lee and Mr. Fang?" Tom asked.

"They are ready to meet their maker and have made their peace with life. It is their choice. They accepted their crimes and their roles as martyrs who will open new frontiers for a superior human race."

The cops froze.

"Tell us, Detective, what have you done for your community?" Edgar asked, drawing his face close to Tom's.

"I keep it simple. I vow to remain sane," Tom replied sarcastically.

Norris turned to Edgar. "What the fuck is wrong with you?"

Tom looked at the surrounding people. Their words had no effect. They had made up their minds. They believed what they were doing was right, no matter what the outside world thought.

"It's no use," he said to Norris.

Edgar smiled. "Good. Detective, you understand us. Norris, I hope you find enlightenment."

"Fuck you," said Norris.

"You will never change," Edgar said, smiling. He put his mask on and turned away.

Ella did the same. She turned to the group and said, "Let's prepare."

Tom's face turned bleak.

17th April 2020
Fortress, Willow's Heart

The hunters separated Norris from the others and threw him into a dimly lit room. The heavy door shut with a loud bang. He stood up and, after dusting his clothes, peered out of the small, barred window. All he saw were trees. Pulling the bars, he tested if they would budge. After a few attempts, he gave up. It was no use. They had taken his phone, wallet, and gun. There was no way of calling for help.

Norris heard a cry. He put his ear against the door. It was Kyle. Anger rose inside him. He had to do something. Norris walked up and down. They had to escape because if they didn't, they would be next to be eaten by wolves. He paused when he heard a thud. The door swung open, and a masked hunter stepped in. He recognized him.

"Don't worry. I don't intend to kill you yet," Edgar said removing his mask.

"What are you doing here?"

"I wanted to see you before you die."

"I wouldn't bet on it."

Edgar smirked. "There is no one coming to save you."

Their eyes met.

"Where is Gail?" Norris demanded.

Edgar's smile widened. "He is around. He is everywhere."

Norris remembered his research on cults. "Is he your leader?"

"He is…divine."

Norris raised his eyebrows. Gail was mentally unstable, probably a murderer, but not divine. Given a chance, Tom would put a bullet in his head. But one thing was clear: Gail had a powerful influence on the Shadow Fraction.

"I would like to talk with him."

"He doesn't have the time to talk with degenerates like you. A dying generation."

Norris stopped himself from rolling his eyes. "How do you know Gail?"

"We have the same origins. We are superior beings."

Norris tried very hard not to laugh. "How come?"

"I come from a family who ruled this valley. They were like kings and queens, respected by their people. Feared by the villagers. Powerful, intelligent centurions who lived over a hundred years."

Norris remembered the information Kyle had gathered. It was true—their ancestors lived a long, and prosperous life. "And what about Gail?" he asked. His eyes shifted to the door momentarily, thinking if he could escape.

"He sees a pure world. A world beyond a simpleton's imagination. A world without fault and disease. He is the spiritual leader of our people."

Norris kept his eyes steady and said, "He killed three kids and a cop ten years ago, and now you have helped him kill three more people."

"Sacrifices are essential. My ancestors taught me that."

"But your ancestors didn't sacrifice people."

"No, they did not. But this endeavor needed human blood."

"Why?"

"Few sacrifices would save many."

"How? How would you be saving people?"

"Our work will open doors for a better generation."

"Better generations? How? What would these people be like?"

"They could survive wars and pandemics, and we would be powerful to bring the world to its knees. This is just the beginning. The first steps toward a better mankind."

Norris was speechless. Was he talking about the nanoparticles that made the victims immune to viruses? He forced himself to keep talking with him. "Why did you pick Neville and Peter?"

"They needed the money, and they hated cops and the system. We needed people to join our cause.

"What did you do to them?" Norris asked.

"We made them better. Stronger. No biological factor could infect them. Anything that attacked their system died. Miracles happen when you pair science with powerful beliefs. It's our way. It's God's way."

"But the coroner's reports said Neville was suffering. Your experiments could have killed him."

"He knows nothing!"

Norris clamped his lips. "But then you killed them. Why?"

"They were of no more use. It was time for them to depart this world. I told you they were martyrs."

His mouth went dry. Edgar had always been selfish and arrogant. It seemed Gail had turned him into a man without a soul. "Who performed the surgeries?"

"Ella has too many talents. All she needed was a place to do her work quietly and a few assistants."

"And Gail used his wife to get more people... into this... cult..."

"Don't use that word!" Edgar thundered.

Norris raised his hands. "Was Gail's wife involved?"

"No."

"Why did Ella save Gail?"

Edgar's face lit up. "Because she saw the light in him. She said the minute she spoke with him; she saw the world differently."

Or both of them are nuts.

"She had lost her own daughter. Maybe she wasn't thinking straight," Norris said.

"No. No. Only we can see the light. We are light-bearers. She saved him because she saw something in Gail. She believed he could save the world. He can save all of us," said Edgar.

"Who created the Shadow Fraction?"

"It was Gail. I told you. He has divine intervention."

Norris controlled his anger. Gail was a murderer. He didn't think Gail was good for society or the Shadow Fraction. "Why do you follow Gail?" he asked.

"He understands me. My needs. My visions and what I want to be. Everyone wanted me to be like them...follow so many unnecessary rules and regulations. But he set me free. He taught me to embrace my darkness."

Norris nodded thoughtfully and recalled his research

about cult leaders. Manipulation was their game. "I would really like to talk to Gail."

Edgar's face became stern. "He is not available."

Another thought occurred to Norris, and he said, "Why did you kill the seven wolves?"

"To mark the dawn of a new era. We are the future. The best of mankind, and we will not bow down to anyone!"

Norris was speechless.

Edgar smiled, "I wanted to face you for the last time. Say goodbye to everyone, including Nightridge."

Norris gawked at him. "What do you mean?"

Edgar smiled wickedly.

"What do you mean?!"

He left without another word.

Time passed slowly. Norris calculated he had been locked up for several hours. He tried not to let Edgar get under his skin and came up with a plan. He stood with his ear to the door. Then suddenly, he screamed in agony. He collapsed to the ground and cried out. The door opened, and a hunter appeared. Norris puked and felt his gut twist.

As dizziness took over, two hunters dragged him to another room. His throat was sore, and he felt nauseated. They put him on a bed. A figure hovered over him, and something pierced his arm. He felt pain, but then all the stress left his body. His heartbeat slowed, and his fear was long gone.

Time flew by, and his eyes wandered around the room. He spotted a window and saw it was almost dusk. He now remembered. His plan had worked. He had purposely gagged himself and screamed to grab the hunter's attention. As he expected, they treated him and left him in a small medical room. He wanted to get out, escape. But he lost his will and his eyes shut.

Norris drifted in and out of sleep.

"Get up! Get up, Sheriff!" said a voice.

He knew that voice. Ethan's face hovered over him. Fear captured Norris. Ethan was gone, dead. Drowned in the murky water of the Nightridge swamp. Norris had failed him. He was responsible for his death.

"No…no, you are not real," he murmured.

"Get up now! Or more people will die!" shouted the voice.

Norris awakened and sat up. The room spun in front of his eyes. He got off the bed and headed for the door. He forced himself to focus and slowly opened it. The passageway was overflowing with hunters. Closing the door, he turned. A bundle of clothes in a corner caught his eye.

Norris felt uncomfortable. He didn't understand how someone could breathe in these masks. They were heavy, smelled funny, and suffocating. The robe that he had found was bulky, and he felt hot. Dressed as one of them, Norris blended amongst the hunters. He didn't know his way out, so he waited for his chance. But he had little time. If the hunters discovered he was not in the medical room, they would start looking for him. He spent ten minutes searching for Tom and Kyle, but he couldn't find them.

Not wasting any more time, he decided to flee and get help. A gong went off, and all the hunters headed toward the hall. Norris slowed his pace. When the hunters vanished, he opened the door to his left. It was a storeroom. Acting fast, he opened the door next to it. Norris found a room and snuck inside. Checking no one was following him, he removed the outfit and jumped out of the window. He dropped on a large rock and hurt his knee. He winced. Getting on his feet, he glanced behind and ran into the woods.

29

THE EYES OF EVIL

18th April 2020 (Present Day)
Willow's Heart

Norris had been running all night. He was tired. Lying on the mushy ground, he was so glad to see Roumoult.

"Move away from him!" said Roumoult, pointing the gun at the hunter.

The hunter lifted the blade to kill Norris. A shot rang. The bullet blew out the hunter's brain. The lifeless body dropped to the ground. Norris felt numb and gawked at the dead man.

Roumoult stepped close to him, kneeled, and placed a hand on his shoulder, "Are you okay, Sheriff?" he asked.

Norris wanted to weep. He thought he was going to die. It was hard to control his tears. Roumoult helped him get on his feet. Norris's heart was racing. He was exhausted and craved a soft, clean bed.

"Norris, are you all right?" Roumoult asked again.

"Yes. Thank you. I am fine. How did you…" his voice faded away.

From behind the bushes, a familiar figure appeared. Mrs. Flores rushed to him.

"Chief! Chief! Good Lord. Look at you!" she cried out. "We should take you to a hospital."

Norris didn't listen to her and hugged her. She put his arms around him.

"I am so glad I found you…" she whimpered.

They parted, and Mrs. Flores looked into his eyes.

"I received your message and got help as soon as I could."

"Where have you been? We have been looking for you all night long!" said Roumoult.

"I have been on the run…"

Norris wiped the sweat from his face. Roumoult was standing over the dead man. Curious to see the face of the hunter, Norris came to stand beside him. Roumoult unmasked the man.

"Do you know him?" he asked.

"Yes, we found Neville's body in his barn. His name is Eddie."

"Are you telling me the entire village is involved?"

"More or less…"

"Oh, that is just great," Roumoult remarked.

Norris noticed a pair of lights on the mountain. "They are coming," he said irritated.

Roumoult followed his gaze.

"Come on," he said, taking his arm.

Norris hobbled.

"We have to hide in the woods…" he said breathlessly.

"You must go to the hospital," said Mrs. Flores.

"No. No. We must find Tom and Kyle. Otherwise, they will kill them."

"Don't worry. John is looking for them."

Norris relaxed his tense shoulders. Of course, Roumoult was not stupid to come here on his own. He had backup. The trio stepped on the rough road and began making their way down the hill. He glanced back.

"Roumoult, we must hide in the…" he insisted, but his voice trailed off.

The moonlight bounced off the shiny roof of the Audi. Norris smiled.

"Hiding in the woods will not help. They have been chasing us for the last three hours. We need to get to the fortress. That is where John is heading," Roumoult explained.

Norris and Mrs. Flores sat in the back seat. He held his aching knee. His arm was not doing great either. He longed to close his eyes and fall asleep. But he had to make sure his friends were alive and well. An engine revved. He glanced over his shoulder. Headlights appeared on the top of the hill. He was about to warn Roumoult when the car started and darted down the dusty road at immense speed.

18th April 2020 (Present Day)
Willow's Heart

Tom wept, but it was no use. The vision of Kyle falling into the void played in front of his eyes like a bad horror movie. They had lost. He was next. In the dim light, he glared at the chains binding him to the wall. The hunters did not need to chain him. He didn't plan to run. It was over. He had let Kyle die. He didn't deserve to live. Tom counted his blessings and sent love to Jenny, his father, and his friends. He had lived a blessed life and was grateful. If this were the end, he would accept it.

The door opened with a loud clang, and a hunter unchained him while another stood on guard. The hunters took him to the hall. It was dimly lit with a few candles in each corner. The Shadow Fraction was waiting. Tom was too tired to resist as they led him to the pillar and secured the ropes around his wrist. The pillar carried a strong metallic smell. They had cleaned Charles's blood and remains, but the smell of blood lingered. Sweat dripped down his face as his heart pounded in his chest. He felt exasperated, and his legs trembled.

Tom prayed. He didn't know why. He asked himself what he had done with his life. Had he lived and enjoyed his life so far? The answer was yes. The thought gave him some peace.

In front of him, there was a painting of a lady, fierce, brave, completely naked, surrounded by wolves. He had seen it before. When he looked down, he saw he was standing in the middle of a pentacle.

The Shadow Fraction stood silently, wearing masks and heavy robes. Their attire still bothered him. Children, men, and women spread around the hall. From their heights, he guessed the children were between six to ten years old. A gong went off, and Tom's body turned numb. Three hunters, one wearing a golden robe with a blue mask followed by two colossal figures in black masks, approached him. It was Ella Morgan.

"You have let the innocent die and freed the criminals. In the eyes of our goddess, you have blood on your hands, and you must pay for your crimes. This would be the day justice will be served. Our goddess will show mercy on your soul if you plead for your life."

The hall became silent. Tom stared at the stone eyes. He felt a sense of fear, remorse, and disgust.

"Plead for your life!" demanded a hunter.

Tom grunted. "I don't give a shit about your goddess or your deranged ways. So, why don't you go fuck yourself?!"

There was no response, but he sensed their hatred and anger. He preferred not to say anything else. It would be in vain. Pleading these maniacs would not get him anywhere. Instead, he put his energy into calming himself down. Death was near.

A shiver ran down his spine as the chanting began. The soothing humming echoed in the hall. Tom bit his lips. Did he really want to die? Wasn't there any way he could get out? The light in the hall was still dim, and he gawked at the mirror above him. They would wait for dawn. He had a few minutes. Could he escape? Suddenly, the group bowed, and it was silent for a second. Tom's heart leaped to his throat. The chants began again.

Outside, the edge of the sun's rim appeared above the horizon, and the first ray of sunlight entered the valley.

Tom gulped. "Okay. This is it."

18th April 2020 (Present Day)
Willow's Heart

The powerful four-wheel-drive chased the Audi that drove through the heart of the valley. On the next turn, the car skidded sideways. Norris grabbed the door and winced as pain rippled through his arm. The black truck was not far behind. His jaw dropped when he saw two headlights ahead of them.

"Roumoult!" he warned him.

"Oh, shit!" Roumoult muttered and switched on the GPS.

The Audi raced ahead, pushing Norris and Mrs. Flores into their seats.

"Damn it! I hate the country," Roumoult shouted.

A second four-wheel-drive headed directly towards them.

"Hold on!" Roumoult shouted, making a swift turn to the left. The Audi cut through the weeds and drove down the rough road.

"What the hell are you doing?" Norris said, leaning forward.

"Trust me," Roumoult replied.

Norris wanted to protest. The car would not get through. But he paused when he saw Roumoult had a map displayed on the screen on the dashboard. It showed a trail. Mrs. Flores shrieked when branches bashed against her window. The car drove down the hill, leaving a long trail of dust. The trucks followed.

"Where is the backup?" Norris asked, almost yelling.

"They should be on their way."

The narrow route widened. Roumoult took a sharp left turn and then swung the wheel to the right, heading back into the wilderness. The car jolted and bounced over the rocks buried in the muddy road. Norris grabbed the car door. Breathless, he feared the worst.

"Norris, can you shoot?" Roumoult asked.

"Yes," he replied, touching his injured arm.

The Audi's exterior bashed against millions of branches

and leaves. The engine roared. Suddenly a group of deer and rabbits jumped in the car's path.

"Oh!" Roumoult cried.

He pushed the brakes, barely missing a rabbit. The little animal vanished in the bushes, and the car quickly gained speed. Norris glanced over his shoulder. Dust clouded the road. The trucks were nowhere in sight.

"We might have lost them," he said.

Suddenly, the path broadened, and Roumoult swayed the steering wheel. Norris held his head. He felt dizzy. Roumoult was driving too fast. The car almost skidded as it returned to the main road. At a distance, he saw the fortress. A loud screeching resonated, and a truck broke through the bushes and followed them.

"They are back!"

"I know," Roumoult replied, giving him a gun.

Norris checked the bullets. Holding the gun in his right hand, he glanced at Mrs. Flores.

"We will be fine," he said.

She smiled bleakly.

Light shone on the Audi, and his eyes became fixed ahead. The second truck was heading straight for them. Suddenly, Roumoult dropped speed.

"What are you doing?" he demanded.

"Mrs. Flores, get down!" Roumoult yelled.

"Oh," she cried out and slid down the seat.

From both sides, the trucks raced toward Audi. Norris glanced on both sides. The trucks were approaching fast, too fast.

"What we going to do?" he shouted.

18th April 2020 (Present Day)
Fortress, Willow's Heart

Tom tried to fight his fear. He had to. There was no choice. Gradually, the illumination increased in the hall. Two hunters wearing horned masks approached him with knives.

So, this is how I die.

From between the mountains rose a large object. It blocked the sunlight and flew toward the fortress. Another black object followed it. The enormous blades of the helicopter cut through the air, crushing the silence of the valley. The illumination in the hall dimmed and fluctuated. The chanting stopped, and heads turned. Tom heard a whirring, and he glanced out of the dusty window.

Amongst the hunters, a figure moved. It bent over and threw an object. Two cylinders rolled across the hall, and white gas began dispersing. Screams echoed. The smoke spread through the hall, disrupting the congregation. Two blasts shook the fortress. Tom tried to free himself. He froze when he sensed someone behind him. He glanced over his shoulder. A figure with a horned mask approached him. Tom tried to move away. The hunter took off his mask, and Tom's jaw dropped. It was a face he thought he would never see again.

"Hey, Tom," Kyle said, smiling.

"You! You are alive!" Tom said happily, coughing. "You are alive!" he screamed.

"Yes. I was lucky. Sorry, I could not save you," Kyle explained, untying him.

Tom's eyes filled with joy. He didn't care. "I am so glad to see you!"

When he was free, he hugged Kyle tightly.

"We have to get out of here!" Kyle said, grabbing his arm and pulling him away from the pillar. The fire and smoke were spreading fast.

"How did you get here?" Tom asked.

"I survived the fall. Then John found me, and I led him to the fortress. I disguised myself as one of them. We had to get you out. Come on. The squad is waiting outside."

Two hunters raged at them. The cops ran in the opposite direction. They broke through a window. Tom landed on his face, and a sharp pain shot through his leg. He cried out.

"Get up! They are coming!" Kyle shouted.

Limping, Tom rushed to the woods. Tom heard the hunter's curse and ran as fast as he could. He came to an abrupt stop when two figures emerged from behind the tree.

"Tom," said John.

Tom's heart swelled. The cops embraced each other. He could not utter a word and tried to control his tears. Just a minute ago, he had thought his life was over.

"Are you okay?" John asked once they parted.

Tom nodded, covering his face with his hands. It was over. The nightmare had finally ended. He turned and saw William. No words were exchanged. He stepped forward and hugged Tom.

The helicopter whirred above them. Two SWAT trucks came to a standstill. The back doors swung open, and armed men and women jumped out. In a matter of seconds, they surrounded the fortress. Still trying to catch his breath, Tom stood with his friends gaping at the two hunters.

"NYPD! You are under arrest! Put your weapons down," shouted John, raising his gun. The squad followed his lead.

Tom knew this was not over. The battle had just begun.

18th April 2020 (Present Day)
Willow's Heart

The Audi bounced. Norris's grip on the gun tightened. He pushed a button to lower the car window. The two trucks were closing in from the opposite direction. He looked back and forth, confused, not knowing who to shoot first.

"You need to tell me what to do!" Norris said.

"That one!" Roumoult said, pointing ahead.

Peering out of the window, he aimed and fired. The bullet hit the windshield. The truck wobbled heading straight for them.

"Whoa…" Roumoult cried out, taking the Audi on to the rough road.

Norris fired again, blowing up the tire. Loud screeching echoed. The truck whirled smashed into a tree.

"Whoa! That was close!" said Norris.

The Audi skidded back on the road, steered around the truck, and raced down the murky road. The second truck sped behind Audi. Norris checked the bullets. Five bullets should be enough, he thought. He noticed something on the floor. A handgun.

"Okay, that worked. Now what?" he asked Roumoult.

A sound echoed, and the windshield behind him shattered into pieces. Norris ducked, shielding Mrs. Flores. Another bang echoed. A bullet struck the car.

"Any other ideas?" asked Norris, wondering if he should shoot back.

"What's this?" Roumoult asked, pointing to the area.

Trying not to raise his head too high, Norris peered at the GPS.

"It's the Field of Ashes."

Roumoult glanced at him as if checking he was not joking.

"Literally?" he asked.

"Literally."

Suddenly, Roumoult turned the car and headed toward the field at full speed.

18th April 2020 (Present Day)
Willow's Heart

The cops waited with guns aimed at the masked men.

"Put your weapons down!" shouted John again.

Tom was armed, but he did not raise his weapon. He just observed the hunters. The helicopters continued hovering over the fortress. Cops stood with shields, helmets, and guns, waiting for John to say the word. Their armor looked strong and thick. But the men in front of them stood straight, wearing nothing but a thin robe. Through their horned masks, they fixed their lifeless eyes on the officers.

Tom feared the worst.

"How many of them?" John said.

"Around thirty," Kyle replied.

"John, there are children in there," Tom said.

John glanced at him worriedly.

"I said, stand down!" John yelled.

The two men did not move.

"You are under arrest… I repeat, put the swords down!" John shouted.

"I have a bad feeling about this," Tom muttered.

"Don't lower your guard..." John said to the squad, "Team B, take cover. Kyle and William go with them."

The team rushed toward the woods.

John took the lead. Tom followed hesitantly.

"Put your swords—"

The windows of the fortress shattered, glass flying in every direction. A dozen hunters emerged, armed with machine guns. Tom's eyes widened as a hunter pulled a gun. Tom pulled the trigger, and the bullet missed the hunter by inches. Shots blazed in every direction. He fell to the grass and covered his ears with John on his side. He lifted his head and saw the bodies of two cops.

"Kill them all!" shouted a voice.

John and Tom looked at each other.

Shouts echoed, and the fearless hunters marched toward the cops. The SWAT team returned fire. A roar thundered as a wolf charged toward Tom. He swung and pulled the trigger, blowing its head off.

"There are wolves in the woods!" he warned.

John stumbled to his feet and fired several shots as he rushed toward the woods. A hunter charged at him and knocked him down. John's gun fell. The hunter pulled out a knife.

"No!" Tom yelled.

Getting on his knees, he fired. The masked man dropped to the ground. John acted quickly and grabbed his gun. A loud bang resonated. The ground shuddered. Tom screamed as a powerful force threw him over. He landed on his face and winced in pain. A ball of smoke rose to the sky. With his ears still ringing, Tom watched with horror as a cop screamed in pain, holding his leg. He rushed and dragged him behind a tree. Gunshots boomed. Amid the smoke and fire, he looked for his partner. John was nowhere to be seen.

"John! John!"

Shots rang to his left.

Team B fired back. Three hunters instantly dropped to the ground. Taking his chance, Tom rushed towards the woods and hid behind a tree. A thick layer of smog drifted in the air. The firing stopped, and shadows moved within the smoke. The cops waited. Sweat covered Tom's face. His right hand was shaking. He heard a rustle and spun.

"Whoa! It's me," John said, raising his hands.

Tom lowered his weapon. "Do not do that!"

He turned to the fortress. They were still out there. As the smoke settled, he noticed two hunters lurking behind a tree. Dead bodies of over a dozen hunters and cops lay on the ground. Dread spread amongst the police officers. Tom didn't realize he had stopped breathing. A gasp drew him back to reality. He turned and saw William, who stood like a statue, with wet dull eyes.

John spoke into the radio: "Take them out the first chance you get."

John's bitter tone astonished Tom. A crow croaked as it flew over the meadow. Tom jumped when two shots rang killing the hunters. He gulped. Pin drop silence returned. The hunters were most likely dead, but no one dared to step out.

John's head bowed. Quietly, he wiped his face with the back of his hand. "Don't leave your post," he ordered.

Silence returned.

"Charlie One. Is the coast clear?" John spoke into the radio, looking up.

A helicopter returned and circled above the fortress.

"Anything?" he asked.

"The coast looks clear," a voice cracked on the radio.

Tom felt a lump in his throat. "John, I know what they have done. But we must try to save the others."

John's face was colorless. His eyes were fixed on the dead bodies. Without another word, he signaled the squad. With their guns aimed toward the fortress, they cautiously marched ahead.

18th April 2020 (Present Day)
Field of Ashes

The sun's rays spread through the valley, engulfing it in an orangish glow. Norris knew they were running out of time. The Audi jolted, and Norris bumped his head on the roof.

"Be careful," Mrs. Flores said.

He glanced behind. The truck was still following them. The car leaped over the bumpy road and skidded. Roumoult grunted, trying to stay in control. The path twisted, and the car glided over the dusty road.

"Oh great, more jungle!" shouted Roumoult as the car drove on the narrow road lined with thick vegetation.

"Where is this…" his voice trailed away as the path suddenly opened.

The car skidded on the dust, heading for a pillar.

"Watch out!" Mrs. Flores cried.

Roumoult swayed the steering wheel, missing the ancient

pillar by inches. The tires whirled over the mixture of dust and ash. Norris was pushed against the seat. He watched in horror with wide-open eyes as the car headed straight for another pillar.

"Whoa," he cried out.

The car changed direction. He grabbed the seat. Like a snake hissing around poles, the Audi raced on the field, leaving a gigantic cloud of dust. The truck was right behind it. The car skillfully navigated right and then left, going around the field. Then in a cloud of mist, it vanished.

Thin beams of sunlight penetrated the layers of floating dust and ashes. It bounced off the particles. The dust hung in midair as if stopped by an unseen force. Roumoult, Norris, and Mrs. Flores sat in silence, listening. At a distance, an engine roared, struggling to move. Roumoult turned to him and picked up the handgun.

"It's time."

Norris nodded and faced Mrs. Flores.

"Don't worry. We will be okay."

"I certainly hope so," she said.

The ancient pillars stood in silence. Symbols of the past and tellers of the future. No bird sang, and no sound came from the valley. The hunter's truck had stopped. They had lost the scent of prey. In the vast region as big as a football field, they searched on foot. They coughed as dust threatened to enter their lungs. Then they heard a beep, and two bright lights appeared at the far end of the field. With their swords drawn, they marched toward the light.

The Audi's ghostly beams cut through millions of particles of dust. A hunter stepped closer, sword in one hand, gun in the other. A shadow snuck up from behind. Norris pounced on him, shunting the hunter into the ashes. He kicked the sword away and picked up the gun. The hunter slammed his fist in his face. Norris dropped the gun. The men were at each other's throats. Norris kicked him in the groin and hit him with his elbow in the chest. The hunter stumbled to the ground. Cradling his arm and feeling agony in his leg, Norris stepped back. The hunter rose to his feet with another gun in his hand. Norris froze. He checked the holster on his waist. It was empty.

"Damn," he muttered.

The hunter laughed.

"You lose, you miserable asshole!"

Norris knew him. Edgar removed his mask.

"You were never fast enough… nor clever."

"I don't give a damn what you think of me," Norris said.

He looked at the loaded gun. Maybe tonight was the night he would meet his maker.

"Well, all that running came to nothing, did it? Why can't you just give up?" Edgar said.

"Sorry. It's not in my nature," said Norris, trying hard to think of a way out. Where was Roumoult?

The dust was settling. An ancient pillar became visible behind Edgar.

Edgar aimed at his head.

"Goodbye, Norris. Honestly, I am not a fan."

"That makes two of us," he replied, feeling his heart race and breath shorten.

Edgar grinned, showing all his teeth. His eyes filled with excitement. A gun clicked. A tiny figure materialized from within the mist.

"I am not your fan either," Mrs. Flores said.

Fire blasted from the nozzle of the handgun. The bullet tore through Edgar's heart. The gun recoiled and threw Mrs. Flores backwards.

"Terresa!" Norris cried, running toward her.

Mrs. Flores was covered with dust.

"Oh, oh... my back... oh," she cried putting the gun down.

"Are you okay?" he asked, helping her sit up.

"I-I... think so," she replied breathlessly. She took a few deep breaths. "Did I get him?" she asked.

Norris smiled, "Nice shot."

"Oh, good. I hope the miserable bastard goes to hell," she muttered.

Norris heard footsteps. The second hunter raged toward them with a curved blade. Norris took the gun from Mrs. Flores. A shadow materialized and hurled the hunter to the ground.

"Ah! You son..." the hunter shouted, getting on his feet.

Roumoult pulled the trigger. The bullet blasted through the hunter's knee. He shrieked and fell to the ground.

"You fucking..."

"Shut up!" Roumoult shouted, pointing the gun at his head, "Another word and I'll blow your head off!"

The hunter turned silent.

Catching his breath, he looked at Norris and Mrs. Flores.

"You guys, okay?" he asked.

Both nodded numbly.

18th April 2020 (Present Day)
Fortress, Willow's Heart

Tom's heart was drumming faster and faster. The cops marched across the meadow. As they moved up the slope, he tried not to look at the lifeless bodies. The squad sprinted to the entrance. Two cops stood on guard as one officer pushed open the door. Low, rhythmic chanting echoed. Blood drained from Tom's face. The cops swarmed into the fortress, surrounding the group standing on the platform. Tom glared at the rest of the Shadow Fraction, who stood chanting, holding hands. Six hunters surrounded the group dressed in colorful robes.

"Stop this at once!" shouted John.

The chanting didn't stop.

"Step down from the platform!" John shouted.

They stopped chanting, and Tom welcomed the silence. Ella removed her mask and glared at him. Tom ignored her, and his eyes settled on the six children who stood in the middle.

"This is over. Please put your weapons down and come with us," Tom said, taking a step forward.

"Tom!" warned John.

Tom raised his hands. "Let's sort this out. Talk about it. Let there be no more death or violence for the sake of the children."

Ella looked Tom in the eyes. "We don't follow your rules."

Tom found it hard to speak. One wrong move, and things could get worse. "Ella. Be reasonable. You have broken…"

"We don't care about your flawed ways. Nothing can stop us. You are unworthy of us. Your world is corrupt and inferior! We live on our own terms, and we step into the next stage of life with honor and righteousness."

Tom's heart was pounding. His voice trembled as he said, "Ella... please. Let's talk,"

"Just...step..." John said, but his words trailed away.

At that moment, the hunters on both ends drew their swords and cut the ropes. A loud thud stunned the cops. The enormous stone that hovered over the platform descended.

"No!" Tom shouted, dashing forward.

John immediately grabbed him. He watched in horror as the gigantic stone crushed the men, women, and children. Screams echoed and then died out. Tom felt as if life had left his body, and it turned cold. Unable to speak or move, the cops stood dumbfounded. The hall rattled, and the ground shook. It drove Tom out of the shock. He looked up as the roof began to crack. The wheel with the mask fell, shattering into pieces.

"Get out... get out!" John screamed.

The crack enlarged, and large pieces of stone fell. John grabbed Tom by the arm, pulling him away. Tom cast a last glance at the platform. Blood flowed out of the gaps between the stones. John didn't let go of him and Tom didn't know what he was doing. Voices surrounded him as he found himself in the open air. They stopped at a safe distance. The cops watched in anguish. Guns fell to the ground. A few cops looked away from the scene. John looked helplessly at the fallen fortress. With his hands on his head, Tom fell to his knees.

30

THE MEANING OF JUSTICE

18th April 2020 (Present Day)
Fortress, Willow's Heart

The Audi came to a stop. Norris knew something terrible had happened. He stepped out and grimaced at the partially fallen fortress. Along with Roumoult and Mrs. Flores, he rushed toward the site. Tom sat on the ground with his head in his hands. Horror filled every cop's features. He marched toward the fortress, but Kyle blocked him.

"Don't…" he said.

But Norris had to. He plodded ahead with Roumoult on his side. The cracks in the ground were unmissable, and so was the smell of blood. He froze when he saw a stream of blood oozing from gaps between the stones. It had stained the entire floor. A woman's bloody hand was hanging by a string of a muscle. The walls were smeared with blood. He looked up, and the roof had broken in half. The wall facing North had partially fallen. Norris turned to Roumoult, hoping he would say something. But he stood staggered, staring at the blood.

The ambulance came, but Tom thought it was too late. Four cops were seriously injured. Seven had died. Most likely, the entire Shadow Fraction was gone. The ambulance was followed by three coroner's vans.

Tom numbly watched as Norris was taken to the hospital. After receiving treatment, the hunter captured by Roumoult was cuffed and sat in the back the police car. The coroners William, Johnathan, along with other volunteers, got ready to retrieve the bodies or whatever was left of them. Tom studied William's face. He had not spoken a word. Tom did not blame him. He wished he had never stepped foot in this valley.

Tom watched the two forklifts clear the rubble so the crane could enter the fortress. John was long gone. Last he heard; he was talking to the captain. He was upset and needed space. Tom didn't stop him. He watched the forklift reverse, and then a small crane turned toward the opening. It vanished into the fortress.

Tom headed for the entrance and stepped into the hall. The CSI unit was already there, gathering evidence. He stood with William and Johnathan. Two construction workers were drilling holes in the rock. The drilling noise was ear-deafening. When it stopped, they attached anchors to the cement. The crane moved forward with thick chains on its nose. The workers linked the anchors with chains and then jumped down from the slab.

With a loud thud and a groan, the stone lifted, and the

crushed bodies became visible. Gasps resonated. They saw the layer of gore and red tissue mixed with broken bones. Tom felt nauseous and turned away. After a moment, he looked at the platform and felt a hole in his chest. Why didn't he just grab them and pull them off the platform? Why did he waste time speaking to Ella? The cops should have overpowered them. It was no use now. They were gone. He hung his head and walked away.

19th April 2020
The Temple, Willow's Heart

Norris grunted. The pain in his leg was persistent, but his shoulder was better than yesterday. He stood facing the shrine. The temple was just as Tom had described. The deputies were searching the area for the infants. He came down the stairs to the underground nursery and stopped in front of the glass door. The cradles were empty, and the cabinets had been cleaned out. The infants had vanished.

Kyle approached him.

"They were right here, Chief! And now there is no trace of them. Someone took them!" He said pacing the floor.

Norris grunted. While cops were at the fortress trying to rescue them, someone had taken the infants. It meant only one thing. A part of the Shadow Fraction had escaped, and since everyone was wearing masks, identifying them was hard. The CSI units were busy checking for trace evidence, but he had a feeling it was all in vain. They had one man in custody, Mr. Rubin Lare. He claimed he knew nothing and refused to comment further. He did not live in Willow's Heart, nor was he connected to the twelve families. Walking out of the nursery, he glanced into the computer lab. All equipment had been smashed.

Disheartened, he climbed up the stairs with his head bowed. Who was behind all this? First, the Shadow Pandemic. It took several lives and threatened everything he loved, and now the Shadow Fraction had emerged. A group driven by beliefs of superiority and suffered from borderline madness. He rubbed his temples.

The people of Willow's Heart were in shock. The news was spreading fast, and so was the fear. Bodies of long-lost tourists were being extracted from underneath the old Garsow Radio Station. The ones the cops could find. He emerged from the cave, and in the fresh air, he felt better. The sky was clear, and the birds were singing. It was a beautiful day, but all he wanted to do was scream.

19th April 2020
Meadow's Cottage, Nightridge

Norris returned from Willow's Heart with Roumoult. Mrs. Flores was making tea while he sat on the porch. A light breeze cooled his face, and once again, peace had returned. He stared at the two vehicles covered with dust parked in his front yard. Maybe he should buy a new car, he thought as he compared his truck with Roumoult's Audi.

His body ached, reminding him he needed to rest. Maybe a vacation. All of them needed it. He heard voices, and Roumoult, William, and Tom joined him on the porch. Each carried a bowl of snacks and placed them on the table. Mrs. Flores stepped out with a teapot and several cups.

"I think we need something stronger than that," Norris remarked.

"No. The doctor said no alcohol," she said and returned to the house.

The men looked a bit disappointed. Roumoult got to his feet and walked to his car. Soon he returned with a small bottle of brandy.

"Nice!" Norris said, feeling happy as he raised his cup.

They mixed brandy with their tea and enjoyed the drink.

"Tom, did the doctor give you a clean bill of health?" Roumoult asked.

"Yeah," he answered.

All heads turned to him.

"You didn't go to the doctor, did you?" William said.

"I am all right, guys," Tom replied wearily.

The men became silent, knowing he was lying.

"I didn't think it would end this way," said Tom.

"No one could have guessed," Roumoult replied.

"Why not just give up? Surrender?" Tom said, shaking his head.

"They didn't believe in the law or the system and hated cops. They didn't think they would get a fair trial. So, they took matters into their own hands," explained Norris.

"How could someone kill their own children?" Tom countered.

"Imagine if they had survived," said Roumoult. "They would be forever labeled as children of murderers... vigilantes... children of the Shadow Fraction. Just think how miserable their lives would be?"

"It was a pact, Tom. They knew what they were getting into," Norris explained, "And they planned well ahead, knowing that each person on the platform could spend their entire lives in jail. Instead, they chose death."

"We can only assume that the anger against injustice, social anxiety, and dogma haunted them for years. Until they joined Gail and his Shadow Fraction. It brought them together. He promised them a better world, making them believe they were understood and welcome. Perhaps a promise of justice. And they joined hands with vigilantes with access to technology that they thought could make them invincible," Roumoult said.

"Whenever something bad happens, humans turn to something to believe in. Some turn to therapy...and unfortunately, these people turned to the Shadow Fraction," William added.

"And then rolled Edgar in," Norris said, sipping his tea.

"Why would Edgar get involved?" Tom asked.

"His ancestors were one of the first families that settled in Willow's Heart. He was driven by ego. A proud man with a deranged sense of justice. He wanted to win, regardless of the cost. I'm not surprised he joined Ella and Gail," Norris explained.

Everyone nodded.

"Why reach out to you?" asked William.

Norris felt his gut twist. "To prove he was better than me. I think he felt he had to prove he was...superior," he paused and gulped nervously. "Of course, he wanted to kill me, eventually. And make it as painful as possible."

The group became quiet.

"Was the entire village involved?" asked Roumoult.

"Not everyone. Eddie had played his part well when we found Neville's body in his barn. But Mrs. Fryer was not a part of the group, and unfortunately, they put Peter's body in her home."

"That was cruel," said William.

Norris shrugged his shoulders.

Soon, they ate dinner in silence and called it a night.

The next morning, Norris relaxed in the chair on the porch again. He had to admit he had enjoyed the company. Roumoult, since he had woken up, was busy on the phone, either talking to his father or his secretary. Now he was cleaning his car. He had washed off all the dust and was now focusing on the interior. The constant whirling of the cordless vacuum was becoming slightly annoying. The windshield was still broken, and the car bore several scratches. His truck was in the same condition. He heard footsteps, and William and Tom stepped out of the house. A Ford drove into the driveway, and John got out of the car.

"Morning, Sheriff, how are you?" John said.

"I am good. Good to see you."

John nodded.

"How did it go with the captain?" Norris asked.

John's eyes lowered, and he bit his lips. "Not good. He is not happy."

"I understand."

"We lost good people…"

"We did," Norris replied, feeling the emptiness return.

Tom stood next to his partner.

"Are you ready to head back to the city?" John asked.

"Yep," Tom replied.

John looked at William. "I think we have everything we

need from the crime scene. Now, it's up to you guys to separate the remains and identify them."

William nodded.

The detectives said their goodbyes and left.

William leaned forward and hugged Norris. "Until next time."

Norris patted his back and nodded. "Sure. Hopefully, when no one is trying to kill us."

William nodded, walked toward the Audi, and got into the passenger seat.

Roumoult stepped forward and shook the sheriff's hand. "Take care."

Norris's face turned grim.

"It will be fine," Roumoult said.

"I am scared and worried."

"I am aware,"

"What is happening to the world?"

Taking a deep breath in, Roumoult wore his sunglasses. "The world has always been a brutal place, and the pandemic has put it on the edge. There are people driving chaos, and then there are people trying to keep the peace. It's a choice, and we have made ours."

Norris didn't know what to say. It was the truth. Everyone chose their own paths.

"See you, Sheriff," Roumoult said.

Norris watched the Audi smoothly reverse and then drive away. Stillness returned, and he wondered if he would ever find peace. He had had enough. Maybe he should retire. The last six months had been devastating.

"Oh, well… they are all gone, aren't they," Mrs. Flores said, taking a seat beside him with a cup of tea.

"I must ask, how did you know where to find me?" said Norris.

"Oh, you know the boy who doesn't know how to comb his hair," asked Mrs. Flores.

"You mean Jack."

"Yeah. I think that was his name. He tracked the location of the nearest tower from where the text was sent. Roumoult figured you must have escaped. While we looked for you, John assembled the squad."

Norris was impressed. "I never got the chance to thank you. You were right about Edgar. I owe you, my life."

"Chief. You don't have to thank me. And what can I say? I am just a secretary," she replied, winking.

26th April 2020
City Morgue, New York

The enormous cement slab took up all the space in the hall where William had conducted his experiments. Several technicians dressed in white scrubs and masks methodically conducted one test after another. In the far corner, broken bones of various sizes sat in dry, steel trays. Little flags and yellow tags marked numerous parts of the slab. William observed the row of clip pads placed against each set of blood and tissue samples. Collecting these remains was hard but identifying them had given him a migraine.

He smoldered with resentment, trying not to think about the last seven days. Although he had not witnessed the mass suicide, the remains told him the entire story. According to Tom, there were at least twenty people in that group. So far, they have identified nineteen members of the Shadow Fraction.

Fortunately, they could match the victims' DNA samples from their homes and belongings. The police had dug up Ella's daughter's body and used the daughter's DNA to identify her remains. Many members were part of the village and linked to their ancestral remains that Norris had found underneath the Garsow Radio Station. The two skulls in found the dungeon where Tom was held remained unidentified. The cops searched the area but did not find any other remains.

William left the hall and rushed down the corridor. On the second floor, he stepped into another vast, cold room. White machines with black screens of varied sizes stood all over the room. He ignored the people around him and marched toward the DNA analyzer. The technician's expression did not change, and William knew she was annoyed at him. Not everyone was as patient as Juliet. He had been hovering around the machine for the last one week. They had tested several samples, and this was the last one. He watched as the technician worked.

"It will take a few minutes," said the technician.

William said nothing and waited with his hands folded. His uneasiness grew. The machine stopped, and on the monitor, a graph appeared. The printer came to life, and the technician handed over the report to him. Relieved that her work was done, she left him alone. He glared at the report. Rage seized him.

"Ah!" he screamed and kicked the table.

The lab came to a standstill, and every technician stared at him.

"Get back to work!" he shouted.

He peeled off his gloves and threw them in the bin. Leaving the lab, he dialed Tom's number. The detective answered after two rings.

"Hey, William."

Anger quivered inside William.

"What happened?" Tom asked, sensing something was wrong.

"He was not one of them…"

"He? Who?"

"The man who started this all! Gail! He was not in the group that died at the fortress…"

"What?" Tom shouted. "Are you telling me he escaped?"

"Yes. There is no trace of his DNA in any of the tissue samples!"

The line became silent.

"He left them to die for him," Tom said.

"Or they created a distraction so that he could escape," William replied, walking past a few people. He rushed to stop the closing doors of the elevator.

"What kind of man would do that? Leave innocent children to die!" Tom spat.

William got in the elevator with two other people. "A man like Gail! After everyone that died. Everything that happened, he slipped away from our hands! Tom, the real criminal escaped!" William shouted.

Two technicians glared at him, but he didn't care. He ended the call and cursed under his breath.

18ᵗʰ May 2020
Field of Ashes, Willow's Heart

Norris stood with his legs apart, and hands folded. His arm was slightly painful, but his knee had completely healed. He was surprised. He thought it would take more time. Kyle came over and stood beside him. Norris had not seen him for a week, but that was understandable.

"I am glad you are alive," Norris said.

"I almost died," said Kyle rubbing his neck. "It was terrible. I fell on the edge of a rock and grabbed it. Over the rushing water, I heard Tom screaming. If I hadn't moved fast, I would have died. I pushed myself and grabbed a dangling branch. I don't know how I did it, Chief, but I climbed out."

Norris put his arm around his shoulders.

"By the time I reached the top, they were gone. I knew they had taken Tom. I found my way to the main road and saw three vehicles. At first, I thought it was the hunters, and I hid behind the bushes. But as the vehicles passed, I realized it was the police. I screamed and waved. Thankfully, they saw me. I lead them to the fortress…"

"You did good," Norris said warmly.

The men marveled at the ancient pillars. They had collected various samples from the field, and to his relief, the remains belonged to animals. It was a part of a ritual, and the cops decided not to disturb it. They found no more wolves in the houses of the Shadow Fraction. Either the wolves died during the shoot-out or escaped into the woods.

"All of them might not be dead," Kyle said, "Someone might live in those woods that stretch over the mountain. They might have more children who are untraceable."

"It is possible," Norris replied.

They stood in silence.

"It's a pity. They are thinking of taking them down. It makes me sad. The pillars are beautiful," said Kyle.

"I know. I have put in a plea to leave them as they are," Norris replied.

Kyle looked puzzled.

"They are monuments of the ancient families who built this village. Let them also be a reminder of the darkness that grew in the hearts of their children that led them to commit the most horrific crimes during the pandemic," said Norris.

Without another word, he turned and left.

18th May 2020
Withering Heights Apartments, New York

The rain tapped on the windows, creating a rhythmic sound. The city lights shimmered from every direction. William stood, sipping his drink. It had been tough. They had identified several villagers who were a part of the Shadow Fraction. The cement slab full of blood had been removed from the lab, and he had returned to his normal routine.

William hated himself for losing his temper when he'd discovered Gail was still at large. He was on the most wanted list, and the cops were looking for him. But William had little hope. Gail could have taken the infants. But where? William knew one thing. One day, Gail would leave a clue, and he would track him down.

He reread the message from Joan. Happy that he had reached out to her, he looked forward to having lunch with her tomorrow. They had dinner two days ago. It was a start, a good one. Although it was his decision to separate, he had regretted it since day one. Of course, he enjoyed his independence, but he wanted to share his life with someone.

The phone rang, and his heart jumped a little. It was Jack. He had been trying to track down the 3D printer and origin of the artificial organ. The NYPD tech department was also trying to follow this lead, but they had other priorities. He pushed the green button, and the video call started. He was not surprised to see Roumoult. Jack and Tom shared the screen.

"William how are you?" said Roumoult.

"I am fine. You?"

"As good as it can get."

William said nothing.

"What have you found?" Tom asked, getting to the point.

"Uh-huh. I am sad to say nothing!" Jack said.

Tom grunted.

"First, I tried to track the printer. It was registered and bought under the name of Ella Morgan."

William rolled his eyes.

"She is dead and of no use to us. I contacted the seller and asked about the invoice. The buyer paid in cash, and there is no way of tracing the money."

"What about the blueprint used to develop the artificial organ?" Roumoult asked.

"I spoke with three experts who know how to develop the coding to create a blueprint for an artificial organ. They confirm it's not theirs. The computers found in the lab under the temple were wiped clean. We never got our hands on the blueprint."

Tom frowned.

"Can someone write it?" Roumoult asked.

"Yeah. I can," Jack muttered.

William was not surprised. Jack was competent and developing such a code would be easy for him.

"What about nanoparticles? Are they the same as nanobots we found in Nightridge?" Tom asked.

"The technology is similar, and they may be connected."

William thought of the artificial organs at the morgue. He feared someone would steal them. Once again, as suggested by Tom, William had contacted the FBI agent who had taken charge of securing the nanoprobes. But this time, he was skeptical. He did not want to share the evidence with the Feds. Every fiber in his body told him the organs would lead them to the real culprit. The Feds would ultimately take the organs, but he had secured several samples.

"I agree. I think the incidents in Willow's Heart and Nightridge are connected," William said.

"Jack. What about nanoparticles? Can you get us more answers?" Roumoult said.

Jack took a long breath. "I will keep working on it. But we need to identify their origin and find out what they plan to do next."

William's heart dropped to his stomach. "Next?"

"Do you think this will stop? After the nanoprobes, they created nanoparticles and tested them on humans to ensure they could destroy biological factors that would make a normal person sick. Then they tested it against every existing virus on this planet. This is just the start. It could lead to the next generation of humans who may not be affected by biological weapons. Do you know what that means?"

William was stunned. Futuristic humans are immune to

viruses and bacteria. It could be the next step in human evolution.

"It's exciting and scary. Can you imagine the possibilities? If we can evolve the human body, we might not die of natural causes. Nanoparticles might replace dying cells, and people might live for centuries. Technology might help us survive harsh conditions. Maybe when our planet runs out of water, and the radiation level rises after the destruction of the ozone layer, such technology could make us immune to it. It could be equivalent to finding the holy grail."

"Jack. Let us stick with the facts," Roumoult intervened.

"All I am saying is we should keep our eyes open. This is not the end. These people, whether or not we like it, are going to keep evolving this technology. And you know what, if they are successful, it could reshape our future. What happened in Willow's Heart or Nightridge might just be the beginning."

1st June 2020
Tom's Apartment, New York

Tom burped, and he felt his stomach bloat. He sat in his untidy living room surrounded by food wrappers, empty cans of soda, and beer. It was bright outside, and the city was lively and noisy. On the news, the reporter announced the new number of COVID-19 cases in New York and the push for vaccination had begun. He was glad that the news about the incident at Willow's Heart had become a distant memory. Tom was struggling to forget that night.

He had nightmares and suffered from insomnia. In the eyes of the NYPD, he had done well. The case was a success.

He had received several emails congratulating him on a job well done. They had held a virtual memorial for the cops who died. Only a few people could attend in person, thanks to the pandemic. More names of dead cops were added to the wall, and their details filed away somewhere in the system. That was how the world worked. Everyone continued to live their lives as if nothing had happened. But not him. He could not forget, and it was making him miserable. To make matters worse, the babies he and Kyle had found under the temple had vanished without a trace. He remembered one name - Lillian Remer. The surrogate mother of baby 3. But the cops couldn't find her. Tom wondered if it was a fake name.

Not wanting to face the world, not even his own partner, Tom had turned into a hermit. He had taken all his cases home and cut himself off from everyone. He rejected new cases and was catching up on paperwork. Jenny tried to urge him to leave the apartment. It didn't work. They spoke with each other every day, and he thought that was all the human interaction he needed.

A knock on the door distracted him. He was puzzled. He had not ordered food delivery, and John was on leave.

"Tom, open up!" said Roumoult.

"What the hell is he doing here?" he muttered.

With a heavy heart, he opened the door and found Roumoult holding a puppy.

Roumoult looked at him from top to bottom.

"What do you want? I am working," Tom said, clenching his jaw.

"Right," Roumoult replied, barging inside the apartment.

"Look… I have a lot to do…"

Shamelessly, Roumoult cleared a stuffed chair and sat on it.

"What are you doing here?" Tom asked, annoyed.

Roumoult folded his legs and made himself comfortable. "Checking if you are done whining."

"I have my own ways... okay? I don't need... whatever this is."

The pup stood up wagging its tail and barked.

"Woof! Woof!"

It jumped off Roumoult's lap, rushed toward Tom, and pounced on his legs. Tom bent over and picked up the cute puppy.

"She remembers you," Roumoult remarked.

Tom patted the pup and handed her to Roumoult.

"I am fine," he insisted.

Glancing around, Roumoult remarked, "Sure, if you say so."

"There is nothing out there for me. I am done! Finished! I think I don't want to be a cop anymore!"

Roumoult stood up. He turned to the pup and said, "I thought he was ready. I think he needs more time."

The pup barked.

"She agrees."

"What are you talking about?" Tom said, putting his hands on his waist.

"Well, I am sorry to bother you. Since you are not interested, I am not at liberty to tell you that William is on to something."

Roumoult headed for the door and opened it.

Tom could not hold himself back. "What is he up to now?"

Roumoult turned. "It's about Angelus's vampires. Remember those?"

Tom recalled a conversation they had about unexplained deaths where the victim's blood was drained out, and they bore several bite marks.

"I remember. But I thought it was a dead end."

Without answering him Roumoult stepped out of the apartment.

"Wait, a minute… what happened?" Tom asked, marching after him.

Roumoult faced him. "Fine. Fine. I am not supposed to tell you, but since you insist. They found a body in an alley. The disfigured corpse scared the hell out of a homeless guy who bumped into a patrol officer. The officer sealed the crime scene and called forensics. Then the body was sent to the City Morgue."

"Okay…"

"At first, William thought the man was caught in a fire because the body was burned, and there was a fire that morning in that alley. But as William examined the body, he found several bite marks and signs of massive surgery. He did a DNA test to identify the man."

The hair on the back of Tom's neck stood up.

"It's Gail."

Tom's eyes widened.

"Something tells me he was involved in more than one radical group," Roumoult added.

"That son of a bitch!" Tom shouted.

"There are more of them out there. As far as I know, the captain hasn't assigned this case to anyone. Since you are not interested—"

"I have to call him! I have to get to the office," Tom cried out, rushing inside the apartment.

"Tom!" called Roumoult.

"What?" he asked, stepping into the corridor.

"While you are at it, don't forget your pants."

Tom looked at himself. He was in his boxers.

"You…" he was about to say, but Roumoult was already gone. "Oh…you son of a bitch! I am going to kill you!" he yelled, shutting the door behind him.

The End

ABOUT THE AUTHOR

H.G. Ahedi holds a PhD in biomedical sciences and is a fictional writer. Reading is one of her favorite hobbies, and she loves watching movies and series while sipping tea. She spends a lot of time writing, and when she is bored with her desk, she wants to hop on a plane and travel the world. As that is not always possible, she explores local Sydney beaches and parks and enjoys a nice cup of coffee.

A note to readers

Enjoyed Shadow Fraction? Please leave a review and share your thoughts about the book. I would really appreciate it and thank you in advance!

OTHER BOOKS BY H.G. AHEDI

STELLA Bridget Williams is an editor who has been forced to give up everything due to her medical illness and pregnancy. Trying to accept her fate, Bridget attempt to make her home in quiet suburb of New South Wales. Things change when she bumps into Lorena Smith who tells her that she saw a murder. Get your free copy here

Black Moon: When Roumoult Cranston drives to Newburgh, a hired assassin awaits him. While trying to unearth this mystery, he discovers a darkness within himself and could be hanged for murder.

☆☆☆☆☆ Written in the style of Sir Arthur Conan Doyle, you find yourself enthralled!

Haunted: When three men commit suicides without reason, the hunt for answers become a frantic race against time. If you are interested in gripping crime thrillers, you should read Haunted.

An Engrossing, Brilliant Plot!
Suspenseful   Keeps you guessing until the last page!

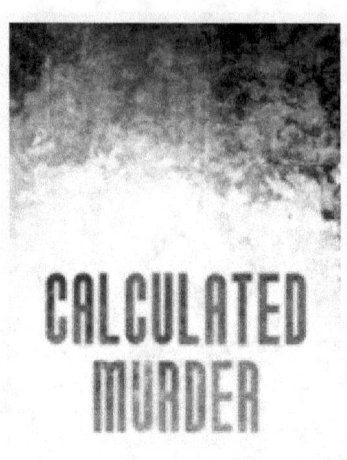

CALCULATED MURDER

H.G. AHEDI

Calculated Murder: If you love scandals, secrets affairs with explosive consequences then you should read, Calculated Murder.

Compelling and well-crafted mystery
Caught in the mysterious plot. The details and the accuracy. A great mystery novel

Transcendence: A soldier trying to survive, a scientist trying to save his world and a dark force that will define them both.
Transcendence is a historical sci fi novella that will keep you at the edge of your seat.

H.G. Ahedi's Transcendence is a bit like an episode of "The Twilight Zone" or a macabre, suspenseful nightmare.

Also an Audiobook

Fall of Titan (Realm Book 1) is action packed, mind bending Science Fiction adventure which is a blend of science, archaeology and magic. Imagine Lord of the Rings, just in space.

⭐⭐⭐⭐⭐ Great read! This book has everything I love in scifi: action, splendid world-building, and aliens. Fans of A. G. Riddle, Michael Crichton, and The Expanse will love this book!

Poseidon (Realm book 2): After the fall all is left is blood and revenge.

In the sequel to Fall of Titan... The wrath of the Orias queen has taken everything from Emmeline Augury. Powerless and hunted by the Orias , Emmeline decides not to yield and vows to kill the queen. But she's facing a being as powerful as the gods themselves. Can Emmeline destroy the queen or will the queen triumph? The answers lie in the wake of the Poseidon.

An Intriguing Plot   Taut Continuation of the Realm Saga   Intense sequel